Her lashes dusted her cheeks, and Tor reached over to push aside strands of her hair from those thick lashes.

She suddenly looked up, and the glint in her eyes lured him closer. Without thinking, he leaned in and nudged his nose aside her cheek, drawing in her perfume, a tantalizing mix of lemon and lavender. He felt her shiver.

When he tilted his head, his mouth grazed her cheek and her lips parted. He brushed them lightly, closing his eyes because the moment demanded he focus on their closeness, the warmth of her skin, the tickle of her hair against his fingers, the scent of her. It all combined with the herbs hanging overhead and the sulfur still lingering from the snuffed candles. A sweet dream. He had never kissed a client before...

Tor pulled a few inches away from Mel's mouth. She gaped at h

Michele Hauf is a *USA TODAY* bestselling author who has been writing romance, action-adventure and fantasy stories for more than twenty years. France, musketeers, vampires and faeries usually feature in her stories. And if Michele followed the adage "write what you know," all her stories would have snow in them. Fortunately, she steps beyond her comfort zone and writes about countries and creatures she has never seen. Find her on Facebook, Twitter and at michelehauf.com.

Books by Michele Hauf

Harlequin Nocturne

The Saint-Pierre Series

In the Company of Vampires

Visit the Author Profile page at Harlequin.com for more titles.

THIS STRANGE WITCHERY

MICHELE HAUF

———

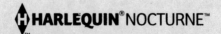

Recycling programs
for this product may
not exist in your area.

ISBN-13:978-1-335-62968-5

This Strange Witchery

Copyright © 2018 by Michele Hauf

Printed in U.S.A.

www.Harlequin.com

Dear Reader,

Crafting a hero and heroine for each new story I write is a favorite thing to do. My brain is always filled with characters. Many I've written about previously in my world of Beautiful Creatures. Others are people that you may never get a chance to read about because they are personal to me. But Tor, the hero of this story, wanted you to learn more about him. He's walked across the pages of a few previous books, and he's always intrigued me. That's the fun part about having voices in my head: I can make them come to life on the page.

And matching a hero to a woman who will challenge him and coax him to step beyond his self-imposed boundaries is another fun task for me. Mel was all too eager, and she barged onto the page with Bruce and Duck in tow. There were times I simply let her have her way with Tor; with you, the reader; with me, the one with my fingers on the keyboard. It was such a thrill to write this story and share the lives of two people who have become a little less imaginary since they have taken up residence in my heart.

Stay weird!

Michele

Here's to you, weirdo.

Chapter 1

The key to disposing of a werewolf body was to get the flames burning quickly, yet to keep them as contained as possible. Torsten Rindle had been doing cleaner work for close to ten years. When a call came in about a dead paranormal found or deposited somewhere in Paris, he moved swiftly. Discreet cleanup was one of his many trades. Media spin was a talent he'd mastered for whenever he was too late to clean up and a human had stumbled upon the dead werewolf. He also dallied with protection work and the occasional vampire hunt.

It was good for a man to keep his business options fluid and to always expand his skills list. And if he had to choose a title for what he did, he'd go with *Secret Keeper*.

But some days…

Tor shook his head as the blue-red flames burned the furry body to ash before him. The use of eucalyptus in the mix masked the smell of burning dog. For the most part. The creature had been rabid, eluding the slayer until it had gotten trapped down a narrow alleyway that had ended in a brick wall. The slayer had taken it out not twenty minutes earlier, and then had immediately called Tor.

Those in the know carried Tor's number. He was always the first choice when it came to keeping secrets from humans.

Thankful this had been an old wolf—werewolves shifted back to human form after death; the older ones took much longer, sometimes hours—so he hadn't needed to deal with it in human form, Tor swiped a rubber-gloved hand over an itch on his cheek. Then he remembered the werewolf blood he'd touched.

Bollocks.

He was getting tired of this routine: receive a frantic call from someone in the know regarding a rabid werewolf who may be seen by humans. Dash to the scene. Assess the situation. Clean up the mess (if extinguishing the problem was essential), or talk to the police and/or media using one of his many alter-ego names and titles, such as Ichabod Sneed from the Fire Department's Personal Relations. Then return home to his empty loft.

Eat. Crash. Repeat.

Tor knew… He knew too much. Monsters existed. Vampires, werewolves, witches, faeries, harpies, mermaids. They all existed. And yes, dragons were known to be real assholes if you could find one of them. A regular human guy like him shouldn't have such knowledge. That was why, over the years, he had striven to keep such information from the public. Because knowing so much? It fucked with a man's mental state.

And then there were some days he wanted to walk away from it all. Like today.

This morning he'd been woken and called to assist with media contacts while a minor graveyard at the edge of the city had been blocked off from public access. Routine cosmetic repairs, he'd explained to the news reporters. The truth? A demonic ritual had roused a cavalcade of vicious entities from Daemonia. Slayers had taken care of the immediate threat, but that had left the graveyard covered in black tar-like demon blood. And the stench!

Tor had spent the better part of this afternoon arguing with a group of muses about their need to "come out" to the public regarding their oppressive attraction to angels who only wanted to impregnate them. Something to do with the #metoo movement. Sexual harassment or not, the public wasn't ready for the truth about fallen angels and their muses. But, being a feminist himself, he had directed the muses to the Council, who had recently put together a Morals and Ethics Committee.

"I want normal," he muttered. He grabbed the fire extinguisher to douse the flames. He refilled the canister at the local fire station monthly. "It's time I had it."

It took ten minutes to clean up the sludgy ash pile and shovel it into a medium black body bag. Fortunately, this werewolf had been tracked to the edge of the 13th arrondissement not far from the ring road that circled Paris. It was a tight little neighborhood, mostly industry that had closed during regular business hours, leaving the streets abandoned and the dusty windows dark. Tor hadn't noticed anyone nearby, nor had he worried about discovery as he made haste cleaning up the evidence. His van was parked down the street.

He hefted the body bag over a shoulder, picked up the extinguisher and his toolbox filled with all the accoutrements a guy like him should ever need on a job like this, and wandered down the street. His rubber boots made squidgy noises on the tarmac. After dousing the flames, he'd rolled down the white polyethylene hazmat suit to his hips. With shirtsleeves rolled up, his tweed vest still neatly buttoned, yet tie slightly loosened, he could breathe now.

"Normal," he repeated.

He'd scheduled a Skype interview early tomorrow afternoon. The job he had applied for was assistant to Human Relations and Resources at an up-and-coming accounting firm in *la Defense* district. About as mundane and normal as a man could hope for. He'd never actually worked a regular "human" job.

It was about time he gave it a go.

The olive green van, which had seen so many better days, sat thirty feet down from a streetlight that flickered and put out an annoying buzz. Humming a Sinatra tune, Tor opened the back of the van and tossed in the supplies. He'd dump the body bag at a landfill on the way home. He'd done his research; that landfill was plowed monthly and shipped directly to China for incineration.

"That's my life," he sang, altering the lyrics to suit him.

Sinatra was a swanky idol to him. Singing his songs put him in a different place from the weird one he usually occupied. Call it a sanity check. The Sultan of Swoon relaxed him in ways he could appreciate.

He peeled off the sweaty hazmat suit, hung it on a hanger and placed that on a hook near the van ceiling. At his belt hung a heavy quartz crystal fixed into a steel mount that clipped with a D ring onto a loop. He never went anywhere without the bespelled talisman. Another necessity for sanity. The rubber boots were placed in a tray on the van floor. He pulled out his bespoke Italian leather shoes from a cloth bag and slipped those on.

"Ahhh…" Almost better than a shower. But he couldn't wait to wash off the werewolf blood. Odds were he had it in more places than the smear across his cheek.

Closing the back doors, he punched a code on the digital lock to secure it. While he sorted through his trouser pocket for the van key, he whistled the chorus to the song that demanded he accept life as it was…*that's life*.

Maybe… No. Life didn't have to be this way for him. He was all-in for a change of scenery.

Before he slid the key in the lock, he saw the driver's door was unlocked. Had he forgotten? That wasn't like him. He was always on top of the situation. Which only further contributed to his need to run from this life as if a flaming werewolf were chasing his ass.

Tor slid into the driver's seat and fired up the engine. Another crazy midnight job. His final one. He would stand firm on that decision. And after getting a whiff of the dead werewolf's rangy scent—someone please show him the way to his new office cubicle.

Adjusting the radio to a forties' swing station, he palmed the stick shift.

When the person in the passenger seat spoke, he startled. "Whoa!"

"Hey! Oops. Sorry." The woman let out a bubbly nervous giggle. "Didn't mean to surprise you. I've been waiting. And watching. You've quite the talent, you know that?"

"Who in bloody—" He squinted in the darkness of the cab, but could only see glints in her eyes and—above her eyes? Hmm… Must be some kind of sparkly makeup. "How did you…?"

"The door wasn't locked. You really should lock your doors in this neighborhood. Anyone could steal your van. Not that it's very steal-worthy. Kinda old, and there's more rust than actual paint. But I'm guessing you have important stuff in the back. Like a dead werewolf!" she announced with more cheer than anyone ever should.

His eyes adjusting to the darkness, Tor could make out that she had long brown hair and big eyes. She smiled. A lot. He didn't get a sense about her—was she paranormal or human? But then, he didn't have any special means of determining whether a person was paranormal or not. Sometimes he didn't know until it was too late. But he did pick up an overtly incautious happiness about her.

Without letting down his guard, he reached across the console to offer his hand. "Torsten Rindle."

"I know!" She shook his hand eagerly. "I've been looking for you. And now I've found you."

If she knew who he was, then she probably knew what he did for a living. Which still didn't solve the issue of *what* she was. Humans hired him all the time to protect them from paranormals. But to find him, they had to be in the know, and also know someone who knew someone who knew him. Who, in turn, had his phone number.

He pulled back his hand and leaned an elbow on the steering wheel, keeping his body open, prepared to move to either defend or restrain. "Who are you, and why are you in my van?"

"It's a rather beat-up old van, isn't it?"

"So you've said."

"Doesn't really jibe with you in your fancy vest and trousers and designer watch."

The watch in question showed it was well past midnight. This had been a hell of a long day.

"I don't need to draw attention by driving a sports car," Tor offered. "And the van is as utility as it gets. A requirement in my line of work. Now. Your name? And why are you sitting in my van?"

"Melissande Jones." She fluttered her lashes as she pressed her fingers to her chest, where frilly red flowers made up the neckline of her blouse. "My friends call me Lissa, as does my family. I'm not sure I like the nickname, but I hate to argue with people. I'm a people pleaser. Sad, but true. And I'm here because I need your help. Your protection, actually."

Tor played her name over in his brain. The last name was familiar. And in Paris, it wasn't so common as, say, in the United States or London. He made it a point to know who all the paranormal families in the city were, and had good knowledge of most across the world. Blame it on his penchant for getting lost in research. And for needing to know everything.

Recall brought to mind a local family of witches. The two elders were twin brothers. And he knew the one brother had twin sons, so that left the other…

"Thoroughly Jones's daughter? A dark witch?"

"Yes, and mostly." She turned on the seat so her body faced him. Her bright red lipstick caught the pale glow from the distant streetlight. Her lips were shaped like a bow. And combined with those big doe eyes and lush feathery lashes? "Can you help me?"

"I, uh…" Shaking himself out of his sudden admiration for her sensual assets, Tor assumed his usual emotionless facade, the one he wore for the public. "I'm not sure what you've heard about me, but I'm no longer in the business of providing personal protection."

"You're a cleaner." She gestured toward the fire truck that was pulling up down the street where the werewolf had been burned. Someone must have witnessed the fire after all. "You also do spin for The Order of the Stake."

Two things that most might know about him. If they

were paranormal. And again, knew someone who knew someone who—

"And you own the Agency," she said, interrupting his disturbed thoughts. "A group that protects us paranormals."

That knowledge was more hush-hush. And not correct.

"Not exactly. The Agency seeks to put their hands to weapons, ephemera, and other objects that might fall into human hands and lead them to believe in you paranormals."

"You paranormals," she said mockingly and gestured with a flutter of her hand that made Tor suddenly nervous. A bloke never knew what witches could do with but a flick of finger or sweep of hand. "You're human, right?"

"That I am."

And she was a witch. A dark witch. Mostly? He had no idea what that meant. And…he wasn't interested in finding out.

"Like I've said, I don't do protection. And I've handed off the Agency reins to someone located in the States. But of most importance is, I really do not want to get involved with anyone from the Jones family. I respect your father and his brother. They are a pair of badass dark witches most would do well to walk a wide circle around." He'd come *this close* to stepping into that dangerous circle a few years back. And he wasn't a stupid man. Lesson learned. "If you need someone—"

"But your Agency protects paranormal objects, yes?"

"It does. The Agency always will, but I'm not doing that sort of—"

"Then you can help me." She bent over and reached into a big flowered purse on the floor and pulled out something that blinded Tor with its brilliance. "I have a paranormal object."

Tor put up a hand to block the pulsating red glow. It was so bright. Like the sun but in a shade of red. He couldn't see the shape or the size, yet knew that she held it with one hand. "Put that away! What the hell is that?"

She set the thing on her lap and placed a palm over it, which quieted the glow to a smoldering simmer. "It's Hecate's heart."

Tor didn't recognize it as a volatile object from any lists he had read or compiled, but that didn't mean anything. There were so many weapons, objects, tools, even creatures that were considered a danger to humans and paranormals alike. The most dangerous had to be contained, or Very Bad Things could happen in the mortal realm.

"What does it do besides blind a man?" he asked.

"Hecate was the first witch."

"I know that. But she's long dead. Is that her actual heart?"

"Yes." Melissande patted it gently. The object pulsed with each touch. "It's said that should her heart ever stop beating, all the witches' hearts in this realm would suddenly cease to beat. Ominous, right?" The red glow softened her features and gave them an enchanting cast. Her lashes were so thick, they granted her eyes a glamorous come-and-touch-me appeal. "But it's pretty indestructible. I dropped it earlier. Got a little dirt on it. No big deal. Though it looks like glass, it's not. It's sort of a solid gel substance."

"You dropped it? Wait." Tor took a moment to inhale and center himself. And to remember his goal: normal. "I'm not doing this. I'm no longer in the protection business."

Melissande's jaw dropped open. And those eyes. Why couldn't he stop staring at those gorgeous eyes? Was it the sparkly makeup that made them glitter, or did they really twinkle like stars? Maybe she'd cast an attraction spell on herself before finding him. Witches were sneaky like that. And how had she found him? Tor prided himself on his ability to blend in, to be the classic everyman. That she had been able to track him down without a phone call…

He wasn't going to worry about this. He'd made his decision. Normal it was.

"I need to get on the road and dispose of the remains," he said, turning on the seat and gripping the steering wheel. "You can leave now."

"I'm not going anywhere. Did you decide *just now* you're not doing the protection thing anymore?"

"No, I—"

"Or is it me? I get that my dad and his brother are a couple of big scary witches. Woo-woo dark witch stuff *is* imposing. But I'm not asking you to work with them."

"I've been considering this decision for weeks. Months," Tor protested. "And it's final—"

"Oh, come on. One more job? I need your help, Tor. I'm just one tiny witch who has an ominous magical artifact stuffed in her purse that seems to attract strange things to it. In proof, on the way to finding you, I gave a zombie the slip."

"Zombies do not exist," Tor said sharply. "Revenants do. But the walking dead are a false assumption. It's impossible to have a dead person walking around, decaying, and actually surviving more than a few minutes."

"Is that so? That's good to know. Still not sure I believe you. But revenants…" She cast her gaze out the passenger window.

And Tor couldn't help but wonder what it was about revenants that gave her pause. Damn it! He didn't care.

He could not care. If he were going to make the transition to normal, he had to get rid of this annoyingly cute witch.

Yet the glow from the heart, seeping between her fingers, did intrigue him. Something like that should be under lock and key, kept far and safely away from humans. And should it fall into the hands of the Archives, whom her uncle Certainly Jones headed? The Archives wasn't as beneficent as they were touted to be. The things they stored weren't always left to sit and get dusty. Tor didn't even want to think about all the nasty happenings that occurred because something the Archives had obtained had been used.

Yeah, so maybe he had stepped into that circle of danger with one of the Jones brothers. Whew! He knew far too much about the ominous power of dark magic. And yet he had lived to breathe another day.

"You want me to protect you and that thing?" he asked. "You know the Agency would take that heart in hand and put it under lock and key? In fact, if you want to hand it over, I guess I could take it right now—"

"No." She lifted the heart possessively to her chest. Tor squinted at the maddening glow. "Can't do that. I need it for a spell that I can't invoke until the night of the full moon."

Which was less than a week from now. Tor always kept the moon cycles in his head. It wasn't wise to walk into any situation without knowing what phase the moon was in. Had tonight been a full moon? That werewolf would not have gone down so easily for the slayer. And burning it would have roused every bloody wolf in the city to howls.

Tor rubbed two fingers over his temple, sensing he wasn't going to be rid of her as easily as he wished. "Why me? What or who directed you toward me and suggested I might want to help you?"

"If I tell you, you'll think I'm weird."

"I already think you're weird. I don't think a person can get much weirder than stealing a dead witch's beating heart and then breaking into a stranger's van to beg for his help."

"What makes you think I stole this?"

"I—I don't know. Is it a family heirloom you dug out of a chest in the attic? Something dear old Granny bequeathed to you on her deathbed?"

"No." She hugged it tightly to her chest. Guilty of theft, as he could only suspect. And he *had* locked the van doors. He never forgot.

"People only find me because someone has given them my name," he said. "And I always know when someone is coming for me, because that's how it works. I want to know how you learned about me."

"Fine. This evening, after I'd gotten home with the heart and sat out on the patio to have a cup of tea—I like peppermint, by the way."

"I'm an Earl Grey man, myself." The woman did go off on tangents. And he had just followed her along on one! "You were saying what it was that led you to me?"

"Right. As I was sipping my tea, a cicada landed on my plate. It was blue."

Now intensely interested, Tor lifted his gaze to hers.

"Cicadas always look like they're wearing armor. Don't you think? Anyway, I didn't hear it speak to me," she said. "Not out loud. More like in my head. I sensed what it had come to tell me. And that was to give me your name. Torsten Rindle. I'd heard the name before. My dad and uncle have mentioned you in conversation. Cautiously, of course. I know you stand in opposition to them. And they know it, too. But they also have a certain respect for you. Anyway, I knew you could help me."

A cicada had told a witch to seek him out for help?

Tor's sleeves were still rolled to the elbows. Had the light been brighter, it would reveal the tattoo of a cicada on his inner forearm. The insect meant something to him. Something personal and so private he'd never spoken about it to anyone.

"How did you know—"

A thump on the driver's side window made Tor spin around on the seat. A bloody hand smeared the glass.

"That's the zombie," Melissande stated calmly. "The one you told me didn't exist."

Chapter 2

Melissande observed as Tor swung out of the driver's seat and darted into the back of the van. Heavy metal objects clinked. The man swore. His British accent was more pronounced than her barely-there one. He again emerged in the cab with a wicked-looking weapon. Actually, she recognized that hand-sized titanium column as one of those fancy stakes the knights in The Order of the Stake used to slay vampires. Was that supposed to work with zombies, as well?

"Stay here," he ordered. Tor exited through the driver's door, slamming it behind him.

Crossing her arms and settling onto the seat, Melissande decided she was perfectly fine with staying inside the nice safe van while the hero fought the creepy thing outside. Zombies didn't exist? The man obviously knew nothing about the dark arts.

A hand slapped the driver's window, followed by the

smeared, slimy face of something that could only be zombie. One eyeball was missing. From behind, Tor grabbed it by the collar and swung it away from the vehicle.

Melissande let out her breath in a gasp, then tucked the heart she still held into her bag on the floor. Growing up in a household with a dark witch for a dad and a cat-shifting familiar for a mom, she should be prepared for unusual situations like this, but it never got easier to witness. Dark magic was challenging. And sometimes downright gross. She was surprised she'd accomplished her task today, securing Hecate's heart. But she hadn't expected it to attract the unsavory sort like the one battling Tor right now. Earlier, that same creature had growled at her and swiped, but she'd been too fast, and had slipped down the street away from the thing in her quest to locate the one man she knew could help her.

Anticipating the dangers of possessing the heart, she had known she might need protection. She couldn't ask her dad, or her uncle. And should she ask her cousins—the twins Laith and Vlas—they would have laughed at her, saying how she'd gotten herself into another wacky fix.

She did have a knack for the weird and wacky. It seemed to follow her around like a stray cat with a bent tail. She didn't hate cats, but she'd never keep one as a pet or familiar. When one's mother was a cat-shifter, a girl learned to respect felines and to never take them for granted.

The not-zombie's shoulders slammed against the vehicle's dented hood. Melissande leaned forward in time to watch Tor slam the stake against its chest. The zombie didn't so much release ash as dechunk, falling apart in clumps, accompanied by a glugging protrusion of sludgy gray stuff from its core. Gross, but also interesting. She'd never witnessed a zombie death.

With a sweep of his arm, Tor brushed some chunks

from the hood. He tucked the stake in a vest pocket, then smoothed out the tweed vest he wore. Shirtsleeves rolled to his elbows revealed a tattoo on his forearm, but she couldn't make out what it was in the darkness.

He was a smart dresser, and much sexier than she'd expected for a jack-of-all-trades human—because she had expected something rather brute, stocky and plain. Probably even scarred and with a gimpy eye. Tor's short dark hair was neatly styled (save for the blood smeared at his temple and into his hairline). Thick, dark brows topped serious eyes that now scanned the area for further danger. With every movement, a muscle, or twelve, flexed under his fitted white shirt, advertising his hard, honed physique. And those fingers wrapped about the stake… so long and graceful, yet skilled and determined…

Melissande's heart thundered, and it wasn't from fear of a vile creature. The man did things to her better judgment, like make her wonder why she had never dated a human before. Maybe it was time to stretch her potential boyfriend qualifications beyond their boundaries.

"Did you get him?" she yelled through the windshield.

Tor's eyebrow lifted and he gave her a wonky head wobble, as if to say, *Did you not see me battle that heinous creature then defeat it?*

She offered him a double thumbs-up.

He strolled around the side of the van. The back doors opened, and he pulled out something, then came back to the front. A shovel proved convenient for scooping dead zombie into a body bag. He was certainly well prepared.

After the quick cleanup, he again walked to the back of the van. Melissande glanced over the seats into the van's interior. When he tossed in the bag and slammed the door, she cringed. The driver's door opened, and Tor slid inside. She noticed the blood at his neck that seeped onto his starched white collar. It looked like a scratch on his skin. If that thing had originally been a vampire, it could be bite marks. Tor slammed the door and turned on the ignition.

Melissande leaned over to touch his neck. He reacted, lifting an elbow to block her. But she did not relent, pressing her fingers against his neck. "I'm not going to bite," she said. "I want to make sure *you* didn't get bitten."

"It's just a scratch. The thing didn't get close enough to nosh on my neck. Sit down and buckle up." He pulled away from the curb as she tugged the seat belt across her torso.

"Was it a vampire?" she asked.

"I'm not sure. Hard to determine with all the decay."

"Zombie," she declared.

"Not going to have that argument again. Probably a revenant vamp."

"I've heard they're rare. And don't live in the city."

"Dead vampires who live in coffins and have no heartbeat? Most definitely not common. And generally not found in any large city, including Paris." He dusted off some debris from his forearm. "Though I didn't notice fangs. And usually decapitation is required. Whatever it was, it's dead now."

"You're driving with me in your van," Melissande remarked cheerfully. "Does that mean you're going to protect me?"

"No. That means I'm going to take you home and send you off with a pat on your head and well wishes. Where do you live?"

Pouting, she muttered, "The 6th."

In the flash of a streetlight, he cast her a look. It admonished while also judged. Such a look made him fall a notch on her attraction-level meter.

"You're not very nice," she offered.

Tor turned his attention back to the street, shaking his head.

"I'll pay you," she tried. "I would never expect you to work for free."

"What's the address?" he asked.

Obstinate bit of...sexy. If he weren't so handsome, she would ask him to stop and she'd catch a cab. She was not a woman to hang around where she wasn't wanted.

After a reluctant sigh, Melissande gave him the street address and muddled over how to convince him to protect her. She didn't know who else to contact. She'd overheard her dad and his brother one evening talking about the various humans in the city whom they trusted. The list had been short. And while they'd both agreed that Torsten Rindle was definitely not on their side, they'd also agreed that he was a man of honor and integrity who could get the job done, and who had a concern for keeping all things paranormal hush-hush without resorting to senseless violence or assuming all nonhumans walked around with a target on their foreheads.

At the time, Melissande had known if she'd ever need help, he was her man. And then, when the whole conversation earlier with the cicada had occurred—well. She never overlooked a chat with a bug.

She hadn't told her dad, Thoroughly Jones, this part of the plan, though he did know her ultimate goal. She'd agreed to take on this task because she knew how much of an emotional toll it would take on her father. And she intended to handle every detail on her own, so he could focus on taking care of her mother, Star, when she really needed the attention.

Poor Mom—she had only just been reborn a few weeks

ago after a fall from a sixth-floor rooftop, and this life was not treating her well.

Melissande's neighborhood was quiet and quaint and filled with old buildings that had stood for centuries. The Montparnasse Cemetery wasn't far away, and often tourists wandered down her street, but were always respectful of the private gates and entrances. She loved it because she had a decent-sized yard behind the house, fenced in with black wrought iron, in which she grew herbs and medicinal flowers. It served her earth magic. Her two-story Victorian, painted a deep, dusty violet, held memories of ages past. But no ghosts. Which bummed her out a little, because she wouldn't mind a ghost or two, so long as they were friendly.

Tor parked the van before her property. The front gate and fence boasted a healthy climbing vine with night-blooming white moonflowers. Opening the van door, she breathed in the flowers' intoxicating scent. "Blessed goddess Luna." Soon the moon would reach fullness. And then Melissande would be faced with her greatest challenge.

Tor swung around the front of the van before she'd even gotten her first foot on the ground. "I'll walk you up," he said as he rolled down his sleeves.

She dashed her finger over the cut on his neck and was satisfied it was just a nick.

"I'll live." He offered her his arm.

Startled by such a chivalrous move, Melissande linked her arm with his, and with a push of her hand forward and a focus of her magic, she opened the gate before them without touching it.

She'd been born with kinetic magic. Sometimes the things she needed moved did so before she even had the thought.

"Witches," Tor muttered as he witnessed the motion.

"What about witches?" she challenged. The narrow sidewalk forced them to walk closely, and she did not release his arm when she felt his tug to make her step a little faster. "You got a problem with witches?"

"I have little problem with any person who occupies this realm. Unless they intend, or actually do, harm to others. Then that person will not like me very much."

"I know your reputation. It's why I came to you. But you're not a vampire slayer, so why the stake to fight the zombie?"

"Revenant." They stopped before the stoop, and she allowed him back his arm. Tor pushed his hands into his trouser pockets. "I like to keep my arsenal varied. The stake was a gift from an Order knight. I also carry a silent chain saw and a variety of pistols equipped with wood, iron and UV bullets. And at any given moment I might also be wielding a machete. Gotta mix it up. Keep things fresh."

"You don't use spells, do you?"

"Not with any luck."

"Good. That's my expertise. Do you want to come in for some tea before you abandon me to be attacked by all the vile denizens that seek the heart?"

"No, I'm good." He winked.

Melissande's heart performed a shiver and then a squeezing hug. Surely the heat rising in her neck was a blush, but she couldn't remember a time when she'd blushed before.

"I'm beat," Tor said. "It's been a long day. Had to talk down a couple muses from going public with their life stories before that werewolf cleanup. Started the day with a demon mess. And capping it off with a revenant slaying put me over the edge as far as social contact." He held out his hand for her to shake. "Good luck finding the person you need for protection."

Melissande stared at his hand for a few seconds, deciding it was the sexiest hand she'd ever seen. Wide and sure, and the fingers were long and strong. She'd like to feel them handle her as smoothly and as confidently as he had the stake.

As she reluctantly lifted her hand in a send-off to her last best hope, she remembered something. "I forgot my bag in your van. It's got the heart in it."

"I'll get it for you—"

They both turned when a growl in the vicinity of the van curdled the night air. Looming before the vehicle was a skeletal conglomeration of bones and smoke with a toothy maw.

"Really?" Tor said. "A wraith demon? What the hell is up with that heart?"

"I have no idea," Melissande offered as she grabbed him by the arm and clung out of fear.

"Go inside," he ordered. "I'll handle this."

"Good plan. I'll start tea." As Tor strode toward the growling demon, unafraid and shoulders back, Melissande called, "Don't forget my bag!"

Tor's strides took him right up to the wraith demon. The thing slashed its talons at him and hissed, "You have something I want, human." It dragged its obsidian talons across the passenger door, cutting through the faded green paint to reveal the steel beneath.

"If it's a wish for a new paint job, you're right, bloke," Tor said.

Not giving the thing a moment to think, he swung out and landed a solid right hook on the side of its head, just below the horn. That was a touchy spot where no bone covered whatever tender innards were contained within the thing. The demon howled in pain.

Not wanting to wake the neighbors, Tor acted quickly. Taking out the stake from his pocket, he plunged it against the demon's chest and compressed the paddles to release the spring-loaded pointed shaft. It wasn't the first line of defense against demons, but it did slow them down just long enough.

From his belt, he unhooked the vial of black Egyptian salt—that he purchased in bulk—and broke the glass outward so the contents sprayed the demon's face. *"Deus benedicat!"* The *god bless you* wasn't necessary for the kill, but he liked to toss that in. Those were the last words a demon wanted to hear as its face stretched wide in a dying scream.

"Bastard!" the thing shouted before its horns dropped off. The wraith demon disintegrated to a pile of floaty black ash at Tor's feet.

Glancing over his shoulder, Tor scanned the neighborhood. No lights on in any nearby houses. And the altercation had occurred on the side of the van facing the witch's house, so he'd been partially concealed. But he waited anyway.

Curiosity always tended to come out in moments of fear. If any humans had witnessed this, he'd know about it soon.

Checking his watch, he verified it was nearing 2:00 a.m. Too late. And like he'd told the witch: he'd had a day.

"Normal," he muttered, and shook the ash from the toe of his leather shoe.

Sure the demon slaying had gone unnoticed, Tor opened the passenger door and grabbed the floral tapestry purse. It was so heavy he wondered if rocks were inside it, and red fringes dangled from the bottom. Girl stuff always gave him pause for a moment of genuine wonder. What was the purpose of so many fringes? And what did women put in their purses that made them heavier than an army rucksack? He'd like to take a look inside, but he knew that a wise man did not poke about in a witch's personal things.

He turned toward the house, then paused. He should take out Hecate's heart and toss the purse on the step. That would solve a lot of problems he didn't want to have. Namely, revenants and crazed demons.

The purse had a zipper. He touched the metal pull—

"Didn't your mother teach you it's not nice to snoop in a woman's bag?" Melissande called from the threshold.

Tor rubbed the tattoo under his sleeve. No, his mother had not.

With a resigned sigh, he strode up to the witch's stoop and handed her the curious receptacle filled with marvels untold.

"Tea?" she asked sweetly. As if he'd not just polished off a wraith demon in her front yard, and wasn't wearing werewolf blood on his face like some kind of Scottish warrior.

"Why not." With weary resolution, Tor stepped up. Pressing his palms to the door frame and leaning forward, but not crossing the threshold, he asked, "Wards?"

"None for you, but as soon as you step inside, I'll reactivate them. Come on. I won't bite, unlike some people."

Tor's chuckle was unstoppable. He stepped inside and closed the door, then followed the witch down a hallway papered in cutout purple and gray velvet damask and into the kitchen, which smelled of candle wax and dried herbs.

Two cups of tea sat on a serving tray, which she picked up before leading him into a living room filled with so much fringe, velvet and glitter, Tor closed his eyes against the overwhelming bling as he sat on the couch. And settled deep into the plushest, most comfortable piece of furniture his body had ever known.

"Right?" Melissande offered in response to his satisfied groan. "I like to become one with my furniture. That's my favorite spot. If you relax, you'll be asleep in two sips."

Tor took a sip of the sweet tea. Not Earl Grey, but it was palatable. "I never sleep on the job."

The witch sat on an ottoman before him, which was upholstered in bright red velvet. "On the job? Does that mean…?"

That meant that Tor had just fended off two crazed creatures who had wanted to get to the heart in the witch's mysterious purse. There was something wrong with that. He couldn't ignore that she was in some kind of trouble. Whether dire or merely mediocre, it didn't matter. When bad things came at you, a person needed to defend themselves. And she didn't seem like someone who knew how to protect herself, even if she did possess magic.

He took another sip of the tea, and his eyelids fluttered. This was good stuff. He'd had a long day. And combined with his growing nerves for tomorrow's interview, his body was shot. His tight muscles wanted to release and…

Tor's teacup clinked as it hit the saucer. He didn't see the witch extend her magical influence to steady the porcelain set in midair, because sleep hit him like a troll's fist to the skull.

Chapter 3

Melissande leaned over Tor, who was slowly coming awake on the couch. He was so cute. Not a high-school-crush-with-long-bangs-and-a-quirky-smile kind of cute (though there was nothing wrong with that), but rather in a grown-up male I-will-save-you-from-all-that-frightens-you manner. His glossy hair was cut short above his ears, growing to tousle-length at the top of his head. She restrained herself from dipping her fingers into those tempting strands. Didn't want to freak him out and send him running when he'd only just agreed to help her.

His face shape was somewhere between an oval and a rectangle, and essentially perfect. Even the remaining smudges of blood at his temple did little to mar his handsome angles. His nose was long yet not too wide or flat. A shadow of stubble darkened his jaw, but she suspected he was a morning shaver and liked to keep as tidy as his knotted tie. The zombie debris smudged on his white shirtsleeves must be driving him batty.

Her gaze traveled to his mouth, while she traced her upper lip with her tongue. The man's lips were firm, and sprinkled with a burgeoning mustache on the skin above. That indent between nose and upper lip was something she wanted to press her finger to. It was called a philtrum, if she recalled her explorations in anatomy (for spellcraft, of course). Maybe, if she was really sneaky…

Tor startled and Melissande quickly stood, tucking the offending finger behind her back. "Good morning!"

She waited for him to fully register wakefulness. He shook his head, stretched out his arms and curled his fingers. Then he patted his chest as if to reassure himself of a heartbeat. His next move was grasping for the large crystal hooked at his belt—she figured it was a kind of talisman.

The man looked around the living room, brightly lit by the duck-fluff sunshine beaming through the patio-door windows—and groaned. "What the hell did you put in that tea, witch?"

"Chamomile and lavender. You had a long and trying day. And you said you were tired, so I knew those specific herbs would help you along."

"Help me along? To where? Oblivion? That stuff was hexed. It knocked me out like a prizefighter's punch. It's morning? Bloody hell. I have business—"

"It's only eleven."

"Eleven?" He stood and ran his fingers through his hair. "I've slept half the day."

"I've made breakfast. You have time to eat and get a grasp on the day."

He winced. The man really did have a hard time coming out of a chamomile-tea sleep. Sans spell. She hadn't added anything to the tea leaves. Honest.

"Appointment's at—" he checked his watch "—one."

"Good, then you've time. This way!"

She skipped into the kitchen, which gleamed from a cleaning with lemon juice and vinegar. It was the coziest place Melissande could imagine to create. The kitchen was a large circle that hugged the front corner of the house. A pepper-pot turret capped the room two stories up, giving it an airy, yet still cozy vibe. Everywhere hung tools of her trade such as dried herbs twisted into powerful protection sigils, a bucket of coal (all-purpose magical uses), abundance and peace spells carved into the wooden windowsills, and charm bags hung with bird feet, anise stars and such. Drying fruits and herbs hung before the windows and from the ceiling. Crystals suspended from thin red string dazzled in all the windows. And the curved, velvet-cushioned settee that hugged the front of the house and looked out on the yard glinted from the tangerine quartz that danced as if it were a fringe along the upper row of curtains.

On the stretch of kitchen counter sat the fruit bowl she'd prepared while listening to Tor's soft and infrequent snores. She had already eaten, because who can prepare a meal without tasting? And really, she'd risen with the sun to collect fading peony petals for a tincture.

Stretching out his arms in a flex that bulged his muscles beneath the fitted shirt, Tor wandered into the kitchen and cast his gaze about. He took in the herbs hanging above and the sun catchers glinting in the windows, and then his eyes landed on the frog immediately to his left, at eye level.

He jumped at the sight of the curious amphibian. "What the bloody—? A floating frog?"

Melissande shooed the frog into the dining area where the table mimicked the curve of the windows and wall. The fat, squat amphibian slowly made its way forward, but not without a protesting croak. He did not care to be ordered about. "That's Bruce, my familiar. And he does not float."

"Looks like it's floating to me." Tor sat before the counter, checking Bruce with another assessing glance.

"He's a levitating frog," Melissande provided with authority.

"I don't think I understand the difference."

"Anyone, or any creature, can float. And a floater just, well…floats. But a frog who levitates? That implies he's doing it of his free will. Not many can do that. Am I right?"

Tor's brow lifted in weird acceptance. He tugged at his tie.

"I hope you like smoothie bowls." She pushed the bowl of breakfast toward him and held up a spoon.

Tor took the spoon, but his attention was all over the bowl of pureed kiwi and pear spotted with dragon fruit cut in the shape of stars and sprinkles of cacao and coconut. "It's…blue?"

"The algae powder makes it blue. Lots of good minerals in that. Do you like hemp seeds?"

"I…don't know." He prodded a small pear sphere that she had cut out and added to the bowl arranged to look like a night sky filled with stars. "It's so…decorative. I'm not sure I can eat it."

"Of course you can. Dig in. It's super healthy, and the dragon fruit is only in season for a short time. I already ate. I have a tendency to graze more than sit down for official meals. When you're finished we can discuss your payment plan."

"My payment plan?" He scooped a helping of the smoothie and tasted it. With an approving nod, he ate more.

"You did say you were on the job last night. I took that to mean you were going to protect me."

She fluttered her eyelashes, knowing she had abnormally long lashes. The action was one of her well-honed man-catcher moves. Well, she hadn't actually field-tested it as a kinetic magic, but surely it had some power.

Tor sighed, and the spoon clinked the side of the bowl. "Really? Using the ole bat-your-lashes move on me?"

"Did it work?" she asked gleefully.

He shook his head and snickered. "I am impervious."

Standing on the opposite side of the counter from him, Melissande leaned onto her elbows and gave him another devastating flutter. "That's very sad that a man has to make himself impervious to a harmless little thing like me."

"You, I suspect, are far from harmless." He plucked out a star of white dragon fruit speckled with tiny black seeds and downed it. Stabbing the air in her direction with the spoon, he said, "I'm not buying the tea story. There was something in that brew. And you *are* a witch."

"Wow, you got that on the first guess."

"Don't patronize me. I know my paranormals. All ilks, from shapeshifters to alchemists, to the feral and the half-breeds. And I know…" He set down the spoon and looked her straight in the eyes.

And Melissande's heart did a giddy dance as his brown irises glinted with such a promise she didn't know how to describe it, only it made her know—just *know*—that he had been the right choice. In more ways than she could fully realize.

"Fine." He looked away from her gaze, clutching for the knot in his tie to ease at it self-consciously.

"Fine?"

He conceded with a headshake that was neither a yes

nor a no. At least, he was trying hard not to make it an all-out yes. "To judge from the events that have taken place since we've met, it is obvious you need protection from—whatever that *thing* you have in your purse is attracting. And I would never refuse to defend anyone in need."

Melissande clasped her hands together.

"But I would prefer you simply hand over the heart and let me place it in safekeeping."

"Can't do that, because I know you won't give it back."

"You are correct. The Agency takes containment and security very seriously. Once we obtain an item, there is no way in hell—or Beneath—we'll let that thing out of hand or sight."

"Then that's a big *no way* on the safekeeping suggestion. And I know you can't take it from me because that would be stealing, and that'll have magical repercussions."

"Yeah? Did *you* steal the heart?"

"I…" She walked her fingers along the counter toward the dish towel and grabbed it, then turned to dust the front of the fridge.

"As suspected. Guess that means I'm on the clock for the next handful of days, eh?"

Melissande tossed the towel to the sink and clapped gleefully. "Oh, thank you! You won't regret it. I won't be trouble. I promise."

"That promise has already been broken. Twice over." He scooped in more of the smoothie. "But this ornamental fruit thingy makes up for some of it." He twisted his wrist to check his watch. "I didn't expect to take on a protection job. I do have other plans, and an online appointment I need to make in less than two hours. I have to go home to clean up and prepare."

"Then you'll come back?"

He finished off the smoothie bowl and stood. "You're coming with me. From this moment, I won't let you out of my sight. Not until our contract is complete."

"We have a contract?"

He held out his hand to shake, and Melissande slapped her palm against his. His wide, strong hand held hers firmly. And if she hadn't been so excited for his acceptance, she would have swooned in utter bliss. Maybe she did a little of it anyway, but she gripped the counter to keep her knees from bending and sinking too far into the silly reaction.

"Yes, now we have a gentleman's contract," he said. "Grab whatever you need for the day. We'll discuss details and logistics later, after I've finished with the appointment. Do you think you can stay out of my hair while I do that?"

"Of course. Although, you've some very nice hair. I almost ran my fingers through it while I was watching you sleep."

"You were watch—" Tor put up a palm. "Don't want to know. Let's head out."

"I'll get my things!"

"Uh…" Tor glanced toward the dining table. "The frog stays here."

"Of course he does," Melissande said. With a snap of her fingers, the door leading out to the narrow side yard opened a few inches. "He'll be going out for his noontime bug hunt, anyway!"

This was not how he'd intended his day to go.

Tor liked to keep to a schedule, which could be significantly different from day to day. But that he planned in advance for the following day's events was key. He was always prepared, even for surprises.

Most surprises, anyway. A cute witch sitting in his van with a strange, glowing heart in her purse? That had been an unexpected one.

He walked into his apartment, followed by the witch, who carried two big bags of—whatever it was witches felt the need to carry with them. *Please, do not let it be rank and slithery spell supplies.* He didn't mind the creepy stuff, so long as it was on his terms.

"I've but an hour before the interview," he said with a glance at his watch. "This is the kitchen. There are food and drinks in the fridge. I'm going to shower and shave. Please, don't touch anything that looks like it shouldn't be touched."

"So that means everything?" Melissande dropped her bags to either side of her feet.

Tor winced as he heard something hard *clunk* against the marble floor. "Exactly. You did bring the heart along?"

"Of course."

"I assume you've hexed it well to prevent those we don't want sensing it from…sensing it?"

"Hexes are dark magic. Of which I am learning. Fast. Although protection requires a ward instead of a hex." She bent and dug out a container from the tapestry bag and held it up. It was a clear plastic container, of the sort women used to store food, which they then placed in their pantries.

"That's…" Tor winced. Really? "Is that a plastic food container?"

She nodded enthusiastically. "I store all my spell stuff in these. They're sturdy, and I have the whole pink set. And it's got a stay-fresh seal on the cover."

First it was a floating frog—make that a levitating frog—and now flimsy plastic kitchenware to protect a foul and officious artifact that seemed to attract the denizens of evil. And he'd yet to learn if that black line that curled out at the corner of each of Melissande's eyes into a swish was intentional or a slip of the wrist.

His initial assessment of the witch was spot-on: weird.

"Ward it," Tor said as he turned to stride down the hallway. He couldn't stand before the woman any longer and not wring her neck. Or try to shake her to see what common sense might tumble out from those gorgeous curly black locks that spilled over her cheeks so softly— "Do it outside on the deck so you don't make a mess in the house!"

"Oh, you have a fabulous deck. So big for Paris. Okay, sure! You take care of your manscaping. I'll be good. Don't worry about me!"

He was beyond worried about the woman who seemed lucky to be alive. And her father was the dark witch Thoroughly Jones? The awesome, fear-inducing magic he knew that man possessed hadn't seemed to have been passed down the family tree, at least not concerning the malevolent confidence dark witches tended to possess. Melissande Jones was a fluff of flowers, glitter and star-shaped fruit who didn't seem capable of wielding a crystal wand, let alone handling and controlling a volatile heart.

"Not going to think about it right now," Tor muttered.

He pulled off his vest, made note of the blood on it and set it aside for the maid to bring to the cleaners. The shirt was a loss. Blood never did come out from cotton. He had a standing order from the tailor and received two new shirts every month. Might he have to change that with a desk job? He looked forward to saving on his clothing bill.

But he'd never see that savings if he didn't get ready for the big interview. Pre-interview, that was. The Skype meeting would allow him to speak to a representative from Human Resources, and they'd likely question his skills and qualifications before granting him the ultimate in-person interview with the CEO. He was ready. Or he would be after a shave.

Removing the rest of his clothes, he wandered into the bathroom and flicked on the shower with a wave of his hand over the electronic control panel by the door. The room was big, and the freestanding shower was positioned in the middle of the concrete floor. Simple and sleek, a U-shaped pipe that he stood under sprayed out water from all angles and heights. No curtain or glass doors. The shower area was sloped slightly so the water never ran onto the main floor. He never liked to be enclosed if he could prevent it.

A glance in the mirror found he looked, if still tousled and smeared with blood and ash, rested. A surprise. Had the witch's tea done that for him? He wasn't buying that it had simply been herbs in that tea. He'd slept until eleven. He rarely slept beyond eight.

"Drop it," he admonished himself.

Because he wasn't the kind of guy who worried. Worry kept a man fixed and stifled. He took action. And sure, he'd been set on leaving his current profession behind and leaping forward into a new, normal life with the grand step of the interview today.

But the witch did need his help. And there was nothing wrong with holding down a job until he found a new one. Not that he needed the money. Nope. He was very well-off, thank you very much. But he was a self-confessed type A, and he knew after a day or two of doing essentially nothing, he'd be jonesing for action. His leisure hobbies were few. So work it would have to be.

"Just don't let it suck you back in completely," he said as he stepped under the hot water. *Ahh...*

Whistling Sinatra's "I Get a Kick Out of You" made him smile. His thoughts went to the frog. Which levitated. Wonders never ceased.

Twenty minutes later, he was shaven, his hair styled with a bit of pomade (he liked it a little spiky but also soft enough to move) and the barest slap of aftershave applied to his cheeks. This stuff had been a gift from the young mother who lived on the ground floor of his building. She sold handmade products online. It smelled like black-cherry tobacco. It was different. As was he.

Now he stood in his long walk-in closet before the dress shirts. They were all white, Zegna, with French cuffs, but the one he touched now had a nice crisp collar. And the buttons down the front were pearl—not too flashy, and small. An excellent choice.

He slipped on the shirt, then pulled out the accessories drawer to peruse the cuff links. A pair of silver cicadas was his favorite. He pocketed them until he'd put them on, which would be right before the interview. Usually, he liked to roll up his sleeves if he wasn't going to be talking to the media or trying to impress an interviewer.

He'd wear the black trousers with the gray pinstripes because they were comfortable for sitting, and he didn't expect to battle vampires or to have to clean up a crime scene, so he needn't worry they would pick up lint and dirt like a magnet. A gray tweed vest and a smart black tie speckled with white fleurs-de-lis completed the ensemble.

As he began to roll up his sleeves, Tor thought he heard something like...

Screaming?

He remembered his house guest.

"Can she not go one hour without attracting trouble?"

Before leaving the closet, Tor pushed the button that spun the wall of color-coded ties inward. The entrance to his armory was revealed. Dashing inside, he grabbed an iron-headed club carved with a variety of repulsion sigils, and then raced out of the closet and down the long hallway into the living room.

Chapter 4

The witch wasn't in the living room.

A flutter of something outside on the deck that stretched the length of his apartment caught Tor's attention.

"What is that?" It hovered in the air above his guest. Long black wings spanned ten feet. Talons curled into claws. "Is that a—? Harpie? I have never—"

There was no time to marvel. Tor pulled aside the sliding glass door and lunged to slash the club toward the harpie currently pecking at Melissande's hair. He noted out of the corner of his eye a salt circle with the plastic box sitting in the center. "Grab the heart and get inside!"

"I have things under control!" Melissande called as she tugged her hair away from the harpie's talons.

The half bird/half woman squawked in Tor's ear, momentarily disorienting him. Her whine pinged inside his brain from ear to ear. A guttural shout cleared his senses, and he twisted to the right and swung up the club, catching the bird in the chest, which sent her reeling backward.

"Inside!" he shouted to the witch.

Melissande gathered up the plastic container and scrambled inside. From within, he heard her begin a witchy chant.

"Curse it to Faery!" he called. That was where such things resided. Usually. Unless this one had come through a portal.

The harpie swooped toward him. Tor dove to the ground, flattening his body and spreading out his arms. The cut of her wings parted his hair from neck to crown.

"*Divestia* Faery!" Melissande called.

The harpie, in midair, suddenly began to wheel and tumble in the sky. And then she exploded into a cloud of black feathers.

"Oh, shoot! I don't think I expelled it to Faery."

Indeed, the thing had disintegrated. But it worked for Tor.

Melissande ran out and stood over him. "Are you okay? Are you hurt?"

"Bloody hell!" Tor pushed up and out of the clutter of black feathers. He eyed the neighboring building, where he knew a very curious cryptozoologist happened to live. The shades were drawn. Which didn't mean much. That kid had a way of seeing things he wasn't supposed to see.

"You've a smudge of black salt here. Pity your vest got torn."

Tor charged past Melissande and into the house. Checking his watch, he abandoned his intent to head out the front door and over to the next building. No time to check on the neighbor. The interview was soon!

He marched down the hallway—then abruptly turned and stomped up to the witch. "Do not move. Do not go outside. Do not even blink. And where is that bedamned heart?"

She meekly pointed toward the kitchen counter.

"Did you have a chance to ward it?"

She nodded. "I used a new dark magic spell."

"Fine." He tugged at the torn tweed vest. Not the first impression he wanted to make to a prospective employer. "I'm going to change. Again. Stay right here."

He turned and stalked off.

"But—"

"Nope!" he called back to her. "Not even!"

The man had changed into a midnight blue vest, combed his hair and now led Melissande back toward his bedroom. This was an exciting turn of events! But she didn't read any sexy, playful vibes coming off him. More like stern frustration as he stretched out an arm to indicate the room they entered.

"I need an hour," he said. "With no distractions. No witches getting attacked on my deck. Not even a peep from that little box of yours."

She clutched the plastic container to her chest. He'd hastily grabbed both her bags and now set them on the end of the bed. This was certainly not sexy or playful, being consigned to the metaphorical time-out corner.

"You can stay in here while I'm online. It's a very important interview. So please, please, be quiet. There's the TV on the wall to entertain you. Keep the volume low. And I've got some books on the shelf."

She noted the books were organized by color of their spines, and they were all in a gradient order, from white to gray to black. Did the man not understand color? Fun? Simple civility?

"Can you do that?"

She met his patronizing glare and huffed. "Fine. The teacher wants to put me in detention for an hour."

"It's not that, Mel—" He sighed. "I just…need this interview to go well. I promise as soon as it's over, you have me at your beck and call."

"What's the interview for?"

"New job. Accounting stuff." He checked his watch and shook his head. "I only have five minutes. I've got to sign in to Skype. I'll come get you when I'm done. Do not come out to check if I've finished. Promise?"

"Fine!" she called as he closed the door behind him.

Melissande plopped onto the bed and crossed her arms. A pout felt necessary. Seriously? He was going to treat her like a naughty five-year-old? She hadn't expected the harpie to come swooping out of the sky, wings flapping and bared yet feathered breasts shocking.

"This heart attracts some strange energy." She tapped the container. "Good thing I had Tor to fight off the bird chick."

Because in the moment out on the deck and under attack, she hadn't been able to summon any deflecting magic. She could do that. With ease. A mere flick of her wrist and a few words of intention would make others walk a wide circle around her, or even push back a potential attacker. But she'd panicked. And in such a state, her magic was useless. Only when she'd gotten inside and knew she was out of the harpie's path had she been able to focus.

Now she gave her kinetic magic a try. A twist of her wrist slid the books on the shelf from one end to the other. "Just so. I seriously have to learn to relax during terrifying moments."

Yet despite her faults, she had managed to obliterate the harpie. And that made her sad. She hadn't wanted to kill the thing, just consign it back to Faery. Truly, this strange new magic she sought was going to take some getting used to.

With a nod, she decided she would concede to Tor's request. The man had a life, and he had agreed to help her. Which meant she had to understand that he must have engagements and things to take care of. He wouldn't be able to stand as her guardian 24-7. And she didn't expect that. Should she?

She was getting nervous that the next few days could prove more harrowing than she was prepared for.

Her only chance to acquire the heart had come yesterday afternoon while searching the Archives for the proper spell. A spell she'd already had, thanks to one of her father's grimoires. However, she'd told her uncle Certainly she hadn't the full version, so he had allowed her to search the stacks.

The Book of All Spells contained every spell designed, conjured and/or invoked by every witch who ever existed (and some by witches who were yet to exist). It was constantly updated as new spells were spoken. She'd browsed that massive volume without intent to copy anything out. Never was an item allowed out from the Archives—it was first and foremost a storage facility—but she'd often copied out spells or spent an afternoon studying an incantation to enhance her magic.

Having already studied the spell, she'd gone into the Archives knowing exactly what ingredient was required to make the spell successful: Hecate's heart. And after a lot of digging and sorting through dusty books, old wooden boxes and piles of unidentifiable artifacts, she'd found it wrapped in faded red silk, tucked between a book on crystal alchemy and a steel box that had rattled when she'd brushed it with the back of her hand. She had absconded with it while Uncle CJ had been talking on the phone. With a wave and a *merci, Uncle!*, she'd told him she'd see him soon.

Fingers crossed that her uncle didn't notice it missing from the Archives. It wasn't as though he did a thorough inventory. He very likely had no idea exactly where the hundreds of thousands of items were at any given moment. Melissande had but to perform the spell and free her mother from the haunting, and then she could return the heart. And in the process of invoking dark magic, she could prove to her dad she had what it took to be a dark witch. Just like him and his twin brother and her twin cousins, Laith and Vlas. Even CJ's wife, who had once been a light witch, was now half-and-half.

The practice of dark magic was a Jones family tradition.

"Whoopee." Melissande sighed.

Was dark magic all it was cracked up to be? Try as she might, over the years she'd never been able to bring herself to pull off so much as a hex. Hexes were strictly dark magic. They fed off negative energies and sometimes required demonic familiars. Bruce was about as far from demonic as a familiar got. That amphibian was light, all the way.

Of course, she was aware that without dark magic, light magic could not exist. It was how the universe functioned. No good without bad. No peace without war. No heaven without hell (if you were a human). No Beneath without Above (for the paranormals). No yin without yang. No black without white. No glitter without ash. Someone had to practice dark magic. And in the hands of her dad and his brother, it was handled with grace, respect and kick-ass power.

Her sister, Amaranthe, had possessed that kick-ass skill. She had once been able to stand between CJ and their dad, TJ, and hold her own. Melissande missed her. But lately it was difficult to feel compassion toward her younger sibling for the havoc and utter terror she currently held against their mother.

And if a nudge from Amaranthe was required to push Melissande toward the dark in order to save her mother's sanity, then so be it.

She glanced to the big-screen TV that hung on a black wall. She shook her head. She wasn't much for mindless entertainment. And the books…

"The 7 Habits of Highly Effective People." She read one of the spines. "The man is uptight. But a cute uptight. And what a swing he's got."

Watching him wield the club against the harpie had almost distracted Melissande from the spell. Well, actually it *had* distracted her. Otherwise, the harpie would have been banished to Faery, and not…dead.

"She deserved it," Melissande muttered. "Can't have harpies flying about Paris all willy-nilly."

Bouncing up to her feet, she ran her fingers along the wall opposite the bed, then opened a door, which she assumed was the closet. A press of the light switch at shoulder level flicked on an overhead row of fluorescent bulbs. She leaned in and peered down the long stretch of closet, which was a small room lined on both sides with immaculate shelves and clothing hung and spaced precisely. Everything was neat as a pin. And all in blacks, grays and whites.

A hint of cherries and tobacco tickled her nose. Mmm…he smelled so good.

Unable to resist the adventurous call to explore, she ventured inside.

* * *

Tor thanked the interviewer for his time and ensured him he was on call for an in-person follow-up.

"We'll call you soon if interested, Monsieur Rindle."

"You've got my number. *Merci*."

Tor signed off from Skype and sat back, clasping his fingers behind his head. A smile was irrepressible. He'd aced it. He could win this job—if the in-person interview went well. Which it would. He was experienced in human relations, having worked spin for The Order of the Stake. The only difference was he'd be talking about human issues to humans. He could do that. He had no doubts about his qualifications, and had successfully bluffed his way through the real-world applications parts.

As was necessary to any sort of spin job, he knew how to take rotten lemons and make spectacular lemonade.

Closing the laptop, he hummed a few bars from "They Can't Take That Away From Me" and performed a side-to-side then forward swanky dance step into the kitchen. He opened the fridge and pulled out a bottle of Perrier. He drank half and set it on the counter. The day had taken a turn. It hadn't started out all that swell, with a tea hangover and the harpie attack. All because of the—

"The witch." He'd forgotten about the witch in his bedroom.

Loosening his tie and humming his way down the hallway, Tor felt a new enthusiasm for this unexpected protection job. The witch needed his help. He was the man who could help her. It would be his last hurrah before entering the corporate realm of humans and all things mundane.

Opening the bedroom door, he stepped inside to find…no witch.

"Hmm…" To his left, the closet door was open. Had

he forgotten to tell her not to touch anything? He never overlooked the details most important to him.

Tor stepped into the closet. "I'm finished—"

The witch, who stood at the end of the closet, turned abruptly, her smile exaggerated and her shoulders to her ears. She wore one of his vests over her red blouse. One of his black silk ties hung loosely about her neck. And in her hand was one of his fedora hats.

"Oops," she managed.

Aghast, Tor took a moment to settle his sudden need to shout an oath. He put up a hand. "I don't even want to know." He truly did not.

He had to force himself to leave the closet, but— "Okay, wait." Turning to face the witch, he planted his feet and crossed his arms. "I really do need to know."

Melissande carefully placed his hat back on the shelf and made a point of aligning it as neatly as it had originally been placed.

"Why are you in here?" he persisted. "Wearing my things? Are you…mentally unbalanced?"

She gaped at him. "I got bored. I don't do TV, and I wasn't interested in your literary choices. And I figured if I worked some magic, it could get noisy. And you did reprimand me to be quiet."

"I don't reprimand—"

"Oh, it was definitely a reprimand."

"So you decided to try on some of my things as a means to…?"

"I'm a curious person," she defended herself. "And your clothes smell good. Cherry and tobacco. Like you, I presume. But I can't imagine that you smoke. That's not very attractive. Speaking of, you are much more attractive than I'd expected."

"Than expected?" He had to ask. She had a way of teasing out his curiosity.

"Sure. I thought you'd have a gimp eye or, at the very least, a scar. You know, with the kind of work you do."

He really did not know, and if he thought about it too hard, he might go down the path she followed. And that scared him more than a raging demon or a squawking harpie.

Melissande tugged the tie from her neck, and he rushed to grab it.

"I'll take that." He carefully folded it and placed it in the open tie drawer. A few adjustments to the other ties she'd obviously touched and moved out of order were necessary. "I'm sorry. The interview went long. The rest of the day I'm all yours. In fact, we need to sit down and discuss a game plan."

"Good idea. But I'm hungry."

"Of course you are, you harpie-banishing, vest-wearing witch. Let's just get that vest off you…"

He helped her slip off the vest, and as he did so, Tor drew in the lush scent of her dark hair. Like lemons, but sweeter, almost candy. It was surprising how the scent attracted him. When she turned to give him an inquiring look, for a moment their faces were but inches apart. Exceedingly intimate. And…he had but to move his hand an inch to touch her hair…

"Right." Tor backed away and hung the vest to distract his straying thoughts. Why was he so confused about whether to reprimand or kiss her? "I keep some prepared meals in the freezer. You might like the poached salmon mousse."

"Sounds futuristically unappealing, but I'm in." She marched out of the closet, leaving him in her lemon-scented wake.

She was a handful of kooky and strange, and she annoyed him in virtually every way. Trying on his clothes? He closed the tie drawer carefully. And yet he couldn't think of a single reason to push her out the door and wash his hands of her crazy. So for now, he'd play along.

At the very least, she was entertaining.

Chapter 5

"If that was a job interview," Mel said while prodding at her microwaved dinner, "I'm guessing it's not your usual protection and cleanup work?"

"It's a one-eighty turn from what I usually do. A job in an accounting firm. Completely normal." Tor had finished his meal and was cleaning the plastic bowl for the recycle bin beneath the counter he'd pointed out to her.

"Huh. But you do what you do so well. I don't understand why you'd want another job."

"I need normal. And let's leave it at that. Deal?"

"If that's the way you want to play it. Do I have to stay here while you're protecting me?" The meal he'd taken from the freezer and reheated in the microwave was supposed to be some kind of wild-caught fish-mousse thingy with lemon sauce on green beans but—ugh. "Don't you ever eat fresh food?"

"That's fresh. The chef delivers it frozen. No time to cook, and I eat out a lot. Lots of fresh choices that way."

"Depends on where you eat. I need to go home this evening and pack some stuff if you expect me to stay here. Not to mention bring along half my fridge. A witch can't survive on tough beans and rubber fish."

She shoved the food tray forward, finished. Hey, she'd given it a shot at least.

Tor took it and, using a brush, began the same meticulous cleaning under the running sink water. "As protector, I follow you," he said. "If you need to go home, that's where I will go. I'll be the one who packs some things. And once you're home, you can add a cloaking spell to that thing." He nodded to the plastic container sitting at the end of the counter. "Apparently whatever ward you put on it—"

"I only had time for a quickie ward before the harpie flew in."

The heart didn't glow now. Through the pink plastic, it merely looked like a hunk of meat. Which was odd to Melissande. The artifact was the real heart taken from Hecate's chest. But when she touched and held it, it felt like glass, save for its rubbery texture. If it needed cold storage and might get stale on her, she had better not only cloak the thing but perhaps also keep it on ice.

She sniffed the air, but didn't notice a rancid smell. "That's a good idea. A cloaking spell will enhance a ward. But I'll need Bruce's help since I'm still new to dark magic. Such skills are a lifetime endeavor. It's always a learning process, no matter the magic a witch practices."

"Does the floating—er, *levitating* frog help with your spells?"

"Of course. He is my familiar," she stated as if he should know better.

She slid off the stool and grabbed the heart. "Let's

head out. I'm hungry, and I've got some fruit salad at home with my name on it."

"Let me grab a few things before we leave. Won't be but a few minutes."

The man strolled down the hallway back to his bedroom, whistling as he did so. He had a long, easy stride that spoke of confidence. Something Melissande was always unsure she possessed. And that was the paradox of it, wasn't it? If you weren't sure you had it, then of course you didn't.

Hugging the plastic box to her chest, she wandered down the hallway, cringing only a little that earlier he'd found her wearing his clothes. Everything had smelled like cherry tobacco. It was a deep, heady scent that had lured her to sniff his clothing. And wearing him on her had allowed her to submerse herself in his world. To feel, for a moment, what it must be like to be Torsten Rindle, stylish protector against all means of evil. She bet not a lot of slayers or cleanup professionals could work the bespoke suit like he did *and* still manage to take out the enemy with such skill.

Tor must have plenty of enemies. She hoped he didn't consider witches enemies. A man like him must work for all breeds and species, so hopefully he didn't discriminate. Yet if he did not, that could also imply he didn't discriminate when it came to slaying one.

Peeking into his bedroom, she spied him zipping up a small bag. He startled at the sight of her. "Oh. Uh…" He glanced to the open closet door.

That man's closet was a fashionista's wet dream.

"I, uh…was thinking I should arm myself with a few extra weapons before leaving."

"Sounds like a plan." She remained in the doorway.

Tor stayed by the bed, peering into the closet.

"So?" she prompted.

He pointed toward the closet, then smoothed a hand down his tie.

"You keep weapons in your closet?" she guessed. "I didn't see any when I was—well, you know."

"My closet is a sort of personal stronghold to me."

"Where you keep all things most important to you."

He winced. "It's not so much that—give me another few minutes." He strode into the closet.

And Melissande followed.

"I said to give me a few," he insisted as he spun to stand before a small panel on the wall he'd opened. She hadn't noticed that when she'd been in here earlier.

"You have a secret weapon stash?" She slipped around him and studied the panel, which consisted of a few round buttons. "What does the red one do? Sound the alarm? Send out the hounds? Alert the dragons?"

Tor sighed and gripped the little door that had concealed the buttons. "It reboots the system should an electrical failure occur due to lightning or power outage."

"Oh." Melissande dropped her shoulders. Sounded a lot like her place. It was an old house in desperate need of new wiring. There wasn't a storm that occurred that did not leave her sitting in the dark, from a few minutes to hours. Not that she minded. Candles were always better than electric lighting. "So show me. Oh, come on— it's not like I don't already know your secret identity."

"My secret—" Shaking his head, Tor pressed the topmost button, and the panel that displayed his ties in neat rows swung open. Inner fluorescent lights flashed on to brightly illuminate another room. He waggled an admonishing finger at her. "No touching."

She sighed dramatically, then conceded with a nod and followed him inside.

This secret closet was as big as the clothes closet. The longest walls, parallel to one another, were covered with a mosaic of weapons. Melissande's jaw dropped as she swept her gaze over pistols, rifles and semiautomatic weapons in all sizes and calibers. The knife section boasted the smallest pocketknife to a machete the size of a man's arm. Garrotes were neatly coiled and hung with precision on the gray microfoam-padded wall. Dozens of wooden stakes were neatly stacked on the marble counter. An entire section featured vials of what she assumed were either spells or vile concoctions designed to injure or even kill. The vials with crosses etched onto the glass must be holy water.

Behind her, Tor took down a handgun and checked the bullet cartridge. "You will not tell anyone what you've seen in here."

"Of course not." She ran her fingers over the smooth matte-black finish of something that resembled a rifle but could also be a crossbow. She wouldn't have the first notion what to call all these weapons, let alone gossip about them.

But thinking about gossip…she really needed to get together with the girls and tell them about her studly new protector. Tuesday was living with the handsome vampire Ethan Pierce. And Zoe had been shacking up with the gorgeous slayer Kaspar Rothstein for years. It was high time Melissande got to brag about a sexy man.

But first she needed a better reason to brag than that she was paying him.

"Can you not touch?"

"Of course I can. I mean, cannot." She pulled back her hand and watched as Tor fit a knife in the inside pocket of his suit coat. A box of shells and another Order-of-the-Stake-issue stake were grabbed and tucked away in various pockets or loops on his attire. "What is everything for, exactly?"

"Vampires, werewolves, demons."

"Mermaids?"

"I have a suffocating lariat should I encounter a vicious mermaid."

He ran his fingers over a small iron sphere that had spikes coming out of it.

"What's that for?" she wondered aloud.

"Dragons. They need to swallow it, and it'll explode in their gut. Messy."

Wow. Melissande had never seen a dragon. He lived an exciting life. Gossip-worthy, even.

"Faeries," he recited as he moved his gaze over various weapons. "Reptilian-shifter. Angel. Kitsune."

"What about ghosts?" Melissande tried.

Tor turned his gaze directly on her. "I don't do ghosts."

"Oh, but—"

"No ghosts," he repeated firmly. And he brushed his fingers over the crystal talisman hanging from his belt. She was about to ask what it was for when he said, "Ghosts are just... No. Now come on. And don't touch that!" he called as he filed out of the room.

Melissande made a point of gliding her fingers along a bayonet-like weapon after he'd called out the warning. She barely slipped out into the fore-closet as the door swung shut. Tor gestured for her to vacate the room, and she felt like she was being directed around like a child. She wouldn't have ruined a thing in that room. How could she, a tiny witch, manage to do that?

"You have trust issues," she concluded as she followed him down the hallway and into the living area and kitchen.

"And you are far too trusting," he countered. "Where's the heart?"

She caught herself before saying *oops*. Holding up a staying finger, she then dashed down the hallway, grabbed the plastic container from the end of his bed—took one more moment to inhale his uniquely sexy scent—then rushed back out to the man who waited by the open front door.

"Don't worry," she said as they exited his place with her bags in hand. "We'll sync onto one another's wavelength. I'm already dialed into yours."

"Is that so? Right."

She turned right as they walked outside and remembered he'd parked in that direction.

"Yes," she said. "You're controlling, precise and closed. I might be able to work with that."

They arrived at his van, and he opened the passenger door for her. "You don't need to work with anything. Just be you. Cloak and ward the heart. Go about your normal—whatever it is you do. And let me do my job. Deal?"

As she slid up onto the seat, Melissande turned and stuck out a foot to prevent him from closing the door on her. "How much is all this going to cost me?"

"We'll come to an agreeable arrangement." He shoved her foot inside and closed the door on her.

The man could be intolerable. But that made her smile. He was a tough one. She would enjoy peeling away his layers to get to the soft mushy stuff in the middle. Because everyone had that mush. Some even wore it on their outermost layer.

She did. And she knew she had to toughen up for the unavoidable trial that would arrive in a few days. She could do this. Her mother needed her. And her father would be so proud.

"Maybe I can learn to toughen up from Tor," she muttered. Behind her, he deposited his supplies in the back of the van and closed the door. "Time to step up, Jones. Your family needs you."

She smiled when Tor got in and fired up the engine. She had made the right choice in choosing her protector. But no ghosts, eh?

That could prove to be an issue.

Chapter 6

"Carrots, celery and an onion." Melissande set the vegetables on the counter before the cutting board and handed Tor a knife. "When you're finished, I'll get the mirepoix simmering for soup. Meanwhile, I'm going to the spell room with Bruce to put that cloaking spell on the heart."

"Please do." Tor grabbed a carrot. "Peeler?"

"Nope, I leave the skin on. It's better for you. Nutrients and all that."

He gave an indecisive tilt of the head at that statement. "What is it that you do, anyway?"

"What do you mean?"

"Earlier, when I said you should go about doing what you do. I— Do you have a job? Will I be guarding you while at work? Or are you just…a witch?"

"Oh, I work! I mean, most of the time. I'm a bit of a jack-of-all-trades, like you. I worked at Shakespeare and Company for a few months. Then I got a gig at the ice-cream shop around the corner. I loved that place. They didn't love me giving out free samples. Oh, and just last month I was taking tickets at the d'Orsay, but the manager fired me for letting in tourists on expired city passes. I'm sort of between jobs right now. Which is a good thing. I'll be focusing my attention on perfecting the spell this week and making sure I've got it ready to go. Which means we'll be spending a lot of time together! Come on, Bruce!"

The witch scurried out of the kitchen on a sweep of fluttering black hair. Tor paused before touching the knife to the first carrot.

Bruce floated through the kitchen, passing eye level with Tor. The frog delivered a judgmental croak. Then he floated out. Or levitated. But wait—wasn't levitation more a nontraveling action? It was floating that moved a person—or frog—from one place to the next. Levitation merely moved an entity up and down. Maybe? He wouldn't argue with the witch about it. She was just weird enough to have a completely rational explanation for it.

And he was just curious enough about her to want to engage in such a chat.

"Right, then."

They'd be spending a lot of time together. Tor wasn't sure how he felt about that. While she was definitely pretty to look at, and wasn't at all a threat to him, he wasn't sure her wackiness could be endured for more than short bursts at a time. He did value his privacy and alone time. He had his…ways. And he didn't like when they were disturbed. Like finding his silk tie hanging about her neck. Even if she had been the cutest thing ever—

Well, she had been.

Tor remembered the time he'd had to protect a celebrity singer from the vampire she'd attracted by mistakenly answering a text she had thought was a tease to drink her blood. That woman had clearly defined high-maintenance to Tor. He would never live down the trips to the beauty salon for seaweed wraps if anyone learned he'd had to accompany her there.

He should be thankful Mel was seemingly self-sufficient and didn't seek the spotlight or have too many friends. He liked to keep what he did a secret. It was a necessity.

He turned back to the task. Chop vegetables? Not a problem. He eyed the length of carrot, took a moment to calculate his slices, then began. She hadn't told him how many carrots to chop. There were at least ten in the bag. And as much celery.

As he chopped, he decided this activity was a weirdly soothing task that occupied his brain in a way that allowed him to focus. So often, he had a dozen things going on at once in his temporal lobe. Where was the dangerous creature? How many? Was he surrounded? Where were the escape routes? Had he loaded enough ammunition? What chemical was required to clean up sticky, tar-like demon blood? And would he get a call for the second interview?

He felt the Skype interview this morning had gone well. And hoped to hear back within a few days for another in-person interview. He'd doctored his résumé as best he could, leaving out the parts where he did spin for a group that slayed vampires and, in turn, spinning his skills to show that he worked with the local news outlets and reported on current events that could impact the residents. Spin was making the unordinary sound ordinary. Vampires? Get real! It's just a bunch of satanic idiots.

And while the accounting firm employed number

crunchers, someone in the human resources department didn't require such skills. So he was safe there. And he could make nice with humans and paranormals alike. Changing a man's mind after he'd witnessed a werewolf tromping through his gardenias in the backyard? Not a problem. Did he know that gardenias gave off an intoxicating scent that was actually studied and determined could alter a person's thoughts and give them illusions? No? Well, it was true.

Fake science worked every time.

Tor took pride in what he did. Every single thing he did. He pushed aside the growing pile of orange carrot cubes and eyed the bag of celery.

Everything.

Half an hour later, he set down the knife after a round of near-tears with the onions.

Mel bounded into the kitchen and set the container with the heart on the counter. When she eyed Tor's work, her jaw dropped.

Behind her, Bruce floated over to levitate above her shoulder. The reptile croaked in the most judgmental enunciation Tor had ever heard.

"That's a lot of vegetables," Melissande declared at the sight of the piles that Tor had heaped onto the countertop on a piece of waxed paper. She noted the empty plastic bags that the carrots and celery had been in. "You chopped them all."

"You didn't say not to."

"True. And…" She bent to study the meticulously chopped bits of orange, green and white. All remarkably uniform. "Did you use a ruler?"

"I have very good spatial awareness. I like things in order."

"I guess you do, Monsieur OCD. It looks like a machine did this."

"Thank you."

Mel didn't really care what she was going to do with a shit ton of veggies all chopped into perfect half-inch squares. This was too wonderful. The man was a marvelous freak. And she could fall in love with him right now if he wasn't holding the cutting knife like he intended to defend himself against her.

"You trying to decide whether or not to stab me with that thing?" she asked carefully.

"Huh?" Tor noted the knife he held, blade facing outward and arm pulled back as if to stab. He quickly set it on the cutting board. "Sorry. Force of habit."

"Right." She pulled a big soup pan out of the cupboard, and with a swish of her fingers, she swept a third of the vegetables into the pot. "Thanks to you, I'll have mirepoix for weeks! I should invite you over more often."

"Always happy to help. What sort of soup are you making?"

"Whatever strikes my fancy. I'll get the veggies simmering then toss in whatever is on hand. I've some gnocchi and chicken stock. Toss in some spices and spinach and there you go."

The man straightened his tie, watching as she went about the motions of adding oil to the pot along with the veggies and a good helping of butter, because life wasn't worth living without lots of butter. She and her family bought all their dairy products from a witch who lived an hour outside Paris. She milked her cows by hand and churned butter and made her own cheese. It was heavenly.

Meanwhile, she handed Tor a couple of plastic freezer bags. "Hold those open for me, will you?" He did so, and she again swept the chopped veggies into the containers with but a few magical gestures.

"Handy," he said, sealing the lockable bags.

"It's just…me," she decided. "Kinetic magic. Never known any other way of life. We witches got it going on."

"I'll say. Makes normal look so…"

"Normal?" She leaned a hip against the stove. "How long have you been in the know with us paranormals?"

"Most of my life. Like you, I haven't known much different. But I feel like it can be better away from all this… supernatural insanity. It's hard to explain. It's something I need to do."

Unconvinced, Mel shrugged. "I'll have you know I'm the normal one in my family."

Tor's eyebrow lifted in question.

"It's all about perspective. Family full of dark witches? Then there's little ole sparkly me." She winked at him, knowing her purple glitter eye shadow caught the sunlight. "Do you know what it's like to be the odd witch out?"

"I actually do. Which, again, is reason for me to want to pursue this job."

"I suppose I can understand that. You need to see if the grass is greener. Trust me. It's not." She turned and stirred the pot. "Too bad for us paranormals. Not having you to have our backs."

"Someone else will take up the reins."

"How will that happen? How did you take up the reins?"

"Monsieur Jacques taught me after I moved to Paris. Well, uh…hmm…it's not important."

He hadn't thought about passing along his knowledge to anyone? Mel felt sure he hadn't thought through the whole idea of normal either. But who was she to overexplain something the man had to learn for himself?

"Did you get the heart cloaked?" Tor asked.

"Yep."

He bent to study the container she'd set at the edge of the counter, cracking open the lid to peer inside. "It looks...like a real heart. Wasn't it more glassy when you first showed it to me?"

"It was. And it's not glowing as much either." She seasoned the ingredients with pepper and her favorite smoked black sea salt. "But it doesn't smell, so I think I'm okay."

"That's your determination of an efficacious cloaking?"

She shrugged. "Doesn't it work for you?"

"Well—okay, I can agree with you on that one. Not like I know much about hearts left over from long-dead witches. What, exactly, is this spell you plan to invoke on the night of the full moon?"

"The full *blood* moon," she said.

"Really? Ominous."

"Right? There's a lunar eclipse on the night of the full moon, which will make it appear reddish-orange. The blood moon portends the closing of struggles and new beginnings. Couldn't be more perfect timing for such a spell, if you ask me."

Placing the bamboo spoon across the top of the pot to keep the brew from boiling over, Mel turned her back to the stove to face Tor. The setting sun beamed through the front window in a cozy orange glow and backlit him in the most delicious manner. He looked less uptight this evening. More amiable. And she still wanted to run her fingers through his hair.

It was easy enough for her to reveal a few things to him. As a means to gaining his trust. Because he still wasn't completely on board with her beyond this merely being a job she would pay him for.

"My mother needs protection," she started, then cautioned herself from saying *from a ghost*. The man didn't do ghosts? What did that mean, exactly? "And since she's only recently died—again—my dad is busy getting her back up to speed with life, so I offered to do the spell and take that worry off his hands."

Tor put up a palm to stop her. "So many questions."

"You know my dad," she offered. "Thoroughly Jones, dark witch, husband to a cat-shifting familiar."

"Yes, and your mother is Star. And she's recently died?"

"Fell from the top of my parents' building. She was…" Couldn't tell him Star had been spooked. "Doesn't matter how it happened. Only that she didn't land on her feet. That's a myth about cats. Anyway. You know how it is with familiars?"

"I do. Mostly. I'm not sure about frogs." He looked about the kitchen, but Bruce was nowhere in sight. "I do know that cat-shifters have nine lives. If they die, they come back to life the same age at which they died."

"Exactly. But they never come back with memories of their former life."

"Oh. That's— I didn't know that detail. Wow, that's gotta be tough. For the familiar and for her family."

"Tell me about it. In my lifetime, my mother has died four times. With each death, she forgets I'm her daughter. That she had two daughters, actually. She died after giving birth to me. Poor Dad had to take care of a newborn *and* a newly reborn wife who couldn't remember him or that she'd had a baby. My sister's birth was event free, thankfully. Mom made it through that one like a breeze."

"You have a sister?"

"Had."

"Oh. Sorry." He splayed his hands before him. "Isn't there a life history of some sort you could record to help get your mom up to speed?"

"Dad does keep a video journal for her. It helps a lot. But it's never easy. Poor Mom."

"And you said she needs protection?"

Mel nodded. "It's a private family matter. I hope you can respect that. But suffice it to say, the spell I intend to invoke should bring an end to her worries."

"Is she aware you are trying to help her?"

A sigh felt necessary. Over the years, Mel had struggled to develop a relationship with her mother. It wasn't easy when she died every five or six years. But she did love and respect her, and knew she was kind and so loving. They had baking and listening to loud music in common. And Dad always said she'd gotten her mom's whimsical nature, even though it had been a long time since he'd seen that in his wife.

"She's getting used to the idea of having a husband and a daughter. Again. It always takes a few months to get her back up to speed," she said, and turned to check the pot. The savory aroma of the sautéed veggies perfumed the room.

"I'm sorry," Tor offered. "I'll make sure you're able to perform the spell. I promise."

"Thank you," she said quietly, unwilling to look at him now.

It was tough talking about her family. They were odd, when most already considered them two shades to the left. In the realm of the paranormal, dark witches were the creepy characters that most feared and walked a wide circle around. Add to that a feline shapeshifter and a family history that had seen centuries of persecution and more than a lot of dabbling with the demonic, angelic and the alchemical arts, and—well, it was hard to fit in with human society, let alone attend a party filled with the usual suspects like vampires, werewolves and, yes, even the glitter-crazed faeries. Mel wanted to prove to her dad that she had what it took to master the dark arts and fit in with the Jones family norm. And she would.

Because it was expected of her.

"It's starting to rain," Tor noted. "You want me to close the door in the living room?"

"Just pull closed the screen," she said. She liked to keep the door open a crack for her familiar. "Make sure Bruce is out first. He loves the rain!"

Tor walked into the living room and she heard him mutter, "Hurry up," then the screen door slid closed on its metal track. The smell of the rain mingled with the soup, and she whispered a blessing.

"Bring hope and peace to the Jones family. Free my mother from her persecution." With a sprinkle of thyme over the surface, she infused the blessing with a snap of her fingers and a blink of hope.

"Mind if I turn on some music?" Tor called from the other room.

"Go for it!"

She heard the radio switch between stations, and finally Frank Sinatra crooned softly. At least, Mel guessed it was the singer; she wasn't up on the Rat Pack, but it sounded like a song from that era. And accompanying him was a man she'd thought hadn't the capacity to relax and let loose.

Mel crept over to the doorway separating the rooms and peered around the frame. Tor stood before the radio, singing softly and…he snapped his fingers and nodded his head in time to the music. His voice was deep and resonant, in sync with the music.

Feeling as if she was witnessing a private side of him, she remained by the door frame, ready to whip back out of sight but unwilling to leave, for this new glimpse into the man was incredible. Tor's voice was deep and mellow, and when he performed a dip to the side, he tipped an invisible hat from his head, before sliding back up and turning—

Mel swung back into the kitchen. A grin stretched her mouth, and she pressed her fingers to her lips.

Now that was an interesting man.

Chapter 7

That was the best meal Tor had eaten in a while.

Now he stepped out of the shower adjacent to Melissande's bedroom and grabbed a bright pink towel to wrap around his hips. He used another pink towel to dry his hair. The witch's bathroom had white walls and white floorboards, yet the ceiling was hung with fragrant herbs tied with bright ribbons——same as the long streams of bright ribbons and spangles he'd had to pass through to enter her bedroom. Seemed to be the theme around here: sparkle witch.

Yet the bedroom he'd walked through to get in here had offered unexpected nonquirky decor. The bare pine floorboards had stretched to the wall facing the backyard, which featured a gorgeous, tall, four-paned window that was topped with a half-circle window. Only the bed, a nightstand and a big plush violet lounge chair furnished the room. Richly colored velvets covered the bed. Candles of all colors, heights and thicknesses littered the floors by the window. A witch necessity, he figured.

But the lack of adornment did surprise him. He'd expected fluff and froof, and maybe even pink and purple on her bed.

Whistling one of Sinatra's tunes about *doing it my way* that had played earlier while they'd shared soup and baguettes, he pulled a toothbrush out of his bag and cursed forgetting toothpaste. He opened the medicine cabinet, which revealed an apothecary's buffet. Not a single brand-name product. Everything was in glass vials or stout little pots with handwritten labels.

He read a label. "Belladonna." It was a volatile herb; he knew that much. "Wonder what she uses that for?"

He didn't want to know, because he knew the herb could be deadly.

"Charcoal." He decided that must be the tooth powder and took down the jar. It was messy, but he managed the job and had to follow with a thorough cleaning of the marble vanity. The black powder had gotten everywhere.

When he looked over the pink towel covered with charcoal, he shook his head. "What kind of houseguest am I?"

Realizing he'd left his clothes bag out in the living room, Tor resigned himself to walking down the hallway with nothing but the pink towel wrapped about his waist. He smelled the intense petrichor, an after-rain scent, as he entered the living room and spied Melissande standing in the open patio door, her back to him.

"Duck!" she yelled.

Tor ducked, dodging a look toward his bag, where he knew a handy switchblade was tucked.

But a sudden giggle had him straightening and assessing the situation. From the backyard came waddling through the patio doorway a—

"That's a duck," he said.

"Got that one on the first try. But I did give you a hint. Did you actually…?"

He put a hand to his hip and stretched back his shoulders. "No."

"Oh, yes, you did. You were taking cover."

"You did tell me to duck."

"That's her name." The witch patted the wet fowl on her white head. "She's my Duck."

"You have a pet duck named Duck?"

She nodded cheerfully. "Though she's not really my pet. I'm more hers. She stops in and checks on me daily." Her eyes lowered to Tor's abdomen, where he hadn't yet dried all the water from his six-pack, and he was feeling a warmth rise in his loins standing before her greedy gaze.

"What's that black stuff?" She bent to study his abs closer.

"Charcoal." He stepped back and placed a palm over the smear. "I forgot toothpaste."

"No problem. You can use anything in the house that you need. Except I suggest you avoid the belladonna."

"Not going to be an issue. I shouldn't ask but…"

"It's for girl stuff," she quickly answered. "You know, for when the moon is full and our cycles are raging?"

Tor put up a palm. "Good enough. I should have never asked."

"Does the fact that we women have periods freak you out, Tor?"

"Nope. Just makes you stronger than you all appear. If I bled for days every month, I'm sure I'd be dead."

"Just so." She wiggled her shoulders in triumph. "I'm

going to let Duck sleep inside tonight. She's got a nest over in the corner."

Tor noted the wooden box stuffed with wood chips and feathers. Cozy.

"As for you…" She tapped her lips as she gave it some thought. "I have a cot folded up in the storage room that I might need help getting down from the rafters."

"I can sleep on the couch. Done it once already. It's a comfy couch. Though I'm still not sure that was because of the comfort, or that I was under the influence of some kind of sleeping spell."

"Oh, darling, if I were going to put a spell on you, you would know. I'll grab you some blankets and a pillow. Uh…" Her gaze again fell to his abs and even lower. "Do you sleep in the buff?"

Generally? Yes.

"I left my stuff by the front door." Tor spun to leave the room. "I'll put something on while you get the blankets."

"Don't get dressed on my account!" she called after his departing figure.

Smiling as he grabbed his bag and headed back toward the bathroom, Tor replayed that hungry look she'd given him in the living room. So he worked out and had muscles to show for it. It was necessary when he sported the kind of résumé he did. But if it caught a woman's eye? Bonus points.

On the other hand, did he want to attract a witch's attentions?

"Maybe?" he muttered to himself. A smile was irrepressible. He wouldn't deny she was attractive, and he did like being around her. And below those bright sparkly eyes were a pair of lush, red lips that did entice him to wonder…

He'd never kissed a witch. Nor had he kissed a client.

Right, then. Back to the real world. Now, what to wear beyond the shirts and silk ties he'd packed?

When he returned to the living room in boxer shorts and a longer dress shirt with unbuttoned cuffs, Melissande gave him a nod of approval and then handed him a cup of tea.

"Uh..." He winced and sniffed at the brew.

She sipped her tea, then offered it to him. "I got you covered tonight. It's not bespelled. And to prove it, you can drink mine. I just took a sip. It's safe."

He accepted the mug, then sat on the couch. Mel settled onto the floor before the ottoman, and the duck waddled over to sit on her lap. The tea tasted different and sweeter. Maybe he trusted it. Maybe not. But it was a great way to end the night. A quiet evening after a day fraught with craziness.

"An evening without trouble," he commented.

"I was thinking the same," she said. "My cloaking spell must have worked."

"Must have? You never seem very sure of your magic."

"Lately it has a strange tendency to not last long," she confessed. "It has no sticking power. That's what my sister used to always say when her spells didn't take. I'm not sure why. Some stuff sticks. The stuff that comes easy and right from my heart."

"Maybe the magic you're not completely enthused about feels that lack of enthusiasm and so...?"

"I've not heard it explained quite that way. It is possible. But I hate to consider it the truth. I mean, I'm not overexcited about the full moon spell. If what you say is true..."

"It'll work." Tor set down the cup and clasped her hand. She startled, but then gave his hand a squeeze. He'd meant it as a simple gesture of kindness, but now that they sat there a few moments, in the quiet darkness, it grew to a deeper connection. More intimate.

And he liked it.

"You know dark magic takes a witch's lifetime to master," she said.

"And you think a few days will be just what you need to perform the full moon spell?"

"No, but..." She sighed. Probably unsure, and maybe even worried.

He could relate. For as psyched as he was to start a new job in the normal world, could he really do it?

He shouldn't go there, to that place of doubt. And he didn't want Mel to see him falter. Besides being unprofessional, it was just too...personal.

"You'll do fine," he said. "I know you will."

And he pulled up her hand to kiss it. For a moment he lingered there, with his lips against her warm skin that smelled like soup and spices and lemons. Kind of a crazy moment. He felt as if the world did not exist. As if it were just the two of them. Alike in the most bizarre manner. And yet so different. Worlds apart.

Normal—according to her strange definition—and wanting to be normal. Could they coexist?

Sunlight beamed through the patio doors and shocked Tor awake. He didn't do bright light in the mornings. That wasn't a weird vampire thing. It was common sense. Any sane human needed to cling to the few rare hours he did manage to sleep.

He swung his legs off the couch, and his bare feet landed on a furry rug before the coffee table, his toes sinking deep into the soft texture. It was fake *something*, with long white nap that felt good beneath his wriggling toes. But he still winced at the sunlight.

Standing, he padded over to the patio door, gripped the gauzy white curtains in preparation to pull them closed—at least until he could gather his wits about him—when he noticed something moving in the yard. It was small and—there was more than one. It couldn't be the duck called Duck.

Tor narrowed his gaze. Frogs didn't move like that either.

Chapter 8

Something crouched near what looked like an iron cauldron under a chestnut tree. Tor started to wonder about the big black pot—how cliché could a witch get?—but his attention quickly returned to the moving thing.

"What the hell? Is that…? No. Really?"

Dashing for his pack, he pulled out the pistol loaded with salt rounds, then spun and pulled aside the patio door. Stepping outside in his shirt and boxer briefs, he wandered across the concrete patio crowded with wicker chairs and potted plants and right up to the edge, where long grass blades hugged the concrete.

The things growled at him. And revealed fangs. And then an ear dropped off one that resembled a dog. Not a normal dog either. This one was big and—half its fur was missing, and the two front legs were bones.

"Zombie dogs?" Tor muttered. "What the…? That's impossible. Zombies don't—" Gulping back the denial, he crouched into defense mode.

There were five of them, in all sizes ranging from a dachshund to what must have been a former wolfhound. They tromped toward him with maws opened to reveal fangs and black ooze dripping to the grass.

Taking aim, Tor fired at the wolfhound as it leaped for him. The salt round pierced the creature's mouth and exited the back of its head, spraying bone in the too-bright air. That alerted the other beasts—and they all charged.

"Holy crap!" a voice called out from behind Tor.

"Stay inside! Close the door!"

Firing at the smallest one that crept along the ground, Tor was startled when Mel touched his back and joined his side. "I said to stay inside!"

"What are those creatures? They're…dead? Oh mercy, the heart."

"I thought you put a cloaking spell on that thing?"

Another zombie leaped toward Tor, but midair, the body fell apart and a crumble of bones landed on the grass.

"I did, but I opened the container this morning to check that it was all right. That must have broken the spell. I wasn't thinking. Like I told you, the dark magic I've been studying never lasts for long. That one is going after Bruce!"

Tor twisted and aimed for the creature that had its jaws open less than a foot away from the slowly fleeing levitating frog. He pulled the trigger. Bones scattered.

"One left," Mel narrated. "I could toss a fireball at that one."

Tor caught her arm just as she was ready to fling whatever magic she thought might help. "Let me handle this. Go inside! And take your frog with you!"

"Fine. But I hardly think zombie dogs are a threat."

At that moment, the final creature scrambled across

the grass and nipped at Mel's ankle, which, thankfully, was encased in leather from the knee-high boots she wore.

"Not a threat, eh?" Tor kicked at the thing, and yet it clung to her boot with tenacious fangs.

"Shoot it!"

He was out of salt rounds. So instead, Tor clobbered the thing over the head with the pistol barrel. That released its hold so he could shove Mel toward the open patio door. The zombie dog followed close on her heels. The patio door slid closed. The dog got its head inside and—

—the torso and legs of the dog fell to the ground as it was decapitated.

Tor gave a cursory glance about the yard. No more threats. And now he spied the holes in the garden, from where the dogs must have risen. Former pets buried in a pet cemetery? No doubt about it. But the witch didn't strike him as a dog person.

A white-headed duck popped its head out from behind the cauldron and quietly quacked.

"All clear, Duck," Tor offered. He made to shove the pistol in the holster, which should have been under his arm, then remembered he had just risen and wasn't suited for this kind of adventure.

"The witch needs more protection from herself than anything." He glanced to the patio door, behind which Mel, clutching the frog to her chest, stood staring at the dead dog's skull. "The full moon can't come soon enough."

Melissande set a smoothie bowl on the counter and a spoon beside it. She heard Tor come back inside, swear as he stepped over the slimy remains of the beheaded zombie and wander into the kitchen.

"Breakfast," she announced cheerily.

"I'll clean up the yard dogs first."

"Zombies," she corrected.

He lifted a finger in preparation to argue her point, but then did not.

Standing before the counter, he inspected the smoothie. It was made with blueberries, chia, dragon-fruit stars, pomegranate arils and a touch of magic. It made the whole dish sweeter, but didn't alter or bespell the eater.

Mel didn't notice the smoothie so much as the man and what he was not wearing. She'd been too frightened when standing out on the patio to notice his attire, but now... His legs were long and muscular and dusted with dark hairs. Powerful thigh muscles flexed with his movement. Even his feet were cute.

"What?" he asked, then dipped a finger into the blueberry concoction.

"You're not wearing pants." She stated the obvious, and then quickly wondered if she should have pointed that out. "But that's fine by me."

"Same thing I had on last night. I don't normally sleep in—I'll be right back."

"Don't get dressed on my account!" she called as he slipped into the living room.

Darn. Why did she keep telling the man to put on clothes? The last time she'd had an opportunity to admire eye candy had been... Mel sighed and shook her head. Just because her dating life was awkward and random at best didn't mean she didn't have some great experiences. But lately she'd been too focused on her family to consider her own needs and desires.

Desires being a key word on the list of overlooked things required to make a person happy. She had a half-naked man in her home right now whom she'd just told to put on pants.

"I didn't tell him that," she whispered back at her conscious. "I would never."

"What's that?" Tor glided back in, now wearing pants and buttoning up his shirt to hide those incredible abs. Of which she'd not taken the time to do a proper ridge count. Stupid. He scooped a serving of smoothie into his mouth, followed by a few more. "I'm going to clean up the mess quickly. I'll finish this decorative meal—" two more scoops "—when I get back in. I'm assuming those were all former pets of yours?"

"No! I don't do dogs. Why would you guess that?"

"They were revenants."

"I thought you said zombies don't exist?"

"They don't. And yet…" Tor shook his head. "You've got me thinking down new tracks lately. Maybe they were zombies. I honestly don't know. Haven't had experience with zombies. But they did climb up from graves in the garden."

"Oh, gross. The former owners must have had dogs. I've only lived in this house five years. I do recall I had to do a major cleaning job to remove all the dog scent and hair from the walls and floors. Smudged this place for days to get out the smell."

"That heart." Tor pointed to the container on the counter next to his smoothie bowl. "Needs to be cloaked, chained up and—I don't know—buried until the full moon."

"I'll recloak it right after you finish breakfast. I'll need a triad to invoke a stronger spell this time. You'll serve as one of the threesome."

"Whatever you need." He scooped in more smoothie,

then grabbed the bowl and the spoon and wandered into the living room to clean up the mess.

Twenty minutes later, Tor returned with an empty bowl, dirt smudges on his face and a grin that popped in the dimples on his cheeks. She hadn't noticed those impressions in his cheeks before. Never thought something like that could appeal to her, but—wow. The dimples seemed to only draw attention to his sparkling eyes. Laughter hid in his irises, but it wasn't something he let loose too often. And that gave his whole cute-guy vibe a hint of stoicism that brewed it all into an irresistible facade.

It was hard not to grab him for a hug so…Mel did just that.

"Thank you," she said, pressing her cheek against his shoulder. He smelled so freaking good. Overripe cherries and sharp tobacco-infused leather. Mmm…

"Just because I buried them doesn't mean they'll stay put," he offered. "I'm fresh out of chlorinated lime to dissolve the bones. If you know a spell that'll fix them in the earth, I'd suggest you perform one."

"I'll look one up in my father's grimoire. I own a copy. You've some dirt on your chin."

She licked her thumb and made to dash it over his chin, but he caught her by the wrist. For a moment, she suspected his stoic need to always be the strong one took flight and was replaced by sudden desire. They stared at one another for what felt so long, but could have only been two seconds. And just when she felt herself go up on her tiptoes—

The doorbell rang. Tor's musculature tightened and he gripped her wrist painfully. Her startled gasp shook him out of warrior mode, and he released his grip.

"Sorry. You expecting company?" he asked.

"No. No one ever visits little ole me."

"Then stay put." He swung around the corner into the living room and reappeared with the salt-round pistol.

Impressed by his ability to switch from cleanup guy to alpha protector, Mel felt her heart thump double time. She'd not asked for a hero, but somehow one had dropped into her life. Everything he did fired all the desire receptors in her body. But she knew now was no time for another hug. Even if a kiss had been *so close* to happening. Not when he was responding to his need to protect.

She peered around the corner, following Tor's strides as he walked up to the front door. He opened the door, pointed the pistol barrel into the forehead of the man waiting on the front stoop and—

"Dad!" Melissande yelled.

She heard Tor mutter, "Ah, shit," and then witnessed her father's remarkable magic fling her protector against the wall and pin him there, feet dangling a foot above the floor.

Chapter 9

The dark witch's grip about Tor's throat cut off his air. But he wasn't going to struggle. Or argue with the man. He had been the idiot to point a gun at his head, thinking it might have been a dangerous intruder intent on harming Mel.

His mistake.

Now he'd pay.

"Who are you?" Thoroughly Jones demanded in a deep and slightly malevolent voice. "Why are you in my daughter's home? And how dare you…" He squeezed his fingers so Tor actually squeaked. The silver rings the witch wore cut into Tor's larynx. "…challenge me?"

Tor could but blink. And hope he'd survive to fight more backyard-garden dogs, should that be what the universe tossed his way.

An aura of sweet darkness surrounded the man with onyx hair who wore velvet and leather and whose blue eyes held wicked secrets that Tor didn't want to know. Ever.

"Dad, don't hurt him! He was only trying to protect me."

"From your own father? Insolent—wait." The witch's eyes narrowed as they took in Tor's face. Tor didn't want to look into them. A witch could read a man's soul. "I know you. You're the shill for The Order of the Stake."

Not a shill, Tor wanted to mutter. *A master of spin, actually.* But he'd best remain silent. Not that he could utter more than a garbled plea. His feet still dangled, and his spine was lengthening. That was not a pleasant feeling.

Thoroughly released him and stepped back, yet Tor remained magically pinned to the wall. The dark witch snickered at his helplessness. His expression was menace mixed with a daring mischief.

"I hired him to protect me," Mel insisted.

Her father glanced to her and assessed her truth, then with a nod, turned back to Tor. With a hissed magical word and a slash of his hand, he released Tor from his exile pinned to the wall. Tor dropped, but managed to catch himself and not go all the way down. But he did drop the pistol on the hardwood floor. He'd leave it there. Witches were tricky, and he knew well this dark witch was not someone he wanted to anger any more than he already had. For he could tap into Daemonia, summon demons and exorcise all sorts of strange creatures.

"Why are you in need of protection, Lissa?" Thoroughly asked while he maintained an icy stare on Tor.

"It's the spell I promised you I'd do for Mom. It required an ingredient that is volatile. I felt the need to take extra precautions for the next few days until—you know."

"I can protect you," TJ insisted. His sneer at Tor indicated his unspoken words: *a hell of a lot better than this idiot.*

"You're busy with Mom. Dad, don't worry about it. I got this. Okay?"

Tor sensed the witch release his breath and saw his shoulders drop as he took another step back and nodded, relenting to his daughter's gentle persuasion. "Right. We did talk about this. You can handle it. I know you can." He offered his hand to Tor. "No hard feelings?"

Tor slapped his palm against the witch's and shook. Their squeeze pressed the heavy silver rings into his skin, and Tor wondered if his bones would take on the impressions. "If you can forgive my rashness, I'll forgive yours."

"Done. I know your reputation. Torsten Rindle, correct?"

Tor nodded.

The man sighed heavily, but with a positive resignation. "You and my brother had a row a few years back. He tends to be impulsive and dangerous with his magic. But…I know your integrity is unwavering. I trust you to protect my daughter."

Melissande embraced her dad from the side and laid her head against his shoulder. He was a tall, dark one, but Tor's gaze was level with his eyes.

"Now that we're all buddies, let's go have some tea and you can tell me why you stopped by," she said. "You never visit, Dad. I sometimes wonder why not."

"You know it's your mother." He wrapped an arm around his daughter's shoulder, and the twosome strolled toward the kitchen. "She's…a handful."

Tor remained by the wall, tugging at his tie, which constricted him more than usual. He felt suddenly unwelcome. It would probably be best to give the two some space. Besides, his throat ached, and he wasn't eager to see what further torture the witch could offer if angered.

"I'm going to do a perimeter check!" he called, and picked up the pistol and stepped outside.

Closing the door behind him, only then did he release his breath. He'd almost had his larynx crushed by *the* Thoroughly Jones. One half of the notorious Jones twins who were Paris's most infamous dark witches. If you were in the know about witches, you knew of them. And a wise man walked a wide circle around their air.

Why had he agreed to protect his daughter? Oh right, because she'd batted her lashes at him, and those big doe eyes had stolen away a smart refusal.

Never before had he allowed himself to be swayed by pretty eyes. And a sexy smile. Not to mention, she sparkled. And she was so seemingly unaware of her cuteness. Or that she was a bit inept with her magic. And the frog and duck. What was it about her menagerie? It was all endearing. And appealing. And...

"What the hell have you gotten yourself into, Rindle?"

Was he starting to have feelings for the wacky witch? That wasn't his MO. He didn't notice women while on an assignment. It had never been a focus for him when his job, and the lives of others, depended on him staying in control.

And yet their proximity was teaching him a different perspective on how to handle client relations. Mel demanded a closer, yet more casual approach. She insisted he let down his guard while also maintaining it. It was a weird dichotomy that made him shake his head.

And he'd held her hand last night. Hadn't wanted it to end.

Was he in over his head?

"Never. I can handle one little witch. Even a sparkly one."

He stepped around to the backyard and decided poking about to ensure there were no more pet graves on the property would be a wise move.

Five minutes of searching confirmed his suspicions

that any buried dead thing had already risen. Tor stood at the back of the yard beneath a fall of lush pink flowers that smelled like women's perfume. No more revenants. Or zombies. Hell, really? Was he going there?

It was possible that zombies did, indeed, exist.

Sliding a hand over the crystal talisman hanging from his belt, he smiled as a pair of squirrels chittered and scampered up the trunk of an ancient chestnut tree that mastered the back corner of the yard. And there was that cauldron capped by a round wooden cover. Dare he peek inside?

The hairs on the back of his neck tightened. And it wasn't from thoughts of what could be inside the iron cauldron.

Tor didn't turn around. He didn't want to. He felt the man's presence as a clutch about his throat. Again. But this time he wasn't pinned against the wall.

"Rindle."

Tor winced as Thoroughly Jones joined his side. The air had changed and felt heavy on his shoulders. And he had the foreboding thought that if he swallowed, it would use up the last of his saliva. The witch tapped a pink bloom, and the stamen released a fall of bright yellow pollen. Much more than was normal.

Witches, Tor thought. Too freaky for his peace of mind. Yet he remained calm. Cool was his forte.

"More than being surprised by having a gun pointed in my face at my daughter's front door," TJ said, "finding you in her home, alone with her, puts up my hackles."

Was the man really going to play the part of threatening father to his daughter, who was a grown woman? She had to be midtwenties, at least. An independent woman who lived on her own and had to be long out of her father's care.

"She found me," Tor said. "She hired me. I'm doing a job."

"Uh-huh."

Tor winced as something tightened about his neck. The man hadn't moved to touch him, but he was working some sort of subtle magic on him.

"Protecting your daughter requires 24-7 guarding," Tor said. "I slept on the couch, if that's what's sticking in your craw."

"Lissa is a big girl. I don't interfere in her love life."

"This is not a—" Tor shook his head.

"Exactly. Even you don't know what this is. I can see the stars in my daughter's eyes when she speaks your name. She's always been flighty and walks a few inches above the earth. *Whimsical* is what my wife calls her."

Tor sensed the dark witch hadn't a clue how to grasp the concept of that word. How Mel had turned out so completely opposite her father was a wonder to him. *Whimsical*, indeed.

"You will ensure no harm comes to my daughter."

"That's sort of how it works, me being a protector."

"Sort of?" TJ turned and lifted a brow. The menace had returned to his gaze. He didn't fit in this garden of sweetness and wonder. Unless you factored in the zombie dogs.

"She's safe with me. I guarantee it."

"You are a mere human."

"I've been around the block. I know things. And I take precautions."

"Yes, your reputation is solid." The witch's gaze dropped to the quartz talisman at Tor's hip. "But why ghosts?"

Unwilling to get into that conversation, Tor crossed his arms high across his chest. "Listen, if you don't trust me—"

"I do. I…I came out here to apologize. I was too hasty

at the front door. But self-preservation is ingrained in us all. I've seen things, Rindle."

"I imagine the entire Jones family has. Of course, Melissande is—she's a light witch." Tor stated the obvious, but he wasn't sure how to approach his curiosity with her father. He wasn't going to come right out and state he thought she was doing something to prove herself to her father.

"She'll come around," TJ said breezily. Now he splayed out his hand before him and the flower canopy shuddered, dropping a storm of pollen onto the grass. "You allergic, Rindle?"

Only to dark witches. "No. Why do you ask?"

"Ghosts," TJ muttered. A quirk of his brow pondered the word, but he didn't say more.

Tor wasn't going to give him anything. Especially not about ghosts.

"I'll foot your bill," TJ suddenly said. "Don't bother Lissa about that."

"Of course."

"You going to be here 24-7?"

"That's how—"

"—it works. Right. My daughter is beautiful."

"That she is. And if you think intimidation is necessary here, I don't really understand. Like I said—"

"Just doing your job." TJ chuckled. "The results of your cooperation with my daughter will surprise us all. Know that whatever you expect to happen? Will not." The witch turned to him completely and held his hand before him, then slowly clenched his fingers into a C shape. And as he did so, Tor felt the grip about his throat again, not touching, but warning. "Don't fuck this up, Rindle."

The grip released and Tor breathed in quietly. But instead of nodding like a chastised little boy, as the witch turned to leave, Tor gripped him by the arm, stopping him. TJ's look could have maimed, and it probably would have if Tor held on any longer, but he wasn't about to back down to magical grandstanding.

"She's doing this for *your* family," Tor said. "Don't let whatever this is between us become a war you don't need to fight."

The witch lifted a brow. Smirked. Then with a nod, he tugged his arm from Tor's grip and strolled out of the garden and around the side of the house.

Tor nodded. "Damn bloody straight."

Mel kissed her dad on the cheek and walked him to the front door. She'd understood immediately when he'd confessed that her mother was a handful. It had been three weeks since Star had died. She'd taken a leap from the top of the building in an attempt to make the neighboring building. It hadn't gone well.

TJ was suspicious of that leap. As was Mel. Could her sister have been responsible?

Of course she had been.

That made invoking the spell under the full moon even more urgent. To once and for all end Star's torment and to put her father's mind at peace. It always took a few months for her dad to ease Star back into the life she had once led. That involved showing her videos of her family, walking her around the house and telling her stories of all the adventures they had had. It was trying and hard on Thoroughly.

The fact that Vika, Melissande's aunt, had offered to spend the afternoon with Star and give Thoroughly a few hours off had been gratefully appreciated. He'd only wanted a few hours to relax, breathe, and sit and hold his daughter's hand. They had both watched Tor poke around in the backyard garden. The bright pink clematis had tickled his skin, and purple foxgloves had brushed his ankles as he'd poked and prodded the soil. At one point, he'd fired his weapon into the ground and a sift of dark ash had spumed up. Taking care of any remaining potential zombies, she'd decided.

"He's a strange one," her dad had said. And then they'd both looked at each other and laughed.

Because really, they knew, in the world of strange, their family ranked right up there. Yes, even in the paranormal realm.

At the front door, her dad pulled her into one of his generous hugs and they stood there for a long time. Mel loved it when his hair covered her face and she nuzzled her nose against his chest, drawing in his earthy dark scent. Most would question his motivations to the dark and the acts he had committed over the decades in the name of his magic. He had done some bad things. Yet just as many good things. He was perfect to her. And she would never let him down.

"What does the protector mean to you?" he suddenly asked.

Mel bowed her head and shrugged. "He's doing a job, protecting me."

TJ lifted her chin with a finger. She couldn't look into his eyes for long without a sigh. "I like him, Dad. He's…different. Like me. I've always been the weird one in the family."

"The black sheep," TJ provided, as they'd labeled her more than a few times over the years. "Be cautious, Lissa. But remember I love you. No matter what you are. Weird or normal. And promise me you'll not get in too deep," he asked of her. "Dark magic must be approached with caution."

"I've watched you over the years, Dad. I know what I'm doing." Mostly. Too late to beg leave of the task now. "Don't worry about me. I'll take care of the problem. Then our family can finally breathe a sigh of relief. Give Mom a kiss for me, will you? I'll stop by after the full moon. I don't want to run into Amaranthe, if at all possible."

"She had your mother shivering under the sink all last night. Your sister seems impervious to my magic. I can't expel her from the house. And I have expelled many a spirit in my lifetime."

"This spell will work," she reassured him. "Its efficacy is increased by blood invocation. And my blood is my sister's, so…" She kissed him again on the cheek and opened the front door. Tor walked around the side of the house. "Thanks for taking care of that last zombie," she called to him.

"Zombies don't—uh…huh," Tor said as he again shook Thoroughly's hand. "Monsieur Jones."

"Do not let any harm come to my daughter," Thoroughly said firmly.

"Absolutely not. She's in good hands. But then, you know that."

TJ eyed Tor up and down and then kissed his first two fingers and drew a sigil in the air between him and Tor. The movement left a brief violet illumination in its wake. He turned and gave Mel a kiss on the cheek, then strode down the sidewalk to the street, where his car waited.

"He's intimidating," Tor commented as they watched the car roll away down the street.

"Tell me about it."

Tor touched his forehead. "Did he just curse me?"

"No, that was a blessing."

"I'm not sure a blessing from a dark witch is such a good thing."

"Oh, it's good. And rare. He trusts you. And that's remarkable coming from my dad."

Tor exhaled deeply. "Then I'll take it for what it was."

Mel tugged Tor inside. "Let's perform the cloaking spell. And this time hope it sticks. We don't need another zombie invasion."

"Zombies don't—"

"Yeah, yeah, whatever." She tugged his hand, cutting off his protest. "Come on, Bruce! Meet us in the bedroom for the invocation!"

Chapter 10

Tor pushed aside the silly bunch of multicolored ribbons and spangles and wandered into Mel's bedroom, a little unsure, but a lot more curious. Whistling a tune about witchy women, he took in everything. The room's atmosphere, with its natural wood and rich scent of herbs and spices, wrapped him with a welcome calmness. The ceiling was scattered with dried flower bouquets of sorts he hadn't names for, though he suspected all had come from her garden. It smelled great. The curved window on the far wall looked out on the lush junglelike backyard. And that plush violet chaise across the room looked like something he could settle into with a book and lose the afternoon soaking in the sunlight.

If a guy did things like that. But Tor did not. He hadn't time for relaxation. He—well, he was leaving his current profession, but that didn't make him any less busy. He expected a call for a follow-up interview soon. And then he'd be back to the grind. He liked to stay busy. It kept him from…

Thinking about things he'd best not consider. Like mistakes and hopes and dreams. Some people were put on this earth to do the creative stuff like make art, build empires, dance and share their feelings. And practice witchcraft.

Others—like him—had to balance that out with hard work and a go-getter attitude that had never served him wrong. He had no definition for vacation. Life demanded. He answered. With a gun in one hand, a machete in the other and…a Sinatra tune tossed in for sanity.

A man couldn't be so hard that he didn't allow in a creative trickle. The songs he sang kept him from jumping over the edge. Singing improved his mood, so he allowed in that bit of creativity whenever possible.

The witch who lived in this house was as creative as they came. And wild and exotic and weird and quirky. And…beautiful. He wondered if her bedroom was reflective of her soul, peaceful and serene, while the rest of the house and the backyard mimicked her outer quirks.

Startled by the frog who floated past his shoulder, Tor stepped aside and watched as it hovered over where Mel was laying items outside a circle that appeared to have been poured out of black salt onto the hardwood floor.

"Come sit over here," she directed. "This is awesome to have a triad. That's probably why the first few cloaking spells didn't stick. I've never done one before. Well, of the dark sort. Live and learn."

"Right, because, you know, there's nothing like fighting revenant dogs in a person's backyard because the spell didn't work."

"I need more practice with this dark stuff. It'll be perfect on the night of the full moon." She closed her eyes.

Briefly, Tor wondered if she were praying her words would come true. He certainly hoped they did. For her sake. And for her family's sake. It was a tough deal they had going on. And if he could help in some small way, he would.

He stood outside the circle where she'd pointed out and observed her collection of items. A crystal knife, a feather, a couple potion bottles of which he really didn't want to know the contents. Three black candles were placed around the circle, nestled into the black salt. And a few crystals in shades of purple, blue and red were scattered beside her leg.

On her head sat the most remarkable tiara. It wasn't a fancy diamond concoction. It looked cobbled together with wire and different-sized clear quartz points.

"You're a princess then today?" he commented.

"Huh? Oh." She tapped the tiara. "It's my spell-casting crown. I made it from Lemurian quartz. It focuses my magic. What? You think it's too haughty?"

"Nope. I like it on you a lot. You could do the princess thing."

She waved off the comment with a dismissive gesture. "I don't think so. Too much fanciness and fuss for me. But you really like it?" She blushed, which pinked her cheeks as if with makeup. So pretty.

"It suits you. But you don't do fancy and fuss? I thought you were the glitter queen."

"Oh, for sure!" She drew a fingertip under her eye, then followed the curve of black sparkly liner that Tor thought gave her an Egyptian flair. "But you know, *fancy* as in *haughty* and *fuss* as in *high maintenance*."

"Ah. Nope, you're not that. Not when you have a cauldron in your backyard. You know that's a bit…"

"Cliché? It is, but I make soap in it and I like to do

that outside because of the fumes. And Duck naps in it. Sit," she said. "Bruce is ready and so am I."

Tor sat, awkwardly finding a position that worked with crossed legs. A bloke didn't sit on floors all that often.

He eyed the frog, who levitated across the circle from him. As far as backyard frogs went, the critter was large. More like a bullfrog. Should he hold the thing, it would cover his palm. Not that he had any intention of doing that. Something about a floating frog creeped him out a hell of a lot more than an attacking harpie or long-dead dogs risen from the garden.

"How does Bruce figure in as a third hand?" he asked.

"Oh, Bruce is my secondhand man. You're the third." Mel placed the plastic container with the heart in the center of the circle. "As my familiar, Bruce helps with all my spells."

He didn't want to know. Really, he did not. And yet…

"Is he a magical frog?"

She tilted such a look at him, Tor swallowed. And then he said, "Of course he's magical. He can levitate. My mistake. Sorry, Bruce. No offense. Can he…? Understand what I'm saying?"

"The question is, does he *want* to?" Mel hid a smirk behind a brush of her hand across her face as she straightened the crystal tiara. So beautiful. "Are you ready?"

"I'm all in." Tor rubbed his palms together. "Just tell me what you need me to do so we can get this show on the road."

"Why? Are you in a hurry?"

"No, but if I hear another knock on the front door, we've ruled out your father, so it can only bode danger."

"I get it. There is a need to keep whatever is picking up on the heart's vibration from feeling that and coming after it."

"Seems like it attracts dead things."

"That makes sense since it's going to bring a dead thing back." Mel spread her palms over the circle and spoke a Latin word that lit the candles. Sulfur briefly tainted the air.

But Tor was still stuck on what she'd said. "This heart is going to bring a dead thing back? Wait. Necromancy?" He put up a firm yet protesting palm. "I didn't get the memo on that particular activity. I thought this was going to be a spell to—well…" He made a thinking noise as he got stuck on pondering this new development. Really, he didn't have any information. And since when had he so blindly stepped into the fray?

Right. When the one leading the charge batted her glittery lashes at him. And she was no less attractive now that she had shown him how dark and desperate her family and lifestyle was. Damn.

"No time for discussion," Mel rushed out. Closing her eyes, she waggled her ringed fingers over the circle. "I've already tapped into the heart's aura. The spell has begun."

She cocked one eyelid open. She had the same deep blue irises as her father. And almost the same chastising look. Though she hadn't mastered the evil, I-can-hurt-you-with-a-snap-of-my-fingers look. She was the furthest thing from evil.

As far as he knew.

Tor swallowed and decided he would get an answer to his question later. And he would. Because bringing back the dead did not sound like a day at the beach.

"Should I close my eyes?" he whispered.

"Whatever makes you happy," the witch answered. "Uh, but…hmm."

"What?" Tor opened his eyes.

"That crystal on your belt. That might interfere with the spell. What's it for?"

He clutched the heavy quartz. "Just protection. It's focused only for me. It won't cause problems with other magics. I know that."

She considered it while he hoped she wouldn't question him further. It was too personal. And he never went anywhere without this talisman.

"Fine. You'll tell me about it when you're ready."

He would never be ready.

"Here we go."

Mel quickly slipped into a fast and focused whisper that streamed words into the atmosphere Tor did not recognize. Her hands moved over the plastic container, sweeping, drawing sigils. Or so he supposed. Her movements did not leave a trail of illumination as her father's had. She used the feather to draw around the entire circle as her chants grew rhythmic. The flames flickered higher and thinner until they were as narrow and tall as each of the candles.

Tor did not necessarily oppose magic. When it was used for good. And while he'd been witness to its use on many occasions, he still could never shake the prickle of unease that rose at the back of his neck when it occurred. Witches could summon power from out of thin air, using elements and familiars. And it was freaky.

"All right," she announced. "Now we all join hands and I'll complete the cloaking."

Tor reached to clasp her hand. It was warm and felt small and delicate in his grasp. The connection ignited a sudden want in him, not so much sexual as sensual. He liked being near her. She surrounded him with a unique air. Soft yet playful. She teased at his staunch need to remain, well, staunch.

When he reached to the left, he realized her request wasn't possible. "Frogs don't have hands."

Melissande sighed. "Do what I'm doing," she instructed.

He saw she had extended her forefinger so the amphibian's front paw or foot—whatever the hell it was—curled over it. Right, then. Tor reached out and the frog slapped his webbed footpads over the tip of his finger. Weird. Just...

He wasn't going to overthink this one.

The witch recited three final words. The candle flames flickered out. Bruce ribbited. And Tor felt a strange and warm jolt shiver through his system. He retracted his finger from the frog, who had hopped onto the box in the middle of the salt circle.

"Complete," Mel announced. She sat back with a sigh, catching her palms behind her. Stretching her feet through the salt circle, she toggled the container on which the frog sat. "No one should be able to see this now."

"I can see it," Tor stated the obvious.

"Yeah, but you can't *feel* it, can you?"

He wrinkled a brow. He supposed those creatures that had risen to seek the heart had felt it as opposed to actually having a visual on it. In some strange manner, it was sending off supernatural vibrations and now... "No, I can't. But I never did. I mean, I'm not— Fine. Let's hope this one sticks. Now what?"

"I'll have to vacuum up the salt, but I'm in no rush. You have any appointments you need to make today?"

"No, but I should run home and pack some casual clothing."

"You have casual clothing?" Her shock didn't sound mocking, but he wasn't sure.

"I do. It's not me though."

"I should think not, Monsieur Proper-British-and-Uptight."

"I'm not uptight."

And to prove his point, he leaned back, but his crossed legs set him off-balance, and he wobbled as he tried to untangle his legs. He managed a graceless sway to the side and caught an elbow on the floor and his hand against the side of his head.

"I've never seen a more uncomfortable relaxed man in all my life," she declared. She leaned to the side, putting their faces close. "What do you do to relax, Tor? Count the ties in your closet? Organize the shirts? Wait. You space the hangers using a ruler, right?"

She was…not wrong. But hearing it spoken with the faintest tone of mockery cut at him. It shouldn't. It had never bothered him what others thought of him. He didn't need to please anyone. So he had some OCD tendencies. Didn't everyone? But for some reason, he wanted her approval.

"Relaxation, eh? I like to sing," he offered.

"I noticed that. You whistle while you work, as well. I had no idea it relaxed you."

"It does. A little Sinatra. Some Sammy Davis Jr., Dean Martin."

"The Rat Pack, eh?" She turned onto her stomach to give him her complete attention. A man could get lost in those big bright eyes for sure. "Have you ever sung karaoke? Do you know they have karaoke parties down by the Seine all summer long?"

"I do know that. In the 5th. I've gone to one or two."

"To sing?"

"What else does a person do at a karaoke party?"

"You do surprise me. I find it hard to believe that you'd let down your guard to sing in front of others."

"You don't know a lot about me," he said.

"I don't. But I like what I'm learning. Singing is so intimate."

"You think?"

"It is for the singer." Her big blue eyes sought his. "Isn't it?"

"I suppose. And the song choice makes it even more intimate."

"What does Sinatra mean to you?"

He shrugged. "Teenage memories."

"Such memories must give you confidence."

"They…taught me that being myself was okay."

"Nice." Mel toyed with the salt grains. "Can we go to the riverside karaoke party sometime?"

"I, uh…"

Was that a date request? Because he wasn't sure how to actually do dates. Not like he'd ever taken the time to woo a woman before. The few times he had stopped by the party near the river had been on the way home from a job, and he'd surrendered to the need for mindless engagement. "Maybe?"

"There's my uptight guy returning to his roots. I can accept a maybe. Thanks for helping me with the spell. Your energy is off the charts, you know."

"Probably because it's nervous energy."

"No, you were initially nervous when forced to hold Bruce's hand, but I could see beyond that small annoyance. You are confident and bold. You may appear to be the average Joe to others, but I can feel all that you are inside."

"Is that so?" Now he rolled onto his stomach to face her. Sunlight glinted in the crystals crowning her hair. Her violet eye shadow sparkled, as did her irises. Sparkle witch. A guy had to love it. "How do you know all that about me? Did you perform some kind of witchy gaze into my soul?"

"I'm not that talented. That's my dad's forte. It's just a feeling I have about you. Kind of like a knowing. You're a good one," she said, then dipped her head. "I have to tell you something. Please don't laugh."

Intrigued, Tor caught his chin in his hand and waited for her to speak.

"It's important I prove myself to my father," she said.

"I had wondered about that after talking to him."

"I've never strived to practice dark magic. That was always my sister's calling. And through the years, I noticed that she and Dad got on much better than I did with him. And now...well, now's my chance to show him that I've got what it takes."

Tor suspected that even if she had what it took to invoke dark magic, she didn't want to. But proving oneself to another, especially a parent, was a strong motivator. He couldn't imagine what it must be like to seek approval from a parent. Though maybe it was similar to seeking approval from a mentor. He'd jumped into some wild situations to learn his various trades. All because Monsieur Jacques, his mentor, had asked him to meet some extreme challenges. A werewolf cleanup here, a trip to a vampire lair there. And how many times had he been handed a book on chemicals and told to learn it? He'd won approval from Monsieur Jacques and moved on to become the man he now was.

"We all do what we have to," he said. "I would never judge you, Mel. Much as dark magic freaks me out, it is a necessity to balance out—"

"—the good," she finished for him. "That's what I always heard growing up. My mom would whisper it as

Dad and Amaranthe would go off to bind a hex or communicate with the demonic realm."

"You haven't told me about your sister."

Mel sighed. "Nope. And I'm not going to either. Not unless you want to start coughing up details about your secrets and personal stuff. Can we agree to not share that which makes us most uncomfortable?"

Most definitely. "Agreed."

Her lashes dusted her cheeks, and Tor reached over to push aside strands of her hair from those thick lashes. She suddenly looked up, and the glint in her eyes lured him closer. Without thinking, he leaned in and nudged his nose aside her cheek, drawing in her perfume, a tantalizing mix of lemon and lavender. He felt her shiver.

When he tilted his head, his mouth grazed her cheek and her lips parted. He brushed them lightly, closing his eyes because the moment demanded he focus on their closeness, the warmth of her skin, the tickle of her hair against his fingers, the scent of her. It all combined with the herbs hanging overhead and the sulfur still lingering from the snuffed candles. A sweet dream. He had never kissed a client before...

Tor pulled a few inches away from Mel's mouth. She gaped at him.

"I'm working for you," he said, not entirely behind the statement, but it was a truth, no matter how conflicted he felt. Why had he made such a move?

Because he'd not been able to resist her soft and compelling allure. Or her crystal glitter eyes.

"Oh right." She glanced aside. A wisp of her hair fell across his forehead. "I suppose."

The moment felt wrong. Like he'd just stepped on a ladybug, crushing her delicate shell. Yet Tor could not deny his curiosity for her, so...he would not.

He slid his hand along her jaw and smoothed his fingers into her hair, gliding over the combs that fastened the crystal crown. He tilted her face up to meet his. The connection of their mouths shocked a fiery heat through his system. It was the weirdest thing, and at the same time, the most incredible experience. He wanted to burn himself on her surprising fire, so he pushed away the ridiculous worry that clients were not to be kissed.

And if he even started to consider the fact that her father was a powerful dark witch—

"No," Tor mumbled against her mouth, but he didn't stop the kiss. She tasted too good, and he wanted too much. It was easier to relate to her without words.

He slid closer, nudging across the salt barrier, and slipped his hand down her back to pull her to him. When she tickled his mouth open with her tongue, he groaned as the intensity of her heat flooded into him. All thoughts grew singular. Want. Need. Desire. Heat. Take. Give. Lush.

The curve of her hip undulated under his palm, and he clutched at her, keeping her there, hugging his thigh. Against his chest, the teasing connection of her breasts alerted him how hard her nipples were. He moved his hand beneath her breast, gently cupping the perfect handful. He was moving quickly and...

"Not right?" Tor managed as he took a breath against her mouth.

"Very right."

With her consenting nod, he pulled her back and dashed his tongue across her teeth. Now her body swayed against his, and he felt her weight push into him, so he relented and rolled onto his back. Her breasts hugged his chest. She straddled him with her knees, and not once did their lips part.

Had he been bewitched? Cajoled by a practitioner of magic into succumbing to base passion? What was wrong with acting on his desires? He could kiss a woman when he wanted to. If she was in agreement. And this woman agreed with every move he made.

His elbow nudged something, and he felt a warmth slide up against his shirt. The candle had toppled and the wax spilled onto the fabric of his dress shirt. Another candle was knocked over by his shoulder.

"Mel," he whispered.

"What? Don't say *no* again. I like kissing you." She gave him a quick kiss. "This is awesome."

"Just… Mel," he muttered. He received another kiss that this time made him smile widely against her lips.

Wrapping an arm across her back, he turned them on the floor until she lay beneath him. Clasping one of her hands with his, he then bowed his head to kiss down her chin and neck. She smelled sweet there, like lavender and spice and the blueberries from breakfast. He nuzzled his face against the top of her breasts, drawing her in, sensing his hard-on was striving for maximum steel. He hadn't put all his weight on top of her. He wouldn't be so forward. This was their first kiss. He wasn't that guy.

Most of the time.

Mel giggled and said, "Is that a talisman on your belt or are you just happy to see me?"

He snickered, but then closed his eyes and bowed his head against her neck. Adjusting his stance, he moved so the heavy quartz talisman nestled against her upper thigh and was not more centered, as it had been. "Slower," he said.

"Why?" she asked on a whisper.

"Because I want it that way." He hadn't thought that answer through; he'd spoken from his heart. It felt right.

It needed to go slow between them, if anything was going to happen. And he hoped it would. "Okay?"

"Well, i wasn't about to let you jump my bones, if that was what you were hoping for."

Tor chuckled and then kissed her quickly. "I wasn't, despite what a certain part of my anatomy might make you believe."

"Oh, so it wasn't just a big chunk of quartz." She tapped him on the nose. "I know you fellas have difficulty controlling your second brain."

"My second—?" Tor rolled off her to lie on his back and laughed. "If that's the way you want to play it."

His cell phone rang, and he tugged it out of his trousers pocket and answered. The caller was Rook from The Order of the Stake, an organization he hadn't worked with for months.

"I'm setting that part of my business aside," Tor said to the man's insistent request. "Really?" Tor blew out a breath. "In the 8th? I can stop by in an hour. But for future jobs, find someone else to do your cleanup work." He hung up and turned to lean on an elbow.

"What's that about?" Mel asked.

"There's a media alert that needs immediate attention. A woman was bitten by a vampire last night, and she's been texting pictures of the bite mark. Local news stations have been calling her for interviews. Rook wants me to nip it in the bud."

"That's what you do, isn't it? Make things all better."

"I help people to believe that what they saw wasn't actually what they saw. Vampires? Come on. What a bunch of malarkey."

"I kind of like occasional bouts of malarkey."

He kissed her quickly. Too quickly. "I favor some good nonsense talk myself."

She beamed up at him. And Tor's heart performed an acrobatic flip.

"Can I come along?" she asked.

"You'll have to. I'm not letting you out of my sight until after the full moon. Grab the heart. We've got a job to do."

Chapter 11

Practically flying behind Tor as he walked down the narrow aisle leading to the inner courtyard of a tony 8th arrondissement building, Mel licked her lips and didn't hide her smile. He hummed a tune she recognized: "Witchcraft" by Sinatra. It was about a man seduced by a woman.

Interesting. And points for her.

After she'd performed the cloaking spell, he'd kissed her. It had been a perfect moment, the two of them sprawled over the extinguished spell. She still had some salt grain marks on her knees, but it was all good.

The man's kiss had been electric. Unexpected. The complete opposite of his outer appearance. It had been hot and uncontrolled. And it was not something she wanted to go too long without getting another one of. And another. What luck that the man she had hired to protect her could also kiss like a charm? She'd suspected a softer inner side to him after hearing him sing and agreeing to hold Bruce's hand during the invocation. Was she invading his stronghold? Tearing down his stalwart defenses? How exciting to even try!

She abruptly ran into the man's back as he stopped before a door. His humming ceased. The gentle squeeze of his hand on her shoulder to keep her from spilling forward into his arms reminded her that he was on a business mission right now. And she didn't want to screw things up for him, so she would remain on her best behavior. Keep thoughts of kissing him longer, deeper and harder out of her brain.

This was going to be more difficult than invoking a dark hex.

"Where's the heart?" he asked.

She patted her tapestry bag.

He pushed the hair from her eyes and over her ear, then looked her up and down. She'd changed into a violet velvet minidress that featured a splash of red spangles at the hem. The dress matched the minuscule red sparkly stars dotting her violet eye shadow. White go-go boots had seemed an appropriate pairing.

"That color suits you," he observed.

"Why, thank you. Your choice of ties is always spot-on."

He tugged at the simple gray tie, which was knotted in a complicated triple layer that impressed the heck out of her.

"Why the sudden assessment of my wardrobe?" she asked.

"If I'm going to keep you within eyesight, you'll have to assume a role once we step behind this door. I work hard to wear a facade. Play a role. It's integral to my work.

You're going to have to play my assistant. Take notes. Make it look good. Can you do that?"

"I don't have any paper."

"Where's your phone?"

"I rarely carry it on me. The EMF energy messes with my magic."

Tor nodded. "I get that. Take mine for now." He pulled a fancy gold iPhone out of an inner vest pocket and, punching in the passcode, handed it to her. "Make it look official. But don't mess with anything."

"Like don't touch anything?"

He rolled his eyes. "Thanks for that reminder. You're going to mess with things, aren't you?"

"I promise to stay on my best behavior. I will be quiet and make it look like I'm taking notes on the phone."

"Good. Should I refer to you at any moment, just play along. Deal?"

"Deal. If I do well, can I get another kiss?"

"I—er." He paused from knocking on the door.

"Sorry," she said. "You don't mix business and pleasure. I get that about you. A big no-no to combine the two. But—well, we did kiss. You remember that, right? When the world sort of tilted…just a little." She looked for some sign of agreement but only got a tightened jaw from him. "Okay…business. Forget I asked. We'll discuss it later. Right now, you're on."

"Thank you." He knocked on the door, and a full minute later the door finally creaked open to reveal wary blue eyes beneath a tousle of blond hair. "Mademoiselle deStrand, I am Inspector Jean-Pierre Cassel. Paris Police. I'm from the human relations department."

"I already spoke to the police. They laughed at me. Loudly." Her face pulled away from the crack between the door and wall.

Tor stuck his toe over the threshold, preventing her from closing the door. "I never laugh at someone who has been victimized, *mademoiselle*. I simply want to ensure you are well and safe. The incident last night with the viral outbreak..." He paused and looked to Mel.

"Viral outbreak?" The woman inside opened the door a bit wider. "No, it was a vamp—"

"Oh, I understand, *mademoiselle*. And I accept your previous statement given to the officers who met with you for truth and one hundred percent validity. That was obviously a separate incident. But as I was reviewing the dossiers this morning, I noticed you were in the vicinity of the hot zone during your attack. The Parc Monceau. Not far from here?"

"Yes, it was just off the bike trail. I met a man who lives directly on the park and has twenty-four-hour access— A hot zone? What does that mean?"

"You met a resident? That wasn't listed on the police report."

"It wasn't? But I gave it all."

"Might I come inside? There's some information I need to record such as your exact location, possible contaminant exposure and inhalation of toxins. It's all to ensure your safety."

"My safety?"

"The virus acts quickly, *mademoiselle*. Have you a will prepared?"

"A will? *Mon Dieu...*" The door closed and the chain slid across the wood.

Tor flashed Mel a dimpled smile.

Mel smiled so widely her cheeks hurt. But when the door opened, she resumed a calm demeanor. She couldn't wait to see Tor work his form of fast-talking magic on this woman.

"Come in," Mademoiselle deStrand said. "I don't know what you are talking about, Monsieur Cassel. As I reported to the police last night, I was bitten by a vampire. He lives in a house on the park. I know you won't believe me—"

"Of course I believe you." Tor pointed to the woman's neck. "I can see that by the marks on your neck. The evidence is clear." He followed her inside to a dark living room, and Mel stayed close behind. The television was tuned to an evening serial. "Oh, this is my assistant. She'll be taking notes for the database."

"The database?" the woman asked, and glanced to Mel. She waved the phone, then started to type random letters into the text program which, if sent, would go to her own phone. "They keep a database on vampire bites? You really believe me?"

"Whether or not I believe in creatures with fangs who crave human blood is not the issue right now, *mademoiselle*. What is—are you feeling well? You look pale."

"I've had my curtains drawn. I don't want to turn into a vampire and I know sunshine is not good—I've been feeling poorly all day. You think I'm pale?" She pressed a shaking hand to her neck.

"It's one of the first signs of the virus. Isn't that correct, Madame Jones?"

"Huh? Oh, yes. First sign. Pale skin. Fear of the light."

The woman gaped. "The virus?"

"There was a leak last night in the park," Tor explained. "A medical transfer vehicle crashed, and a container holding a dangerously virulent biotoxin was crushed. The virus went airborne. And from our canvass reports of the immediate area, you seem to be the only one who was outside at the time."

"But the vampire was…"

"Yes, the vampire." Tor turned to Mel. An elegant arch of his eyebrow didn't so much convey doubt but rather a sort of astute knowledge. He was talking babble as far as Mel could determine, but it did sound feasible. He focused his attention fiercely on the woman. "Are you sure the person you say assaulted you wasn't instead trying to infect you with the virus? Did he take you into his house?"

"No, he, uh…pointed out his mansion as we were strolling in the park."

"Alone?"

"Yes, of course—it was after midnight. The park was closed. Do you think he was trying to infect me?"

She swiped a hand down her throat, covering the obvious bite marks. Mel thought whomever had bitten her had been sloppy. Most vamps lick the wound following the bite, and their saliva would cause it to heal within twenty-four hours, leaving no visible sign they'd punctured flesh. That wound looked torn and ragged. Infected, even.

"A virus?" the woman repeated slowly.

"It can be delivered in many ways," Tor offered. "Through saliva with a cough or sneeze, airborne release such as the crash, direct injection with a needle, exposure while trekking through an infected country. Even a sloppy puncture and then touching the bloodstream with an infected item, such as, say, a set of fanged dentiture."

"That sounds like an elaborate method of doing something so harmful. And if you say there was a crash—"

"Staged, yet contained, we believe. A skillful ploy carried out to spread the virus as a means to test its virulence. But you shouldn't tell anyone I gave you that information. This has not been released to the public. The area has been cleared and decontaminated. All are safe.

Except those who were there last night between eleven and one a.m."

"I was leaving the nightclub and having a walk home when I met the man. He was so charming. A walk in the park sounded perfect. It was just after midnight. Why didn't the officers I spoke to last night mention the crash?"

"This is an active investigation, *mademoiselle*. The few facts we had at that time were not confirmed until early this afternoon. Has anyone come to you with a request for testing?"

"Testing? No."

"Good. Such a request could only be a ploy from the people who released the virus. And they are not the good guys. You should sit down. You look—" Tor glanced to Mel. "Don't you think she looks unwell?"

"Most definitely." And Mel made a show of putting her hand over her nose and mouth and taking a step backward.

"I have been feeling woozy." Mademoiselle deStrand sat on the couch.

Tor rushed to sit beside her. He took her hand, and the woman gazed at him with desperation.

And Mel could only be impressed.

"What was the viral incubation rate?" Tor asked her suddenly.

"The what?" Mel asked.

Tor nodded insistently. "You know…"

"Oh! Oh right, the virile incubation rate." She made a show of clicking away at his phone, but it had already gone back to the password screen and the time blinked at her. "The data says a thirty-two-hour window from time of release into the air." She winked then, because she'd impressed herself with that speedy reply.

"Thirty-two hours?" The woman clutched Tor's thigh. "What does that mean? I thought it was a vampire…"

"I would never question what you believe happened, *mademoiselle*, but you must know there are types who like to use the persona of such a creature to disguise their disgusting crimes. If you've been infected, you need emergency care. Stat."

"Stat," she whispered, lost and swallowing.

"Are you sure you saw fangs?" Tor pressed. "There is a perp we've been after who wears fake fangs. He bites the person before rubbing a vile compound into their skin. It's a weird cult. Science gone wrong. We had a death a month ago."

"Death?" The woman stood and gripped her throat. "No, I don't want to die."

"But if you insist that it was merely a vampire…" Tor started.

"No, I—I *thought* it was. He was so handsome. And when I saw he was going to kiss me, he— I saw his fangs."

"Handsome." Tor again glanced to Mel.

She returned an authoritative nod. "The usual MO."

The woman gasped. "I can't believe it."

"Vampires don't exist," Tor said. He smoothed his palm over her hand reassuringly. "You're a smart woman, *mademoiselle*. You've been traumatized. And with the virus exposure, you've not been in your right mind. I'm so sorry. You've been manipulated on a diabolical level. But as I've said, I know you are smart."

The woman nodded.

"Vampires do not exist," Tor repeated. And once more he said softly, as he stroked the back of the woman's hand, "Vampires do not exist."

"Of course they don't," the woman replied.

Mel tucked the phone in her pocket. Mission accomplished.

"I'm going to order a car to pick you up and transfer you directly to Emergency Care. Perhaps I should call an ambulance." Tor stood and reached inside his vest, then looked to Mel. She walked up to him and slyly slipped him the phone.

"No ambulance," the woman on the couch ordered. "I can't afford that bill. You really think I should go in?"

"It is imperative. You've been exposed."

"But you're not wearing a mask, and neither is she. Aren't you afraid of being near me?"

"Not at all. It is a blood infection. Once it gets in your system, you can't infect another person without direct exchange of fluids. You're not going to spit on me, are you?"

She shook her head, obviously baffled. Her shoulders dropped as she sank into the realization she had been a victim of something much worse than a mere bite.

"My team can be here within the hour," Tor said. "You'll need blood tests, and an antidote."

"And that will save me?" The woman clutched his arm.

"Of course. But I'll ask you to keep this hush-hush with the media. We are close to tracking the perp's hideout. If the right information got out to the wrong person... it could ruin the work we've accomplished on this case. When you feel better, we'd appreciate your cooperation. I'm sure you'll have all the evidence that will lead us directly to him. Your help will prove invaluable."

"Really? You're such a nice man. Why didn't you show last night when I was being interviewed by the other officers? They were so rude to me."

"I was out on the perp's trail. So sorry. Sometimes our personnel feel they can handle an issue that is far above their expertise. But I'm here now. And I'm going to take care of you."

"Oh, *merci*." The woman hugged Tor and he patted her shoulder.

He winked at Mel.

A flush of warmth to her neck and cheeks stirred up thoughts of kissing him again. The man could lie his way into her heart any day.

After a car had arrived and whisked away the woman to the ER, Tor made the required phone calls to the major media outlets to inform them the victim had been off her meds and had been transferred to Sainte Anne's for psychiatric care. *No vampires here, people.* They bought it.

They always did.

He'd call Rook back, too. A vampire living in the Parc Monceau? Possible. But more likely, the asshole had told deStrand he lived in one of those fancy houses when he did not. The Order of the Stake would further the investigation.

He started the van and turned onto the main road. Mel, on the passenger seat, practically bounced with enthusiasm.

"You were amazing! But where are they really taking her?"

"First stop is the ER at the Hôtel-Dieu. I have a man on the inside. He'll take her blood and make it look official to Mademoiselle deStrand. He'll give her some directions for rest and what to watch for regarding contracting the virus, like sudden death." He chuckled. "I love that rogue-virus routine. It works every time. And no one dares speak about it because they've been such a help to the Paris Police Department."

"That was crazy."

"The crazy part was the vamp who left the evidence. Did you see that wound? Idiot. I don't have any intel on vamps in that area. And if there were, they'd be elite, very cautious of their actions."

"It is a ritzy part of town. Which could be why the vamp led her there? To throw suspicions off his tracks?"

"It's a possibility. Look at you, thinking all procedural."

She wiggled with pride on the seat. "But the woman…"

"She'll be fine in a few days, after the bite marks go away and the placebo she's been given miraculously keeps her from dying."

"But if the wound wasn't sealed correctly, she could transform."

"She'll get a vamp saliva antidote. Works like a charm."

"I've never heard of such a thing."

"It was developed by The Order of the Stake. New technology."

"Cool. You are a valuable asset to our world, you know that?"

"What? Doing spin to cover the idiocy of stupid vampires?" Tor shrugged. "Anyone can do it."

"But has anyone been doing it as long as you have? Does anyone have all the knowledge you have of the paranormal species that live in the mortal realm? Very few humans are in the know and aware that having such knowledge must be kept hush-hush. You're special, Tor. I can't believe you want to walk away from this."

"I'm not special. I might even be the unfortunate one who had this knowledge dumped on me. Doesn't matter. My mind is made up."

"I think you should reconsider. What happens when you're not around to reassure an obvious victim of a vampire bite that she was instead exposed to a dangerous virus?"

Tor chuckled again. "I bloody love that spin." The sun was setting and he was hungry. "You want to stop for something to eat?"

"I'd like that. Can we call it a date?"

"I, uh…" He stepped on the brake at a stop sign.

A date was something he couldn't manage while on the job. Should he have kissed her back at her place? Obviously it had given her ideas about what could conspire between the two of them. And much as he'd considered it…

"Can we just call it getting something to eat?"

"Oh sure." Disappointment was evident in her voice. "I'm up for whatever."

Tor drove on, but he noticed out of the corner of his eye that Mel seemed let down. She wasn't bubbly anymore. He didn't want her to take things the wrong way. And what was wrong with making her feel good and being nice to her? Kissing her didn't mean he had to have sex with her. He'd been in the moment. Had reacted and…

Yet he wondered now what that might be like. Kissing her again. Taking it further. Just…letting whatever they wanted to happen happen.

She was beautiful. If weird. And smart. If kooky. And she needed his protection. If only for a few more days.

And then what?

If he stepped into the normal, he'd have to leave the world of the paranormal behind. And with that, Melissande Jones.

Chapter 12

At her suggestion to check out one of the more touristy places to eat in the 5th, they now walked side by side as they both nursed ice cream in cups. He had chosen vanilla. No surprise there. And she had picked her favorite, cherry and chocolate. Before that, they'd eaten a meal of roast chicken and carrots at a little outdoor restaurant.

Now they strolled past the famous Shakespeare and Company bookstore that she had worked in for all of three weeks. They stocked some esoteric books on the occult and magic, of which she would occasionally find a gem. Of course, while working, she'd tended to get lost in the books and ignore the customers. A person always thinks a bookstore would be a great place to work, but really, it's the biggest candy shop in the world. And who wants to be interrupted by customers?

The evening was still young, though the streetlights had flickered to life, competing with the alluring shades of twilight and the flash of passing headlights. As they walked toward the river, the scents of roasted meats and vegetables gave way to a bitter perfume of tarmac and motor oil.

Tor stopped and leaned his elbows on the concrete balustrade. Below, the river was calm until an oncoming bateau mouche filled with tourists disturbed the water. He set his empty ice-cream cup on the balustrade and turned around, facing away from the river, rolled up his shirtsleeves and then propped his elbows behind him.

"I don't get you and your family," he said, his gaze strolling down her miniskirt and to the go-go boots. "I know there are some things that you don't want to talk about. I'm cool with that. I have my own secrets."

"Secrets are your thing."

"That they are. I proudly wear the title of *Secret Keeper*. But help me explain how someone like you can exist in a family that practices dark magic. *You're* the weird one?"

Mel shrugged. "That I am." Half her ice cream remained, and she scooped for a big chunk of cherry.

"But your dad is all dark and demonic, and you did mention something about your sister practicing dark magic. And yet from what I've gleaned about you, you sway more toward the light and…"

"Unicorns and glitter?"

He chuckled. "Unicorns are vicious."

"How do you know that? Have you ever—have you seriously seen a unicorn?"

His dimples popped into his cheeks as he bowed his head, but then looked up at her with a telling smirk. "Maybe."

"No way! I would kill to see a unicorn. I mean, well, not kill an animal. Maybe a cabbage. Anyway, what was it like? Where in this realm did you see a unicorn?"

"I can't say. It's a trust thing."

"Secrets."

"Exactly. And it may or may not have been…free."

"Oh no." She caught a palm against her thundering heartbeats. "Was it captive? Please tell me it wasn't in chains."

"Can't say. My clients' secrets are my own."

"Now I'm going to worry about that poor unicorn."

"No one should ever worry about a unicorn. They're tough. And they possess some incredible magic. It's ineffable. But back to the light witch, who makes masterpieces out of fruit, collects an odd menagerie of pets and likes all things that sparkle." He pointed to her eyes.

Mel's glittery eye shadow had given her away. She turned and leaned against the balustrade next to him. Cars passed by slowly, their drivers taking in the sights. A double-decker bus with passengers on the top open level snapping pics parked across the street to let on new travelers. "Believe it or not, I'm actually the black sheep of the family. Isn't that crazy? Of course, I don't mind being the weird one."

"You are weird."

"Why, thank you. You've a touch of the weird about you yourself. What about you? Do you have family? How did you ever develop this relationship with our world of the weird and strange?"

"I…don't have a family."

"Tor, that's so sad. But everyone has a family. Parents, at the very least. Did something terrible happen to them?"

He exhaled, winced, then said, "My mom died after giving birth to me. She was only seventeen. I wasn't put up for adoption and ended up in a home for boys just south of London. Grew up there."

"That means the people in the home were your family."

"Not really. I never developed a close relationship with any of the boys. And the nuns and staff were—well, you've heard rumors, I'm sure. They were a tough bunch. Though Miss Thunder had her moments."

"Miss Thunder?"

"She was the Science and Physical Education instructor. She was also the barracks chief and general hard-ass. But…every Sunday afternoon when the nuns were praying and singing and doing all that religious stuff, Miss Thunder would sit outside her window, listening to old Rat Pack tunes spinning on an ancient record player inside her room. Smoking a joint."

"And how do you know that?"

Tor smirked. "She taught me how to inhale properly."

"Wow. And that's how you developed your love for the old songs?"

"Most definitely. I'd sit there for a couple hours with Thunder. She wouldn't say much except that I was an odd boy. Very odd. Then she'd hand me the doobie and I'd take a toke and laugh. The nuns never found out. I always marveled at that. But then, they tended to walk a wide circle around me."

"Because you were odd?" Mel asked.

"Because I would point out the presence of…" Tor exhaled and shook his head. His thumb stroked the quartz hanging from a belt loop. He dismissed something she wanted to hear, Mel felt sure. "Anyway, I left when I was fourteen. Moved to Paris when I was twenty. Been doing fine ever since."

"Have you always been interested in the paranormal?"

"I wouldn't call it an interest, initially. More like it

was always around me, so I simply didn't know anything else. And... I don't want to talk about this. It's too..."

"Sorry. Secrets. We'll change the subject." Not what she wanted to do, but she respected his need for privacy about his personal life. "Did my dad give you the don't-touch-my-daughter speech?"

Tor turned a half grin on her. "Basically."

"Are you going to do as he asks?" She fluttered her lashes at him.

"Should I?"

She shook her head. "He's all bluster. Trust me."

"I'm not so sure of that. My throat still aches. You know your dad could take me out without even touching me."

"He could. But he won't. He would never do something that would upset his daughter."

"What if his daughter had an issue with the guy?"

"Well then," Mel said dramatically. Then she shook her head. "I would never ask such a thing of my dad."

"Yeah, I'm sorry. I know you wouldn't. That's not you. You're not a dark witch."

"Just like you're not a normal man. If you insist on seeking a job in the normal world, you're trying to be something you're not, Tor."

"Just like you, eh? Miss Light Witch going for the dark?"

He had her there. And, like him clamming up about personal issues, she didn't want to talk about it. Or she did, but she didn't know how. Wasn't sure he was ready to hear it all. She didn't want to scare him off, having already dodged the necromancy concern he'd brought up earlier.

"I'm just trying to do my best," she offered.

"I can relate. I've never been one to follow the rules or listen to what's best for me. I live in the moment. And right now, the moment calls to me." He held out his hand and she clasped it. "I think there's something you should see. Come on."

Curiosity giving her a giddy shiver, Mel walked alongside Tor. They strolled on, hand in hand.

"You got the heart?" he asked.

She patted the bag she'd slung over her shoulder. Good thing the heart wasn't heavy. But it wasn't light either. The guy could offer to carry it for her. Then again, she wanted to keep it close, and she wasn't sure she trusted he could handle the magical energy attached to the thing.

"Know what's ahead?" he asked, as he took her empty ice-cream cup and spoon and tossed them into a bin as they passed.

Mel didn't—but then she heard the music. "Really? Is that the karaoke party?"

Tor spread out his palms before him in invitation, and a dimple popped into his cheek. "All work and no play…"

"Your name's not Jack, and for that I'm glad." She picked up her pace toward the stairway that descended to a wide cobblestoned patio that edged the river below. "This is so awesome!"

The riverfront was alive with people dancing to the sounds of a remarkable trio singing to a famous pop song. The party stretched along the cobblestones. Mel bounced on her heels.

"I just remembered this place," Tor said. "And you did say you like karaoke."

"I love it! Can we dance, too? This song is so catchy."

"My lady." Tor offered his hand and then led her into the fray. The twosome immediately picked up the beat and joined in the crowd as they sang the chorus to cheers and encouragement from the singers with the microphone.

Mei didn't know any official dance steps, but she didn't need to. Just to follow the music and let her body react is what her father had taught her when they'd go to the rooftop and blast some music in the summertime. Her sister had never been interested. And it was one of the rare times Mel had actually garnered her father's undivided attention.

Tor spun her in a circle as her laughter spilled out. He had some moves. His hips and shoulders were loose, which was surprising for his muscular build. He was sinuous and graceful, with a touch of funky. What a treat to see him let loose like this!

Pumping her fists up and down, Mel guessed she was doing an approximation of the "mashed potato." Hey, she was in the zone.

When Tor suddenly pulled her close to him, their eyes fixed on one another's. Mel sighed. If he kissed her, that would make the night perfect. It didn't matter that they were surrounded by so many others. She just wanted…

The song ended with a raucous cheer from the crowd. Someone tapped Tor on the shoulder. "Your turn, *monsieur*?"

"You're on, Sultan of Swoon," Mel said.

"I guess I am." He kissed her quickly on the cheek, then took the microphone and stepped over to the karaoke machine to select a song. The time period plunged back to the mid-twentieth century, and a saxophone led Tor into a croon. The crowd took on the vibe, and a few swayed in pairs as Mel stepped to the edge of the dancers to watch her protector work his human magic.

She snapped her fingers and nodded to the beat as Tor performed a soft-shoe step and twirled and crooned to her.

Sinatra had nothing over Tor's cool dimpled smile

and ease of the moment. He was in his element. Confident and sure.

And Mel wondered if a woman could fall in love faster than taking a trip down the sidewalk. How silly was that? She wasn't in love with the man. He'd only kissed her once. Twice, if she counted the cheek kiss just now. And she did. But she certainly had tripped into something weird and spectacular, and utterly enchanting.

At the end of the song, Tor leaped into the crowd and tagged another, who went on to select a slow tune that demanded couples pair up. Tor bowed to Mel and again offered his hand. She took it and he pulled her to him.

"You have an amazing voice," she said.

"Thank you. It makes me happy to sing."

"Memories of Miss Thunder?"

"You bet."

"It makes me happy to watch you sing."

"An intimate glimpse into the weirdness of me. I'm glad we came here. In the middle of this crazy, anxiety-ridden week, I needed this."

He hugged her closer and turned her to sway on the cobblestones amongst the others. Tor moved with a sensual ease that enticed her to match him, to follow him, to fall into him. And she did, plunging into his scent and his hard chest and his direct way of guiding her deeper into that experience.

Was she a fool to tease the possibilities? They were so close, she never wanted to part from him. The singer's words grew fainter as their connection pulsed in her ears and throat and heart. He had her; she had him. Together they alchemized an intriguing match. Mel didn't want to lose a moment of this remarkable experience, dancing with a human who was protecting her from the denizens who would seek the heart in her bag...

The bag.

She'd set it down by a stone step when he'd taken her hand and led her into the dance. The next turn around, Mel searched the steps and—yes, there it sat. Her red tapestry bag with a dead witch's heart inside, sealed within a plastic container and warded and cloaked to the nines. With the cloaking spell at work, no one should sense what was inside. She hoped. Her dark magic was anything but exacting or lasting. *Please, let it improve, and quickly.*

When the next song began, in yet another slow and sensual beat, Tor leaned in. "Another?"

"Yes, please."

If they closed the place down dancing, Mel could not be happier. And experiencing Tor's entire demeanor change from ultrastiff and always on, to the relaxed, smiling charmer who held her as if only they two existed was a dream.

This was natural magic at its most intoxicating. Gladly, she surrendered to the spell.

When the dancers clapped at the end of the song and the new singer launched into a rap beat, Tor tugged Mel toward the steps and they sat. He tilted his head onto her shoulder. "I like dancing with you. We seem to pick up each other's intentions easily."

"I was thinking the same thing." And snuggling next to him was not something she would trade even for a whacked-out heart that could save her mother. He was just so…much. Manly and handsome, and charming. Sighing, she wrapped a hand about his arm and nestled closer.

"I forget about the real world while singing," he said. "It's been a while since I've had such a good time."

That she could be the one to give him this experience set her heart to a pace even faster than it was already beating. Turning to face him, she asked, "You said you live for the moments. What does this moment beg of you?"

"Focus," he answered. A pulse of his jaw muscle made her wonder if he'd slipped back into protector mode. But his smile discouraged that worry. "On you."

Dimples rising in what she was beginning to note was an indication of his playful side, he leaned toward her and she met his kiss. Clutching her shoulder, Tor deepened the kiss and pulled her close. He invaded her with a delicious intent. The world slipped away. The only time passing was marked by the flutter of her heartbeats. He mastered her with his gentle hold and his seeking mouth.

Don't let this end, she thought. And then it did as he bowed his forehead to hers and they gasped in one another's joy.

"Will you sing another song?" she asked.

"If they'll let me."

Mel turned to grab her bag and—it wasn't there. She dipped to peer around the side of the stairway, but there stood a garbage bin and no sign of the red tapestry bag. Had they sat on a different stairway? She glanced across the crowd of dancers and toward where the singer bounced to his funky rap. Another stone stairway was close to the bridge, but they hadn't come down that one.

She gasped. "It's gone."

"Right?" Tor said. "What a way to get rid of the stress. We should do this again soon."

"No, the bag." She clutched his hand. "My bag with the heart in it is missing. I set it right there."

"Ah, hell." Tor's body stiffened, instantly moving from relaxed to alert. His eyes took in the crowd and then traced along the riverfront. "It was red with big flowers?"

"Yes. I wonder if the cloaking spell dissipated? Or

maybe it was a thief taking advantage of an unwatched bag."

"There!" Tor pointed up toward the street level.

Mel sighted a man walking swiftly, her bag slung over his shoulder.

"Let's go!"

Chapter 13

Tor grabbed Mel's hand and they soared up the stairway to street level. Here at the edge of the 5th the traffic was lighter, but the streetlights were also spaced farther apart, darkening their path. Half a block ahead, they saw the dark-haired man turn a corner.

"I've got this!"

Tor took off, leaving Mel to follow. She reached the corner and saw Tor take another right into what must be an alleyway. She heard shouts and what could only be described as a fist meeting flesh and bone. Creeping toward the turn, she snuck a look around the side.

Tor struggled with a man who snarled and lashed out with deadly knives in each hand. But what was most deadly were the fangs jutting from his mouth.

"Vampire?" Mel muttered. "But how could he know what was in the bag?" Had her cloaking spell been—again—ineffective? What was up with her magic lately?

The tapestry bag sat on the ground ten feet away from the men's struggle. Mel slipped around the corner and crept over. When her fingers glanced onto the wooden bag handle, she saw the glow from within. She picked up the bag and peered inside. "Why is it doing that?"

She hadn't a clue how the thing worked, only that it was necessary for her spell. It hadn't glowed since the night she'd stolen—*borrowed*—it from the Archives. When the dead things had risen from her backyard, it hadn't been glowing.

Curious.

"Watch out, Mel!"

Dodging the oncoming vampire body, Mel stepped to the side and pressed her back to the brick building. Tor lunged and grabbed the creature by the shirt. He wielded a stake high in the air. Just as he swept down his arm to stake the vamp, his opponent kicked him in the shin, setting Tor's trajectory off course and felling him to one knee with a painful groan.

The vampire dove for Mel and gripped her by the shoulders. She clutched the bag to her chest. She wasn't afraid of a vampire. Even if he did flash his fangs—one of which was chipped.

"Divertia!" Her repulsion spell sent the vamp flying away from her. His shoulders hit the wall and he slapped his palms to it.

"A witch, eh?"

"How do you know about the heart?" Mel demanded.

"Heart?"

Tor stepped before Mel. "That's enough chatting. You like to steal things, flesh pricker?"

The vampire snarled. "There's something in that bag I need."

"But you didn't know what that something was?" Mel

called from behind Tor. She bounced on her toes but couldn't see over his broad shoulders.

"I know now that it's a heart." The vampire stood and curled his fingers into claws. "It called to me. And I take what I want."

"It can't call to you," Mel muttered from behind Tor. "It's warded. And cloaked!"

"Oh, it called." Fangs bared, the vampire again lunged for Tor.

Tor bent, plunging the stake upward. Mel saw the vampire's fangs graze Tor's neck, drawing blood, and then the vamp shoved him to the ground as it stumbled backward. The stake had found a place in its heart. Yet the creature didn't turn to ash as it should.

"Heh, heh." The vamp pulled the stake from its heart and tossed it to the ground. "This is not over!" He took off.

Tor, falling to one knee before her, slapped a palm to the brick wall to catch his breath.

"Aren't you going after him?"

He stood and gripped the bag she held. "This is not warded."

"Yeah, I get that. Sorry. Vampire getting away? And why didn't he ash?"

"Because it's a bloody revenant. And—hell." Tor stood and marched down the alleyway. "Let's go home. It's been a long day."

After a shower, Tor walked out of the bathroom to find Mel asleep on his bed and snoring. Her white vinyl boots were strewn on the floor. The flowered bag was hugged tight against her chest, her knees tucked up and her mouth open. He hoped she didn't drool on his Egyptian-cotton pillowcase. Then again, he did have a maid.

Smiling at her easy fall into slumber, he snuck into the closet and pulled down an extra pillow and blanket for himself. Wandering down the hallway in boxers and bare feet, under his breath he sang a lullaby he knew Sinatra had once performed. "Lay thee down, now and rest, may thy slumber be blessed."

In the living room he eyed the leather sofa. It did not look at all inviting. He'd purchased the boxy, hard item because it went with his masculine, streamlined decor. And his decorator had suggested it suited his personality. In the four years he'd lived here, he'd probably sat on it half a dozen times.

With a sigh, he lay down and confirmed the utter hardness of his night's rest. As a consolation, the cushy pillow provided a saving grace.

He hadn't gone after the vampire because it wouldn't have proven fruitful. The creature had been revenant. Not even a stake could kill an already-dead thing. That particular breed of vamp needed to be beheaded in order to be ashed. And he hadn't been packing a machete.

And the key question remained: Hadn't the cloaking and ward worked? How had the vampire been attracted to the heart? Tor had held a frog's hand for that spell.

Mel's spells seemed to work, for the most part. But so far none of her wards had lasted for long. Was it because she wasn't an expert with dark magic? How would she accomplish the greater spell under the full moon if even a small warding wasn't effective for her? The woman had very big plans for that night.

"Necromancy," he muttered. The word sank into his gut like a spiked iron ball. He'd forgotten to ask her more about that unsavory development. Had he known that was part of the plan, would he still have taken the job? "Probably."

Because lush lashes and big doe eyes. Sometimes a man couldn't resist. And maybe, just maybe, she possessed a sort of lash magic. Anything was possible with witches.

Tugging the blanket over his face, he dropped into sleep almost immediately.

When the phone rang, Tor startled upright, winced at the pull in his back muscles and slapped around for his cell phone. Dragging himself up with a groan, he spied the phone over on the kitchen counter. The daylight beaming in through the deck windows shocked him completely awake as he wandered to the kitchen. It was morning? He noted the time of eight thirty as he answered.

The man on the phone sounded pleased. It was the very same one who had interviewed him via Skype a few days earlier. "You're one of three final candidates for the job, Monsieur Rindle. We'd like you to come in for a face-to-face on Monday at 8:00 a.m."

"I'll be there," Tor confirmed. He pumped a triumphant fist. *"Merci, monsieur."*

Hanging up, he again pumped the air and then moaned as his shoulder muscles screamed in protest. "Damn couch. Whew!" He sat on a stool and leaned forward, catching his palms against his temples.

He'd gotten a second interview. Of course, he hadn't doubted he'd aced the first interview. He was excellent at the verbal volley. And face-to-face? He was even more confident in that.

"What's the hubbub?"

A tousle-haired witch wandered into the living room, yawning and stretching her arms above her head. She still wore the violet dress she'd had on yesterday. She walked over to the kitchen counter, and Tor noticed her smile grew to a teasing smirk.

"What?" he asked.

"You're not much for pants, are you?"

He'd forgotten his lacking night wear. Boxers were comfy to sleep in. The woman should be lucky he wasn't naked, as was his usual sleeping mode. On the other hand, maybe he should label that unlucky?

"Not for sleeping in," he commented. "And the hubbub is that I got an in-person interview on Monday."

"Hey, that's awesome." She leaned forward, catching her elbows on the counter. Her eyes glinted with morning sunshine. Unicorns and sparkle? Or lash magic? "The day after the full moon."

"The day after the—ah, hell. Really?" Tor rubbed a hand through his hair. "I wasn't thinking about that."

"That's okay. On Sunday night I'll invoke the spell. All will be well. Your employment with me will be complete. And you won't have to deal with me, or the Jones family, anymore. Monday morning comes around and you get to step into the normal human world of mundane and boring office work."

"That's life," he said.

Sunday night he'd escort the witch to whatever spell-invocation ritual she required, stand guard and make it happen. Monday morning he'd arrive at the accounting office ready to slay the interview.

The only part that didn't sound ideal was the not-dealing-with-Mel part. She'd grown on him. Sort of like a fungus. But still, he liked her close.

"I might need another shower this morning," he muttered. "That couch was like sleeping on a rock."

"None of your furniture appears conducive to comfort. You must have hired a designer."

"How do you know?"

"They tend to make a man's place look manly but

never consider that our bodies like soft, comfy things as opposed to leather and wood." Mel shuddered. "But your bed is a dream to sleep in. And it smells good, too."

"It...smells?"

She leaned across the counter and whispered into his ear, "Like you. All manly and macho. Are you sure you don't smoke a pipe?"

"Positive. It's my soap."

"Well, I love it. Delicious. Want me to make some breakfast while you shower with lots more of that soap? I might be able to find something edible in your cupboards."

"You won't. The stocks are low. Grocery delivery isn't until Saturday. I'll shower quick and then bring you home. Then maybe...you can make us some smoothie bowls?"

"Love to."

Tor wandered down the hallway. His cell phone rang, and he stopped in the doorway to his bedroom. It was his contact at the Hôtel-Dieu ER, where he'd had the vampire victim sent.

"What's up, Jean-Paul?"

"That woman I did the usual runaround on yesterday?"

"Thanks for that. You know I'll pay you."

"Of course you will. It's not easy making up a blood test and disposing of the evidence without some asshole in administration getting onto my ass."

"I know. It's a fine line, but you walk it well. So why the call?"

"There's been a strange complication."

Mel noticed when Tor pounded his head against the door frame leading into the bedroom. Whomever he was on the phone with had not given him good news. Closing the fridge door, she wandered down the hallway to find he had entered his closet and was selecting a shirt and tie.

"No shower?"

"Change of plans."

"Emergency?"

"Of a sort. The woman bitten by a vampire? My contact at the ER did the usual blood work on her and let her believe she'd received an antidote against a vampire bite—which it was not."

"But it was."

He pulled on his shirt and paused, giving her a good view of his abs. "You're missing the point, Mel."

She liked when he called her that. Everyone else called her Lissa. Mel felt more personal.

"I didn't miss it. I know the story. We want her to believe there are no vampires. So what's the sort-of problem?"

He flipped up his collar and threaded a tie around his neck. She stepped up and took command of the silk tie, and he let her.

"The sort-of problem is that Jean-Paul checked the blood. It actually showed a rare strain in her system that only Jean-Paul would have recognized because he's an expert on vampire DNA and bodily fluids. She was bitten by a revenant."

"The same kind of vamp you staked and set free last night?"

"Yes, and I did not set him free. I didn't have a means to slay him. You need to behead those bastards."

Mel stuck out her tongue in disgust and twisted the silk around a length that hung to his chest.

"And since the antidote vampire saliva that Jean-Paul usually injects at the bite sight isn't effective against revenants—because they're dead vampires, and there's no way to inoculate against death—we've got a potential transformation on our hands. Not cool."

"Which means you're getting all prettied up to go slay a potential vampire."

"I wouldn't call this pretty."

"I would." She fluttered her lashes up at him. He brushed the hair from her face, and she realized she'd crawled right out of bed and wandered in for breakfast. "And look at me. This hair hasn't seen a comb and I desperately need a toothbrush."

He leaned down and kissed her forehead. "You are beautiful, Mel. The more tousled the better."

"Really?"

"Really. Is it good?" He patted his tie and frowned.

She shrugged and gave up on the mess she'd created. "I have no idea how to tie a tie."

He patted at the bow she'd formed as if wrapping a package. "Apparently." With a few flips and tugs, he produced a tight square knot. Then he grabbed a pair of pants and nodded toward the control panel. "I need a machete."

"Doesn't sound like a picnic." Mel punched the top button and the door swung open. "I thought you weren't a slayer?"

"I'm not." Tor entered the weapons closet and she strolled in, gliding her fingers along a sword boasting a decorative hilt that gleamed gold. "I'll give Rook a call on the way there. This should be his target. Damned Order of the Stake needs to learn how to clean up their own messes. Hand me that stiletto. I like that one."

He took the blade from her, flipped it and caught it expertly. "You'll have to come along."

"Does that mean I get a weapon?"

He winced. "Don't you have magic in your arsenal?"

"Oh. Right. Of course I do. When it sticks."

"About that—"

"No time! You're in a hurry."

Tor grabbed a wicked machete and led her out into adventure.

Chapter 14

Mel did as she was told, and waited in the van while Tor walked through the courtyard toward the victim's home. He shook hands with a man wearing a black leather duster coat who had been waiting for him. Must be Rook from The Order of the Stake. One of her good friends, Zoe Guillebeaux, was in a long-term relationship with a knight recruited by the Order. She knew the Order was a bunch of human men who had taken vows to defend other humans from vicious vampires. Supposedly they were discriminating and only went after the bad vamps, but Mel had her suspicions that when in the heat of the moment, any mortal man might plunge a stake through the heart first before asking questions or determining benevolence.

She winced to think that Tor was going inside to, in all likelihood, stake the woman she had met yesterday. Mademoiselle deStrand had been an innocent victim, bitten in an attack. And to top that off, the police had laughed at her, and then later she'd been manipulated by Tor to believe that what she'd thought was true had not been so. It wasn't right.

On the other hand, the sensible, protecting-the-masses side of things, this matter could not be ignored. If the human had been bitten by a revenant, she would not develop like a normal vampire, one who could blend in with society and exist alongside humans. She would become feral and, well…dead.

"The poor woman." The clutch Mel had on the door handle was turning her knuckles white. It was so difficult not to run out and stand up for the woman's rights. She whispered, "Just stay put." Tor knew what he was doing. This was his turf.

Her determination lasted four seconds. The urge to help another was so strong, she pushed open the door and dashed out. She got halfway up the walk to the courtyard and stopped abruptly, turning back to the van. "Forgot the heart!" Rushing back to the vehicle, she grabbed the bag.

What would be a good spell to hold back two vampire slayers while she determined if the woman had transformed to vampire and was indeed a threat? She had a motionlessness spell that could fix a person in place for a few seconds. That required nothing more than a few words of invocation and… "Charcoal dust," she muttered. "Left my spell supplies at home. Shoot!"

Locating the door to the woman's home and seeing it was open, Mel rushed up and peered inside. The room was hazy due to the drawn shades. She could hear voices around the corner. An agitated woman who…snarled?

Mel rushed down a hallway, bag banging the wall as she did, which alerted Tor. He stepped out from a room and grabbed her by the shoulders. "I told you to stay in the van."

"She didn't ask to be bitten," Mel argued. "You have to hear her out. Maybe she won't transform."

Tor's jaw pulsed. Then, without a word, he turned her toward the open doorway and, hands still on her shoulders, pushed her forward to stand in the threshold. The bedroom was decorated in blue and white chinoiserie. The knight, with a bladed collar glinting at his neck, held a stake high above the creature who cowered against a dressmaker's dummy, clutching at the torn fabric stomach.

The woman Mel had seen yesterday was no longer. She had changed to a snarling, fanged thing who drooled blood and spat at the knight. Her eyes were…white.

"She must have died last night or early this morning," Tor stated over her shoulder. "She's a revenant vampire now. You still want us to keep her alive to live such a life?"

Mel swallowed. She was too late. Or not. Was there some way to save the woman? She did not know of a way to reverse vampirism. But she didn't know everything. There could be something in one of the books at the Archives. Yet if she had died…

This whole nightmare of dead things coming back to life was enough to break Mel's heart. Was the woman's condition because of the heart she carried in her bag?

She shoved backward and pushed around Tor. "Do it," she muttered, and then ran down the hallway and out into the courtyard, where she gasped in fresh air.

From inside the apartment, she didn't hear any sounds of struggle, but she knew. Her entire body cringed when she suspected the woman had taken a stake to her heart and… Tor hadn't brought along a machete for no reason.

When the man she respected and trusted brushed quickly by her, she didn't speak. He was in a hurry, headed to his van, and she wasn't going to interfere this time. A minute later he returned to the courtyard, unfolding a black body bag. His eyes met hers. His jaw pulsed. Stern and focused. No whistled tunes this time.

She closed her eyes, wrapped her arms across her chest and wandered back to the van, where she tossed in the tapestry bag and climbed up onto the passenger seat. Five minutes later, Tor returned, hefting the body bag, folded in half, over a shoulder. She shuddered.

The knight cruised out behind him, looking not at all disturbed. Just another day at the office.

Which it was to him.

How could they be so utterly unfeeling?

Mel clutched herself tighter. Two days would bring the full moon. And an immense challenge to her tender heart. Could she accomplish such a vile task?

Tor slid into the driver's seat and fired up the engine. Mel sat on the passenger seat, legs bent and arms wrapped around them, head bowed to her knees. He had tried to warn her to remain in the vehicle. Women. They never listened when it was important.

Yet he couldn't disregard the heavy emotional vibes emanating from her right now.

"Sorry," he offered as he backed out and navigated the traffic on a route toward the river.

"You were doing your job."

"She was beyond hope, Mel."

She nodded and turned her head to face the passing cars outside.

"I'll take you home. I need to run some errands alone."

"I do need to shower and change. I'll be good for a couple hours."

"I know you will. But you'll stay in close contact with me on your phone, yes?"

"I don't know where it is. I have one, but I never use it."

Not a surprise, coming from the natural witch who grew her own herbs and spell concoctions outside on the patio, and whose familiar was a frog, and who also claimed to be owned by a duck.

"There's something that bothers me about all this," he said. Because much as he should not prod at her sensitivities, this needed discussion. "The cloaking spell we did on that heart. It seems to have not worked. The vampire last night and—"

"The heart didn't attract that vampire to the woman. And it wasn't the same vampire who stole my bag last night. I don't think. I didn't see the vamp who attacked the woman, but the one last night had a chipped tooth. But that's besides the matter." She tilted her head against the seat and declared "I don't know why my spells are not working. I was calm. Not nervous. There must be something wrong with me."

"I don't— I can't speak to your magical skills, but I also suspect the woman's attack had nothing to do with the heart. Yet the vamp that stole it was called to it, even though it wasn't sure what it was stealing. You say he had a chipped tooth?"

Mel nodded, then hugged the bag to her chest. "What do you want me to say? I'm baffled by this."

"We've got to figure this out, Mel. Tell me everything," he said. "Especially the part about you needing to raise the dead. We never did discuss that. Please?"

With a heavy sigh, she turned on the seat and tilted her head against the headrest. She'd slipped off her boots and looked beautiful with her tousled hair, rumpled clothing and rosy cheeks. He wanted to kiss her, but he didn't want to drive through any traffic lights. But man, a kiss would make him feel much better right now.

And when had he decided thinking with his heart instead of his brain was acceptable? He had to stop doing that, or something would go wrong.

"The spell requires I raise the dead in order to protect my mother," she explained. "It's complicated and…" She shook her head. "All you need to know is that there will be a dead…entity on the night of the full moon."

"Why does your mother need protection again?"

"She's being tormented by…someone."

"What aren't you telling me, Mel?"

"I'm telling you as much as I can. Mom's in trouble. It's the reason she died a few weeks ago. She was so frightened she ran off the rooftop. Dad wants me to believe it was a miscalculation on her part, but I know better. Something spooked her. Dad picked up her little kitty body from the ground and took her home to recover."

Tor couldn't imagine living such a life. Being married to a woman who could change to a cat, but then who could also die and come back to life? How many times had Thoroughly Jones witnessed his wife's death? And Mel? She must have experienced her mother's repeated deaths through the years.

"What if your mom died and…no one found her?"

"She'd come back to life and have no clue about her former life. Would probably wander about lost for days. Naked. Maybe longer if we couldn't find her. Dad had her tattoo his phone number and address onto her ankle after death number three. She's had to use it once, but it took her a couple days to figure out it was a number to call. He made her go back and tattoo *call for family* on there, as well."

"That must be tough for the entire family. But necromancy? How is that supposed to help your mom?"

"It's dark magic," she said, as if that was the norm. "Listen, I know it's freaky to you, but not to me. You have to understand, practicing dark magic carries a certain weight in our family. Both my dad and his brother are dark witches. And CJ's twin sons—my cousins—are dark, as well. Vika was light, but she's come over to the dark side."

"Vika is CJ's wife," Tor stated, recalling the family trees of the Paris witches. "I know something about her having a sticky soul?"

"Her soul attracts lost souls that are unable or unwilling to cross over." She sighed and looked aside. "Most of them, anyway. But not all."

"Victorie Saint-Charles is her full name," Tor said, referring to his mental database of the local paranormal families. "And doesn't she have a sister or two who are also witches?"

"Libby and Eternitie are both light. Libby is married to a former angel."

"That must be interesting."

"Reichardt is cool. He's no longer angel. He got his soul back when he found his halo and now—well, he's kind of like you."

"Like me?"

"In the know, but human. Yet not afraid to step into the fray and fight for what's right."

Tor turned left, but also tilted his head so she wouldn't see his frown. Stepping into the fray was everything he was not about lately. Or at least, he was striving for that out-of-the-fray lifestyle. "You know I have the interview on Monday."

"Right. Because you're going to try to be something you're not."

"Maybe it's something I need to be."

"It's not," she said with confidence. "But you'll never know until you give it a try. Too bad though. Paris really needs a guy like you, stepping into the fray and all. You're a good man, Tor. As upset as I am about that woman's fate, I think you did her a favor by staking her. There was no hope for her."

"There wasn't, and *I* didn't stake her."

"No, I suppose the knight did that part." She sighed.

She'd seen him carry in the machete. Tor had been the one to decapitate the revenant. That was the only way he could get through such an act, by calling her a revenant and not a human. There had been no humanity left in her. She'd been a creature, a dead thing destined only to vile and evil acts, end of story.

"Rook's looking into the local vamp scene for me today. Also checking out the Parc Monceau, where the woman's attacker claimed to live. I'm not sure I believe that. This is the Order's concern, but since I've stuck my fingers in it, I want to stay in the loop and learn what Rook learns."

"Rook was the guy in the leather coat," Mel stated. "I've heard about his girlfriend, Verity. She knows Zoe, who is a good friend of mine."

"Zoe and Kaz," Tor said. "Kaspar is a friend of mine."

"Really?"

Tor nodded. "I connected him with the Order when he was a teen. Made sure he found his way when he needed some guidance."

"Well, look at you, all helpful and kind."

Tor smirked. "Introducing the guy to the world of

vampires and slaying? Not sure that was kind. But he's a good man. We're here."

He pulled up and parked before Mel's home. He would watch until she got to the door and then leave to dispose of the body.

"Ah, nuts. I'm going to really need your protection now," Mel said.

"What? Why?"

She nodded toward her front stoop. On it stood a man with long dark hair and a serious glint to his eye.

"Your dad's back again? What does he want? To finish me off?"

"That's not my dad." Mel got out of the van, dragging the tapestry bag along with her.

Tor swore and turned off the engine. This was even worse than the dad. Certainly Jones, of the twin brothers, was the stronger and darker of them. And he and Tor had once already gone to heads.

"Protection," he muttered. "But for whom?"

Chapter 15

Mel's uncle marched down the steps and grabbed her by the shoulders. She didn't have to see the anger in his eyes; she had sensed it when stepping onto the sidewalk. The concrete hummed with his dark energy. And while that was normal, the anger tingeing that darkness was not.

"Monsieur." She felt Tor's hand go to CJ's on her shoulder. "If you don't mind, I'll ask you to take your hands off this woman."

CJ reared at that statement but did take his hands off her, slamming them to his hips. "Who the hell are you? And—wait. I know you. You're the bastard spin doctor who fucked up my spell against tribe Monserrat."

Mel managed to step before her uncle as he lunged. She wasn't about to repel him with magic, because that would bounce right back at her. Painfully. His body was covered with tattooed wards and repulsion sigils for just such a purpose. But neither was she willing to let the big boys battle it out in full view of the entire neighborhood.

"Uncle CJ, what a nice surprise. What are you doing here? You never visit." Though she didn't want him to answer. *Please, don't answer.*

"You know damn well why I'm here, Lissa."

"Maybe if you'd just tell her," Tor said. "She's had a rough morning."

"Is that so?" CJ crossed his arms and eyed her with the searching gaze she knew could read her like a book. It didn't take him more than a few seconds to pull out one of her secrets. "Revenants? Since when are revenants in Paris?"

"I don't know," Tor offered. "But The Order of the Stake is on it, as well as myself."

Mel felt Tor's confident hand on her shoulder while his other hand gripped the handle of her bag. She let him have it. Now to get inside and away from her uncle.

When she took a step toward the house, CJ moved quicker, blocking her. "Where is it?" he asked.

Tor slung the bag over a shoulder and took a step to place him immediately in front of Mel. "Where is what?"

"She stole Hecate's heart from me," CJ announced sternly.

"You—stole it?" Tor narrowed a condemning look at her. "I knew it."

"I borrowed it," she corrected. "And I only need it for another two days, Uncle CJ. I promise I'll bring it right back as soon as I'm done with it."

"What reason do you have for needing such a volatile artifact?" CJ defied her with his intensity.

Mel glanced to Tor. She hadn't given him all the details. And she wasn't about to. "Can we talk, CJ? Alone?" She nodded to indicate that Tor should take the bag with him. "Why don't you go check the garden out back for... you know."

"Sounds like a plan." Tor bowed to CJ. "Monsieur Jones. I'll have my ears open for trouble. Your niece is my client. I've been charged to protect her—from whomever should mean her harm."

CJ mocked the man as he took off around the side of the house with the heart in the bag. And Mel blew out a breath, thankful to, at the very least, have that out of the way. Though surely CJ must sense the heart. Maybe?

"Come inside," she said to her uncle. "Didn't my dad tell you what I have to do?"

"He did, but he didn't mention any of the items required to complete the spell." CJ followed her inside and closed the door. "Why the bodyguard? Oh. Mercy. Of course. That's what it does. Is the heart attracting the undead?"

"Depends on your definition of *undead*. They seem pretty alive when they come rushing toward me with claws or spittle drooling from their mouths."

"Lissa, Lissa, Lissa."

"Yes, I know. I should have asked, but you never would have allowed me to take the heart out of the Archives."

"No, I would not have."

"Even if it meant helping my mom? It's required for the spell. I can't complete it without the heart. It brings up the dead, CJ. You know that's very necessary. And I had to take it days ago when I was visiting you because— well, I saw an opportunity. I didn't want to keep it so long. And I really did not expect it to attract…things. But there you go."

"Where is it now?"

"I'm not going to tell you that."

"The spin doctor has it, doesn't he?" CJ strode down the hallway, and Mel hustled after him.

In the living room, he peered out the patio door at Tor, who leaned against a support beam under the trellis, his back to them, bag in hand.

"It's in that bag," CJ declared. He gripped the door pull.

Mel slapped her hand over his. "CJ, you have to let me complete that spell. My mother's life depends on it. Your brother would never forgive you—"

He put up a palm to stop her tirade. "Don't try that with me, young lady. I've been around far too long and been to too many dark places of the soul to allow anyone to pull fast-talking on me. I know the situation. I…" He blew out a sigh. "This is magic at its darkest, Lissa. You're not accomplished enough to control it."

"Yes, I am. My dad believes it, too. And I'm going to prove it." She hoped. When would her dark magic decide to kick in and prove effective? "I couldn't let him do this. He's got enough to worry about what with Mom coming back into her new life and my sister hanging around."

"Your sister," CJ hissed in a whisper. "Vika did try her hardest to get her soul to stick to hers."

Vika was her uncle's significant other. They'd been together a long time without the marriage certificate; a piece of paper wasn't important to them.

"The family appreciates her trying," Mel said, "but there's only one way to fix this, and that requires the spell and subsequent release. You know that."

"One of your father's specialties. Release. It's kind of you to take this on for him. He is always in a tough place following your mother's deaths. I'm sorry. But if the heart is attracting dead things, you should cloak it."

"I have. A few times. It never seems to stick." Mel winced and didn't meet her uncle's gaze. "It's dark magic

I've used for the cloaks and wards. I'm still getting a handle on it."

"It shouldn't require getting a handle—ah." He ran his fingers back through his hair. "You've never practiced dark magic before."

"Well, of course not. But don't think I'm not capable."

"I'm sure you are."

She wasn't too sure he was being honest.

"But, Lissa, the only way dark magic will answer to your beckoning is with a sacrifice. Hell, didn't TJ warn you about that?"

"A sacrifice?"

"It's the reason your cloaking spells haven't been effective. The dark magic you put out slips off things as if they were greased. If you want it to stick, you need to sacrifice to—well, Hecate would be fine—to prove your worthiness of the dark."

Mel gaped at him. She'd never heard of such a thing. Her father had done such? And Amaranthe? She couldn't recall her sister ever—oh, wait. That one time when they'd been eleven. Amaranthe had eaten her familiar's heart. Still beating.

"The salamander heart," Mel whispered.

"Your sister." CJ nodded. "I remember that. It doesn't have to be a grand sacrifice. But it must prove your willingness to be open to the dark arts. Where's that familiar of yours?"

"Bruce? No." Mel couldn't keep the tremble from her voice. If Bruce were in the vicinity, she hoped he took cover. Because if CJ got a look at him, he'd surely bind the amphibian and hand him over to her for a snack. "He's my familiar. I would never betray his trust that way."

"Then you have to find another means of sacrifice.

And quickly. The blood moon is soon upon us." He crossed his arms and turned to study Tor, who still stood outside, back to them, observing Duck waddle about the yard. "And the day after the full moon, the heart gets returned to the Archives."

"If there's anything left of it. I mean—" Mel avoided his questioning gaze. "Yes. Promise." She crossed her heart, a binding that all witches took very seriously. "And Tor is protecting me, so everything is good."

"That man is not an ally."

"Nor is he a foe."

CJ lifted a brow. "True enough. But he got in my way a few years back—"

"He's helping the Jones family now. Accept that."

"Very well. But he is merely human. I'd be much more accepting if you had someone with actual skills or magic to protect you."

"Tor has skills. He knows his way around a weapon and how to keep his clients safe. You know that well. He protected that vampire tribe from your dark magic."

"Indeed." CJ rubbed his jaw. He'd lost to Tor, but he should have never taken on the entire tribe in the first place. Her uncle wasn't always kind or benevolent. In fact, his magic was often malevolent.

"I looked in your eyes outside on the steps. I saw the new female revenant," CJ said. "Is that about the heart, as well?"

"The revenant vampires are a different situation Tor has been dealing with. A human woman was bitten and— she had to be slain. We're not sure those vamps' presence in Paris are related to Hecate's heart."

She was pretty sure they were. But Mel had a hard time assigning blame to the innocent woman who'd been victimized.

"I don't like this. It's too sketchy. Maybe I should do the spell."

"I can do this, Uncle CJ. I have to do this. I know Amaranthe the best." She splayed her palm so he could see the scar on it. "We had a bond like no one else in this family."

He nodded. The man was a twin to her father, and his sons were twins. They each had a bond that was inexplicable. Though she and Amaranthe were not twins, they had formed an equal bond through a blood ritual when they were little. A cut on each palm, some magic words and the desire to never be apart and to always have one another's back. Was such a bond unbreakable? Death had broken her physical bond to Amaranthe. And spiritually, she had not been able to communicate with her ghost. It seemed only her mother could see and hear Amaranthe.

But she would do what she must to reaffirm their bond. Even if it killed one of them. Again.

CJ peered out the patio windows. "What is he doing out there?"

Tor was now prodding the toe of his shoe at the edge of the garden where the dirt had been pushed up. "Uh, I had an issue with zombie dogs."

"There's no such thing as zombies, Lissa."

"You see? You and Tor do have a common bond. You both have the same belief. But trust me, when the dead rise from their dirt beds, I call it like I see it. Zombies."

CJ scratched his head. "Disturbing. I'm going to look into that. And I'm going to have a few words with the man digging through your clematis."

Mel caught her uncle by the arm as he headed toward the patio doors. "Just chill, all right? He's helping me.

He didn't want to, but he is. Don't do anything to piss him off."

"We'll see." He shrugged out of her grasp and headed outside.

Not a day ago, Tor had stood in this same spot and had felt the same creep of dread crawl up his neck as the other half of the notorious Jones twins had come out to the yard to give him a piece of his mind.

He'd expected a conversation with the dark witch. The time a few years back when he had successfully defended a tribe of vampires against CJ's dark magic, Tor had not spoken personally to the man about it. The witch had been so enraged, he'd charged off before Tor could offer his side of the story. He'd been hired to protect clients. He did his job well. Even if they were vampires.

Vampires were not inherently evil. Most humans would not be able to pick them out of a lineup, and some might even have vampire friends without knowing it. They blended in, and they insinuated themselves into the mortal realm because they chose to do so. They did not need to kill for blood to survive; a drink every few weeks sustained them. And transforming a human to vampire was not a requirement to get that sustaining blood.

Tor straightened his tie as the witch approached him from behind. A glance to the house confirmed the bag he'd tucked behind a wicker chair was barely visible.

"Listen, bloke," Tor started. "Your niece hired me to protect her, and I'm going to do that."

"Lissa is *paying* you?"

Tor nodded.

"Don't take any money from her. Send me your bill. Got that?"

"Of course. Thank you." And her dad had offered the

same. He'd sort it out later. "I promise you I will be the first to make sure that annoying heart is back in your hands on Monday morning after the spell is completed."

"Funny, I would have thought you'd keep it for your Agency."

"I'm not head of that organization anymore. Dez Merovech has taken it over, and as it is, the Agency has its hands full. Hecate's heart belongs in the Archives. That's where it will be returned."

"I appreciate that. The Archives is a repository for dark magic. Your Agency is still so young, untested with handling such vile objects."

"We fare very well. You'd be surprised the objects we have in storage. And apparently, under much better security and surveillance than in the Archives."

The witch lifted his chin at that dig. It had been deserved. Tor was tiring of being confronted by pissed-off dark witches. He wasn't working for them. Mel was his client. And he would defend her against her own family if he had to.

"Lissa is no expert on handling such magic," CJ said. "I don't want to stand back and let her do this alone, but I respect her decision to take it over when it might have been left in my brother's hands."

"She knows what she's doing. And if she doesn't, I'll be there to pick up the pieces."

"Yes, well, we've figured out why her cloaking spells have not been effective. In order to access dark magic, a witch must show it she means business."

"And how does Mel go about that?"

"That's for her to figure out." CJ narrowed his gaze on Tor. "Do you really know what you've gotten into, Rindle?"

"Of course. I've handled it all, from vamps and weres,

to harpies and unicorns. And now mother-freakin' zombies. Trust me, I've got this one covered."

"Yeah?" The witch's gaze averted to the talisman at Tor's hip. "What about ghosts?"

Chapter 16

Seething from what Certainly Jones had told him, Tor marched around the side of Mel's house, stomped on a climbing vine that tried to trip him up, and took the front steps in a leap. Once through the front door, he stalked down the hallway to find her standing before the fridge holding a bunch of celery.

"What part about *I don't do ghosts* did you not understand?" he asked.

Mel's jaw dropped open. The celery hit the counter, and she clasped her hands before her. "Tor, I couldn't tell you that part."

"Why? Because you're keeping secrets? Because you have to do something weird and strange to make your dark magic take hold? What else haven't you told me?"

"I've told you everything. At least, everything that I could. I didn't think it was important to mention the part about my sister being a ghost because, well, first, I thought you'd figure it out. And second, if you didn't, it wasn't important because you wouldn't ever have to deal with her, anyway. And I don't know what your deal with ghosts is. You only said *I don't do ghosts*. How's a girl supposed to interpret that vague statement?"

"Vague?" Tor resisted fisting his fingers, but it was a struggle.

The nerve of her to keep important information from him. And he had generously agreed to help her, even after he'd decided against doing protection work.

When she started to speak again, he put up a palm between them. "Enough. Let me state this one more time, loudly and clearly. I. Don't. Do. Ghosts."

"I got that, but—"

He shook his finger at her. "No. No more *but*s. If you can't be truthful with me and respect my one small caveat, then I'm out of here."

He swung around and sailed down the hallway. Expecting her to rush after him, he fled out the front door and slammed it behind him.

He marched out to the van without turning around to see if she'd be peeking out the window at him or yelling for his return.

She had broken a rule that he had adhered to for years. And he couldn't conceive of relenting now.

Mel turned toward the counter and caught her head in her hands. Tor had every right to charge out all angry and alpha. Which is why she hadn't run after him. She'd wanted to. But her only excuse would have been because she felt desperate and had lied to keep him on the job.

She hadn't lied to him; she just hadn't divulged all the details.

He wasn't going to protect her anymore?

She glanced to the plastic container sitting next to the celery on the counter. Ugly things had surfaced, attracted to that heart.

"What if they come for me?" she whispered.

Jerking her gaze to all the windows, she looked for moving shadows in the grayness caused by the setting sun. She might like to think she was strong. She might even think she could invoke the dark magic required to save her mother's life. But she wasn't brave. And any courage she had had just marched out the front door.

Bruce came into view, hovering near her left shoulder.

"What are we going to do, Bruce? He left. I don't have a big, strong man with weapons to protect me should something evil and dead charge through my front door. The doors! We've got to batten down the hatches."

Bruce moved over to the chair in the dining room.

"Right!" After slapping her palms together, Mel began to move furniture. A few magical words and gestures lifted the heavy chairs, which were carried down the hallway to park before the front door. And…she'd have to blockade the kitchen door and the patio, as well as the spell room. "We've got our work cut out for us, Bruce."

Tor tossed the body bag with the revenant body into the incinerator and then kicked the machine's on button that burned the contents to ash. A brand-new revenant didn't ash, remaining in human form with death. Rather, a second death, since the person actually died as they transformed to vampire.

The majority of vampires—a good ninety-five percent of them—were alive. They did not die when bitten and then transform to vampire. The vampire taint was passed to the victim and then, with a massive blood exchange, they also became vamp.

No death. Hearts still beat. Blood still flowed.

Revenants were literally a dying breed amongst the species. Because it was difficult for anything that had already died to maintain life for long after death. But they could, and they did manage to blend in with humans surprisingly well. Save the obvious smell of decay and their voracious hunger for blood—that hunger being the only thing that kept them resembling aliveness and able to stand upright instead of falling apart like…

"A zombie," he muttered as the flames flared before him.

Two different things, revenants and zombies. And he'd never believed zombies were real until he'd seen the dogs in Mel's backyard. They existed. And he didn't like it one bit.

The dead witch's heart possessed some vile energy. He should have taken it from Mel that first night and been done with it. And now? Now the whole world had become a shit storm of dead things.

He walked out of the salvage yard, punched in the digital code to lock the gates and met the knight waiting at the back of his van with arms crossed. "You know all the spots, don't you?" Rook asked.

"For disposal? That I do." Such knowledge would never afford him a real job. A normal job. But a bloke didn't need such expertise to sit behind a desk in a cubicle. He couldn't wait for that to happen.

"This was a tribe," Rook said as Tor went about removing the hazmat suit, hanging it up in the van and replacing his shoes. The usual after-disposal routine. "And I'm not sure we got them all."

Rook had called Tor an hour earlier. He had been fighting revenants in the 18th. Tor had made it there in record time and had joined the knight. They'd slain eight vampires in a dark warehouse. Tor was confident no one had witnessed their actions. But he wasn't sure the vampires had actually been nesting in the warehouse or if they'd just been trapped by the UV lights set up in a stand outside the building. Some local-artist exhibit was photographing graffiti on a time control, and the lights had been left on all night without supervision.

"What's up with revenants in Paris?" Tor asked. "Aren't they rare? And don't they prefer unpopulated areas? Those things were wild, bloke. As close to animal as a vamp is going to get."

"Yeah, I don't know." Rook winced. "The knights haven't seen any revenant activity in over a decade. And those we just took out were all drones." He closed one side of the van doors at Tor's gesture. "No leaders present that I could determine. Mindless, yet hungry. Something is directing them. And I'm not sure I buy that it's an old witch's heart in a box."

"Why not?"

"It doesn't fit with the woman attacked the other day. That was purposeful. She was lured to the park and bitten."

"Might have been the leader, creating new blood. That last one I burned was new, unable to ash with second death."

"We can be thankful the older ones do ash. I don't understand revenants," Rook said. "They don't survive long in a city. They are monsters. But they don't decay like a zombie and can live undead for a long time. Years, even. To risk coming into the city was stunning."

"Can they procreate?"

"No. It wouldn't have made sense for them to change the woman with hopes of her birthing vampire children. Revenants don't work that way. They all begin as humans, who then die and are brought back to life with the blood exchange. But to be safe, maybe we could get that heart under lock and key?"

"It's needed for a full moon spell. Then it's back to storage."

"So the next day will be spent tracking dead things. Joy. The Order ranks in Paris are currently me, Kaz and Lark. And at the moment, both Kaz and Lark are on a business trip to Romania."

Business trip? Such a euphemism was something Tor would use in his own fast-talking spiels. "Seriously? Romania? That's about as cliché as it gets when it comes to vamps and slaying."

"I don't write it—I just slay what needs slaying."

"So it's just you and King in Paris right now?"

"King is…"

Tor didn't need an explanation. The elusive founder of The Order of the Stake had recently been discovered to be vampire. Really. A vampire had founded the Order that slayed his own kind. King had been lying low. Though his knights had stood by him. Hell, he really was a former king of France, and despite his questionable authority, his Order did do a good job at slaying the vamps who needed slaying.

"I'll help when I can," Tor offered, "but I'm quitting the business."

"Quitting?" Rook laughed. "That's like me saying I'm going to pull on some yoga pants and start teaching classes outside in the park."

Not a stretch for the knight who had been practicing yoga for centuries and was a yoga master.

"I'm serious," Tor said. "I've had enough of this crazy shit. I want…"

"You'll never have normal, Tor. Trust me on that one.

The things you've seen, known and done cannot be unseen, unknown or undone. There's not a talisman big enough in this realm to make that happen."

Tor clasped the quartz that hung from his belt. Rook knew what it did for him because he was the man who had introduced him to the witch who'd charmed it for him.

"Don't we pay you enough?" Rook asked.

"It's not the money. I have more than I'll ever need. It's…peace of mind."

"Protecting innocent humans from the weird shit doesn't give you peace?"

Tor sighed. It should. It did.

And it did not.

"If not this, then what the hell are you going to do with yourself?" Rook asked.

"I have an interview in a few days. Office stuff. Normal human cubicle stuff."

Rook grasped his throat, mocking a choking motion, and stuck out his tongue.

"Have you ever tried the normal?" Tor challenged.

His cohort shrugged. "I'm no longer immortal. Gotta beware the vamp fangs as much as the next human. As for normal? What's so great about that? If you ask me, I'd much prefer knowing than not knowing. And like I said, it's too late to put that genie back in the bottle. Not unless you have a memory-loss spell. Which I'd highly recommend if you're serious about this career change. Because you can give normal a try. But you'll always know what's out there."

Again, Tor touched the crystal, its heavy weight reassuring. It had taken away his ability to see ghosts. A memory-loss spell? It was a good suggestion.

"I guess a man has to do what he has to do," Rook

conceded. "It'll be tough not having you to call on when we need you."

"You'll find someone to replace me. I haven't been doing much work for the Order the past few years anyway."

"Sure, but whatever you do, be careful. You can walk away from this life, but I'm pretty sure this life won't allow you to walk away without keeping one eye over your shoulder."

Which was another fact Tor knew. Would he always be running away from that which he had once so freely run toward? *Could* he do normal?

"Will you at least consult with me on this revenant issue?" Rook asked.

"Of course. I won't leave you a lone slayer standing amidst a bunch of wild vampires. It's just this witch who hired me to protect her—"

"Now I get it. You've got a pretty little witch to protect, eh?"

"She hired me, Rook. It's a business deal. Which..." How quickly he forgot. "...I ended earlier today."

"Uh-huh. You don't sound pleased about that decision. You want my advice when it comes to pretty witches?"

The man's girlfriend was a witch. A very pretty witch.

"I'm not sure."

"Doesn't matter, I'm giving it to you. If she makes you smile, then don't ignore that. It isn't often guys like us get to simply smile, is it?"

Tor considered the strangeness of an easy smile, and before he could agree, Rook said, "She means something to you."

"She's kind and beautiful and—"

"Sexy?"

"Weird."

Rook chuckled. "Those are the best kind."

He hadn't expected that agreement, but now Tor smiled broadly and turned his head down to hide it from the man he had only ever been serious with, or stood alongside to slay vampires, or worked out a game plan with for media spin with the Order.

"So should I destroy your phone number?" Rook asked.

"Not until after the full moon."

He should get back to Mel—ah, right. He'd stormed out on her. Had given her his walking papers after learning she'd not told him a ghost was involved in the job.

He slid a hand over the talisman, clutching it.

"You want coffee?" Rook asked. "I'll buy."

The two men got into the van cab, and Tor navigated toward the city center near the river. He'd handled things wrong with Mel. He shouldn't have stormed out on her. He shouldn't have been so mean. He should have explained himself.

He should have. He should have. He should have.

Now what was done was done. And he had not ended it properly. Not in a way that sat well with his morals or his soul.

Stopping at a light, he swiped a palm over his face, leaned back against the seat and closed his eyes. His fingers tapped impatiently on the steering wheel.

He'd never quit a job before. Even when he'd faced insurmountable odds, such as the cover-up of a werewolf gaming den where they'd pitted tortured vampires against one another to the death. There had been dozens of crazed vampires left behind in a warehouse located in the center of the city. It had to be cleaned out and sanitized, and he'd had to field more than a few calls from the local police, fire department, news stations and even the EU-OSHA.

Not to mention the werewolf pack that had returned to challenge him. He'd stood before them all, shown them his mettle and talked down the pack from angry retaliation, as well as handled all the city agencies with a flair that sometimes even impressed him. He walked away cut, bruised and sometimes near death, but he always survived.

To do it again and again. And always because he knew if he didn't do it, no one else would.

So why couldn't he allow himself to even be close to a woman who may or may not have an instance where he would be in the vicinity of a ghost? The ghost incident that had pushed him over the edge had been years ago. He'd moved on. There was no way to change what had happened. He should fear nothing.

"Tor?"

"Huh?" He pulled across the intersection, driving toward the Rue de Rivoli, where Rook said a late-night coffee shop was located. "Sorry, man."

"You're distracted. Is it the pretty witch?"

"She's a client. Was a client."

"Was?"

"I…don't work with ghosts. You know that."

"Uh-huh. Who's protecting her now?"

Tor cast the man a glance. He knew the answer to that one.

"Ghosts are assholes," Rook offered. "But I've never known you to back down from a challenge. You surprise me, Rindle."

"You shouldn't be. I'm over it all. The life. The weirdness—"

"This side of normal is a hell of a lot more interesting

than the one you think will change your life. Pull over. I'll run in and grab us a couple."

Tor did so, and Rook got out, closing the door behind him.

"This side of normal," Tor muttered.

He clenched the steering wheel. Normal. Normal, normal, normal. Why was it proving such a hard concept to grasp? And when had he backed away from a challenge? That wasn't him. While he'd avoided anything that reminded him of that horrible night, he—well, he could avoid it forever. But that would be...

"A lie," he whispered.

He couldn't run away from his truths. Because to hide was like being haunted all over again. A constant haunting that would always cling to him, and never relent. He'd seen ghosts since he was a child. Had never feared them, even thought they had intrinsically guided his life to exactly where he stood this day. He'd never seen his mother in ghostly form but had always sensed when she was near, with the presence of a cicada that would show up in the most unexpected times and places.

A few winters ago, he'd found a cicada in an old house, tucked between two books. It had peered at him with wise eyes. And the books had been titled *Always with You* and *I Love You to the Moon and Back*.

His mother's way of saying she had his back. She had never left him.

And now Mel and her family were being tormented by a ghost in such a personal way. A family member sought to harm Star? That was terrible. He could imagine the grief and pain associated with it.

And that was the part that tore at him. He knew that emotional pain.

Rook opened the door and handed him a coffee that

warmed Tor's fingers when he wrapped them about the cup. He noticed the elaborate artwork on the paper cup and realized it was a floral line drawing featuring flowers and one very prominent...cicada.

The knight put up a boot on the dash and leaned back. "You think about what I said?"

"Yes," Tor muttered, knowing the man had ulterior motives. He tapped the cicada.

"Good. Then drop me off and head back to the witch's home."

Chapter 17

At the sound of a knock on her front door, Mel startled awake and sat up from the floor. She'd fallen asleep? It was dark in the house. Down the hall, in the kitchen, a candle flickered softly. Bruce levitated before her. She peered at him through her goggles.

Another knock. The frog tensed.

Gripping the crystal athame in her left hand and the carrot shredder in her right, she turned onto her knees to face the door. "Who is it?" she called out cautiously.

No response.

Bruce ribbited.

"I *did* ask," she shot back at the amphibian.

Another croak in response.

"Not loud enough? Do zombies *have* ears? They could have fallen off."

She clutched the shredder against her chest and peered around the side of the inverted easy chair. Her heartbeats thundered. Something lurked on her front step. And yet, would zombies have the courtesy to knock?

Calling louder, she said, "Who's there?"

"It's Tor. I'm sorry, Mel! Can I come in?"

"Tor? Oh yes!" She pulled at the huge easy chair before her, but it didn't budge. "Hang on! I'll be right there!"

Using the kinetic magic she'd employed to stack the chairs before the doorway, she now managed to shift the barricade as a tangled mass about a foot away from the door.

The door opened, and Tor popped his head inside. "I know it's late but—what the bloody mess?"

"You can slip through!" she called. "Climb over the furniture."

He did so, and stepped awkwardly onto a wooden kitchen chair, finessing the obstacle course until he landed on the easy chair before her. Seated, he bent before her—she was still on her knees—and tapped the plastic goggles she normally wore when cutting onions.

"I'm afraid to ask," he said.

Tugging down the goggles and tossing the grater aside, Mel felt her fears evaporate. Yet in the process, her anxiety gushed to the surface, and she began to cry anew. She didn't want to, yet it was impossible not to.

Tor slid off the chair to kneel and pulled her into a hug. He kissed her head and wrapped his arms about her. "I'm sorry. I shouldn't have walked out on you like that."

"I thought I was alone," she said between sniffles. "And you don't know how I attract the weird stuff to me. I was afraid something would get through to attack. And I'm not sure if zombies would knock or just crash through the windows. I did the best I could. But I'm not very brave. Oh!"

He pulled her up with him as he sat on the chair, and

Mel bent her legs and snuggled against him. Hugging his hard chest, she clung and sniffled. Her anxiety lessened as she focused on the slide of his hand across her back, a soothing move. She was safe in his arms. Her protector had returned.

"So you barricaded yourself inside?" he asked.

"Bruce helped me. But I don't have many weapons. I'm not into guns and garrotes like you. And when I'm upset, my magic always malfunctions. That's why I couldn't clear the chairs away now."

"I'll put them back for you. It was wrong for me to walk out on a job. But more so? It wasn't right to leave you alone when I know you need support. I'm here now. To protect you."

She looked up at his face. Minute stubble darkened his jaw. His hair was tousled. He looked as though he'd had a tough day. Yet truth glinted in his eyes. She believed him. He'd needed an escape, some time to work out his apparent issues with ghosts.

Ghosts. No avoiding that topic any longer.

"If you stick around to the end, I can't promise there won't be ghosts," she said. "At the very least, one."

"I wish you would have told me about that from the get-go. But that's neither here nor there now. If there's a ghost, I'll have to deal."

She nuzzled her head against his firm bicep, drawing his warmth into her bare arms and legs. She hadn't realized how cold and small she'd felt barricaded on the floor. Now she could relax. "Tell me about you and ghosts. Did you say you could see them?"

Tor hooked a hand along her thigh as he pulled her closer. He tilted his head back and exhaled. His heartbeat was steady. Fierce. A warrior in suit and tie. Mercy, but she adored him.

"I can see ghosts," he finally confessed. "I have been able to see them forever. At least, since I was about five or six and started to realize that the imaginary friend I would talk to wasn't so imaginary, and it was like those spirits the little boy saw in that movie, *The Sixth Sense*. Only then did I realize I saw dead people, too."

He tilted his head forward, and his lips pressed the crown of her head. She sensed that he wasn't keen on revealing this information, but he wanted to. In his way. So she didn't barge in with all the questions bouncing inside her brain.

"I never thought it was a problem until it did become a problem. I grew up believing there were always extra people around the dinner table that the other kids in the boys' home couldn't see."

"That must have been startling for you."

"Yes, well, the first few times, when I mentioned the extra guests and wanted to know why they didn't get served, the nuns were having none of that crazy talk. And Miss Thunder was never there at the dinner table with a joint to relax my apprehensions. I learned to keep that information to myself if I wanted to eat."

"It makes me sad that you were an orphan. How old did you say your mother was?"

"Seventeen when I was born. She died in the hospital a day later."

Mel's heart tugged. "I'm sorry."

Tor stretched out his arm and rolled up his sleeve to reveal the tattoo on his inner forearm. The candlelight from the kitchen glowed softly into the hallway, and for the first time Mel saw what it was. She traced the intricate artwork. The wings were so finely crafted, it appeared as if the insect might lift off and fly away.

"Most cicadas have a seventeen-year life cycle," he

said. "They come out of hibernation for a short time. Bring new life into the world. Then die. I got this in memory of my mother."

"It was a cicada who told me to look for you," she recalled. "That's the universe at work."

"I believe that. My mother has always been in my life in the form of cicada sightings. Once I even saw one in the wintertime."

"Wow. She's a very strong spirit."

"But I've never actually seen her ghost. Not that I would recognize her if I did. I was never given a photo or description of her. It's something that has always bothered me. Did I get my brown eyes from my mother? And who was my father?"

"I'm sorry that you never got to know your parents, Tor."

"I've never known anything else, so that's my normal. There are times I feel I'm being directed by an unseen force. And…I like to think it's her. It's never pushed me in the wrong direction. It's what made me return to you now. Earlier, I saw another cicada. On a coffee cup, of all things."

"Some souls lost in this realm are very powerful. Too powerful," she said with a sigh.

"So." He sighed heavily. "That's the story on me and ghosts. And why I'm a freak about working with them." He tapped the quartz crystal at his belt, and Mel was almost going to touch it when she pulled back. A talisman was a personal thing. Only if invited would she touch it.

"When I was in my early twenties and had moved to Paris from London, I met a woman who also saw ghosts. She'd been from mental institution to mental institution, and was living on her own, but barely clinging to sanity. She was haunted by some vicious entities for reasons, I believe, that had to do with her growing up as the daughter of a murderer. Anyway, she wasn't crazy. Too much. And I understood her. We became friends. Never dated. It wasn't like that. Charlotte was more a sister than someone I'd want to date. Then she had to move. Whenever the media got too hot regarding her father, she'd pack up and change addresses.

"Five years ago we met again after not seeing each other for some time." Again he tapped the crystal. "She spoke of the voices that wanted her to kill herself."

Mel clasped his hand. She could feel his pain as a shiver wrapping her spine. The Jones family had been dealing with their own ghost issues. It was not easy. And it was real, as strange as that was for most to believe. Ghosts were not friendly little white blobs. Or sheet-covered spooks. Some could be vicious, homicidal, and could even influence a living person's mind.

"I was supposed to meet her one night for supper," Tor said, "but by that time I was working for The Order of the Stake. I got called to a job, so I was late by four hours. I went immediately to her place because she'd texted me a dozen times. I hadn't paid attention to the texts. It was a particularly busy night talking to the media about—I forget. Probably vampires. I'd turned off my phone to focus."

He drew her closer and gripped her tightly. Clinging as she so wanted to cling to him. A minute shiver traced his torso, and the reverberations hurt her heart desperately.

"Anyway, when I got to her house…" He tensed. "I found her in the bathtub, her wrists slashed. She'd been dead an hour. If I hadn't been late, she might still be alive. It was my fault."

"No, it wasn't. You couldn't be there for her all the time. And ghosts can be nasty. Evil. Malevolent… Oh."

Now she realized how hard it had been for him to re-

turn this evening. His issue with ghosts *and* not being
there to protect the girl? It was happening all over again
for him. And she had dragged him into this.

Oh, Mel, what have you done?

"After that night I made a strict no-ghosts rule. I went
out the next day and found a witch to charm this talisman so I couldn't see ghosts. And so they could not make
contact with me. They're still around me, I'm sure, I just
can't see or sense them. And since then, my life has been
going as well as it can."

"Until I dragged you back into it all." She sat up on
his lap. "What kind of a person am I? I can't ask any
more of you."

"But you have to. That's why I returned. *Had* to return.
This has become more than a job, Mel. I care about you.
You can ask anything of me. And you should. I want you
to. I want you to—well, I like you. Those kisses we've
shared? I want it to be a beginning."

"You don't know how much I'd like that, too. But if
that happens, I'll be stirring up all your issues."

"Maybe they needed a good stir." He kissed the crown
of her head again.

"But you were ready to walk away from this part of
your life. And look what I've done. I feel terrible."

"Don't ever feel bad for coming into my life. I'm a better man for it. And for now? This is what I do. I protect
others from harm. And if I can't stand up to one little
ghost—hell, you said there might not even be ghosts."

"Amaranthe, my sister, has only been haunting my
mom. She's in my parents' home. Mom can see her, but
Dad and I cannot. Though we can both sense her. Yet
we see when Mom is being tormented, both in human
and cat form. I don't think Amaranthe's ghost will show
tomorrow night at the crossroads when I need to do the

spell. Because I'll be raising her dead body, not her ghost. Right?"

"You're asking me?"

"Well, if I give it a good think, I suspect I'll actually be summoning a zombie."

"Zombies—" Mel touched a finger to his mouth to stop him from what she knew he was going to say, but Tor took her hand away and finished "—do exist."

"Since when did you have a change of heart?"

"Since I had to fight the zombie dogs in your backyard. They were not revenants. Revenants are solid and don't suddenly drop off body parts. I am now officially on the zombie bandwagon. But really? You're going to raise your sister as a zombie? That wasn't in the initial instructions to me. Of course, you gave me no details. So why should I be surprised?"

"It's what's required for the spell. And now can you understand why I volunteered to do this instead of allowing my dad? Can you imagine if he had to raise his own daughter from the grave?"

Tor blew out a breath. "But you're her sister. It's going to affect you just as much as it would your father. Can't you have your uncle CJ do this?"

She shook her head. "I've got a connection to Amaranthe that no one else has. See here." She opened her palm and he traced the scar. "Amaranthe and I performed a blood-bond spell when we were little. If anyone is going to raise her from the dead, it has to be me. Of course, now that Uncle CJ said I have to make a sacrifice, I'm not sure what that should be."

"A sacrifice?"

"It's the reason my cloaking spells haven't been taking hold. When a witch wants to perform dark magic, he or she makes a sacrifice to prove their commitment to the art. I remember Amaranthe ate a salamander heart when we were tweens. Poor thing was her familiar. I don't know what my dad did, and I'm not sure I want to know. It doesn't have to be like killing a sacrificial lamb. I have to sacrifice something important to me. And I need to do it soon so I can get the mojo I need to work the dark magic."

"What's important to you?"

At that moment Bruce levitated down the hallway, and both paused to watch him pass into the kitchen.

"I'm not sacrificing Bruce," Mel said. "Or Duck. Or any living being. That's not my style. I'm not sure what would work. A lot of things are important to me. My house, my life, my light magic, my love for nature. Heck, even my love for karaoke. But I don't think promising never to sing karaoke again would fit the bill."

"Probably not." Tor stroked the back of his forefinger along her jaw. "I'll help you. Just tell me what you need, and it's done."

"You're so good to me. I will tell you if I need help. But first, I have to figure out what's most important to me."

"And fast."

"And fast." She pressed a palm over his chest. Now his heartbeats were calm and reassuring. Lost in his steady brown eyes, but searching for an anchor, she said, "Tell me you're out and I'll understand."

"I'm in. And you can't change my mind."

"Thank you." She kissed him. "I owe you a lot for this."

"Actually, your dad and your uncle are now footing the bill. Both told me I wasn't allowed to take money from you."

"Oh really? I'm not going to argue with that."

"So are we good?" he asked. "I mean, beyond the work situation. I know I hurt you—us—by walking away. I was…"

"Dealing with your own stuff. I get that. And yes, we are good. But we'll be even better if you can help me move this furniture back into place. Bruce is no help at all when it comes to heavy lifting!" she called into the kitchen.

"Got it. You stand out of the way, and I'll do it all. Where is the heart, by the way?"

"I put it in the fridge." She shrugged in answer to his lifted brow. "Wasn't sure if spoilage would be an issue, though I doubt it. It wasn't in cold storage at the Archives. Don't worry. I performed another cloak and ward on it, just to be safe."

"The same cloak and ward that had an efficacy of about three hours?" he asked with a dimpled grin.

"The very same. I'll figure out my sacrifice before morning. I have to. Just think—tomorrow night this will all be over. And then Monday morning you can start your new life."

He stood from the chair and slipped his hands down her shoulders as their gazes locked. "A new life," he said. "I want that. But what if I want to keep some of the old in the new?"

"Like what old stuff would that be?"

"Well, she's not exactly old."

"She?" Mel wriggled when she realized he was talking about her. "I'd love to stay in your life. If you could manage a witch in your normal world."

"I don't think I'll ever be completely free from the paranormal world I've grown up in. It will be a challenge to keep it apart from the normal stuff, but I think it'll be worth it."

"If you think so."

"I...have been told I should employ a memory-loss spell."

"A—what for?"

"Rook suggested it. It'll make me forget things. If I'm going to enter the normal world, I can't know what I know now."

"That seems drastic."

"Extreme measures. For my sanity."

He'd obviously considered it, and the man was usually very sure about his decisions. She shouldn't say anything. She wouldn't.

"Of course," she offered as calmly as possible. "It's your life. You do what you have to do."

She kissed him again, quickly, and bounced into the kitchen to put away the grater and goggles. If she'd told him the truth, that she would be lost along with his abandonment of all things paranormal, she might lose his newly given trust.

But really, that man could only exist in her world. *His* world. She knew that. Would he come to realize it? Before he decided to forget it all?

Chapter 18

"Did you have any furniture stacked up in the back of the house you want me to put back in place?" Tor asked Mel as she walked down the hallway.

"I didn't blockade my spell room."

"I've seen that side of the house from outside. Isn't it all windows? Like a conservatory? Anything could have broken through—" Tor decided that stating the obvious wasn't going to help matters. He was here now. He could protect Mel.

And he wouldn't run away from that responsibility again.

"I know. Not very efficient at battening down the hatches. But I ran out of furniture. Come on—I'll show you."

As they entered the spell room, which was a long conservatory attached to the side of the house, Tor fell into a state of wonder. With a snap of her fingers, Mel lit a few candles placed in sconces along the walls. Above them, centered over a stretch of stone table, a candelabra was lit, giving the room a soft, cozy glow. Vines grew all over the windows from the outside, so the night sky was blocked in most places, but the moon shone through, high above, full and round.

Tomorrow night would see the moon's apex. *Showtime*, Tor thought. And he was going to stand by while Mel raised the dead. That would be interesting, for sure. Out of his comfort zone? Nothing doing. But still, it was going to try his bravery.

It would be worth it to help Mel.

The room smelled fresh and summery. Plants in terracotta pots were positioned all along the tiled floor. One wall was lined with shelves and vanities that were stocked with vials, bottles, jars, candles, rocks, more plants, books and—well, everything witchy Tor could imagine.

He smoothed a hand over a massive pink stone table that stood as high as his thigh. The top surface was about four feet square, and it had no legs; it was a solid chunk of rock. He jumped up to sit on it. "Must have taken a crane to get this piece in here."

"I'm not sure," Mel said. She tapped a bit of dried flower that hung from a copper rack over the pockmarked wood table that abutted against the pink stone. Must be her main spellcrafting table. "It's rose quartz. It was here, in that exact spot, when I moved in."

"A witch lived here before you?"

"I think it was a geologist. The whole house, when I did a walk-through before buying, was filled from floor to rafters with pretty stones and crystals. I suppose the owner decided that piece was too big to move. Must have cost a fortune. It feels great, doesn't it?"

Tor pressed his palms to the cool stone and shrugged. "It's a rock."

"Oh, dear, no." She moved to stand before him, and Tor spread his legs wider so she could step right up to him.

Mel slid her fingers along the pink stone, and then with those same fingers, she tapped his heart. He clasped a hand over hers. "Rose quartz is a stone of the heart. It's filled with love and compassion. Self-worth and confidence reside in this stone. And passion."

He wasn't sure about all that, but he was on board with the passion bit. And the way her lashes lowered when she said that, dusting her candlelit, glitter-covered skin, was devastating to his desires. Lash magic. He was bewitched.

Tor bent to kiss Mel. Her mouth was soft and giving, so lush. The moment felt right. Maybe? After today's argument, he wasn't sure. "Is this all right?"

"Why would you ask such a thing? Of course it is."

"Less than an hour ago you were barricaded in your house because you thought I'd abandoned you. I'm sorry."

"I forgive you."

Croak.

Tor startled at Bruce's interjection. He'd not noticed the familiar had levitated so close to them and now hovered but a foot from their heads.

"That did not sound approving," Tor said. "Would you give me a break, Bruce? You can trust me. I like your witch. And I promise you I will protect her and never do anything to harm her."

The frog stared at him a moment. And Tor could only hope he'd get an approving ribbit or whatever was the amphibious offering of acceptance. Instead, Bruce turned and floated off.

"What was that?" he asked Mel.

"I'm not sure. But I'm inclined not to overthink it. Now kiss me and show me just how much you're on my team."

"Team Mel?"

"I like when you call me that."

"I can call you whatever you want me to."

"I like Mel because it's what you want to call me." She pushed up onto the stone table and landed each knee beside his thighs.

Tor slid his hands up her back as her kiss forced him downward to lie across the smooth quartz. Her kisses were passionate and searching, and for a moment he simply lay there, allowing her to do as she wished. Her body hugged his as she snuggled against him. Her hair spilled over his face and neck, and he breathed in lemons and lavender.

Attempting to loosen his tie, she cursed. "Your knots are thwarting my lusty desires. How did you get it like this?"

"It's an Eldredge knot. One of the more complicated knots, but it makes me happy to accomplish it."

"You are a man who likes a good challenge."

"Always. And I would never purposely thwart you. Promise." He gave the tie a shuffle, which loosened it, and then he pulled it free with more than a few twists and tugs.

"I think you practice knot magic," she said.

"Is there such a thing?"

"There's a magic for everything. Tasseomancy, aleuromancy, crystal divination, pyromancy. I'll have to show you my lithoboly skills sometime. Freaks out Bruce."

"I'm not sure I want to know."

"Some things are better left to the imagination. But it does involve rocks raining down from the sky." She slid a hand down to his belt.

"Your talisman against ghosts," she affirmed.

"Lillian Devereaux spelled it for me years ago. You know her?"

"I don't, but I've heard of her. Pretty sure that witch has been around for centuries."

"She's quite the flirt."

"Is that so?"

"I never kiss and tell. Hey, she did me a favor. I can't see or sense ghosts when I've got this on me. And they can't touch me. I never take it off."

"But you know it doesn't repel them. Just makes it so you can't see them."

"That works for me. Are we going to discuss the miraculous powers of my...talisman..." He pumped his hips against her thighs playfully. "Or are we going to make out?"

"I vote for making out." Mel unbuttoned his shirt and her lips landed on his bare skin, following with kisses as each button was released. "This hot, hard chest of yours. Mmm..."

Her tongue traced his nipple, and Tor hissed at the sudden and remarkable shock of pleasure. He gripped her hair, his fingers getting lost in lush, soft curls, and pulled her up to kiss her deeply. He needed to taste her want and desire. And he wanted her to know the flavor of his.

The intense need to become as close to her as possible had him pulling her tight against him. Their tongues danced. Sighs mingled. The tickle of her lashes against his skin felt like the best kind of magic.

"I want to do more than kiss you," she said.

"Me, too," he said on a wanting groan. "Mel, you don't make it easy to resist you."

"Why resist?" She pushed up from him, her soft hair dangling onto his bared chest. She was on top and in control, and he didn't mind that at all. "I can make you do as I say." A waggle of her brow combined with her lash magic to completely enchant him.

"With witchcraft? I have no doubt. But you don't have to resort to sneaky tactics. I'm on board with whatever happens next."

"Good." Her eyes twinkled. She tugged his shirt out from his pants. "Because I have plans."

She bowed her head and kissed a trail down from his neck to his nipples, and took her time with the sweet torture of sucking them, then licking and lashing at them.

Tor sucked in a gasp. Her mouth on his skin did not allow for clear thought.

Above him, the chandelier glinted with golden candle flame. The air swirled sweetly with herb and flower scents. Briefly, he wondered if the vines climbing outside the windows concealed their tête-à-tête from the neighbors' view. The shrubbery was probably high enough.

Mel unzipped the fly of his trousers, and her hand slipped inside to caress his hard-on. The contact worked like a torch to his desires. Tor groaned with soul-deep pleasure.

"You know, I never use a wand," she commented, and kissed him below the belly button. "But this one I'd like to get my hands on for a test drive."

"Nothing magical there," he commented with an intake of breath as her next kiss was placed on his briefs, right there, on the swollen head of his cock. Though now that he considered it, something magical might happen if she continued her efforts. And he wouldn't be able to contain the results, that was for sure.

"Are you comfortable?" she asked, and then snapped the elastic band of his briefs.

"I…was." He winced, wondering if she intended to snap him again.

"I mean, this rock you're lying on."

"I thought it was a passion rock? Isn't it going to make this all glowy and magical?"

"I don't think we'll glow." She tugged down his pants and boxers. "But magic will happen. I can promise you that."

"Yep…that's…nice grip, witch."

She chuckled and ended it with a lash of her hot tongue over the crown of his cock. Tor closed his eyes. Something hot stung his chest and he winced, but he didn't think on it too long as the wicked, wet heat of Mel's tongue traveled the length of him, slowly, firmly and oh, so…

Another hot sting splashed his shoulder, and now he realized what was happening. The candle wax was dripping from above. And…he almost asked Mel to stop so they could move, but now she sucked him deeply and—fuck, that was good.

He grasped a hank of her hair and didn't push or cajole, but merely anchored himself to her as she expertly lured his body to a rigid, trembling frenzy. He was going to come. And she was still completely dressed.

Wax fell in torturous droplets from above. And… none of it mattered as he saw vivid colors behind his closed eyelids, and the tension in his groin burst. His hips bucked on the pink stone. Mel's hands slid up his abdomen.

And the witch whispered, "Now that was magical."

Crouched over her protector on the rose-quartz table, Mel had never felt more powerful, more in her body and so in touch with her feminine core. Her entire body tingled with the pleasure that she had just given Tor. And she wanted to feel it as viscerally and with such an abandoned thrill as he just had.

But her knees were killing her.

Sliding off the rock table, she tugged up Tor's pants, and he—still breathing heavily and in a sex daze—clutched them at his waist and followed as she grabbed his free hand and led him down the hallway.

"The big pink rock was fun," she said as she entered the bedroom. "But now we're going to do it the comfortable way."

"I'm all for that." Tor dropped his trousers, stepped out of them and flung himself onto the bed. The thick, fluffy comforter slapped over his face and he pulled the blanket about him. "Man, this is soft! It's like a nest in here! You girls get all the good stuff."

Mel leaned over and tapped his erection, which had softened a bit, but was still a mighty wand. "We most certainly do get to play with the good stuff." She kissed his abs and moved up to his chest where— "What's this?"

"Wax." He pulled her up to kiss him. "The candles were dripping on me, but I didn't want to move because what you were doing…"

He kissed her deeply and rolled her to her back, effectively wrapping them into a blanket burrito.

Another drop of wax on his shoulder alerted her. "You should have told me you were in pain."

"It was a good pain."

"You like a little *Fifty Shades*, eh?"

"I don't know what that means. Suffice it to say, I'm not going to lie still if you think dripping candle wax all over me is a good time, but like I said—whew! Now it's my turn." He bowed to kiss her breast through her top. "Okay if I help you out of some of these clothes?"

"Please do."

He untangled them from the blanket and helped her off with the blouse, and when he saw her bra, he bent to study the side embroidery on the yellow and black mesh concoction. "Bees?"

"I love bees."

"Even bees on your boobs?"

Mel giggled as he nuzzled a kiss along the cusp of the lacy cup. A flick of his fingers released the front clasp, and her breasts were freed from their confinement.

"I can still see an impression of the bee here," he said. A kiss to the side of her boob lingered and gave her a good shiver. "You women and your fancy underthings. Who sees them but you?"

"You're seeing them now."

"True. And I do appreciate the effort."

"And if we're going to talk obsessive clothing choices, I know a guy with an OCD closet that'd give a psychologist a wet dream."

"Speaking of wet…" Tor slid his tongue from one breast to the other, forging a slick, heated trail on her skin. When he suckled at her nipple, Mel dipped her head back into the pillow and closed her eyes. She grasped for the sheets, but her fingers only caressed air. It felt so good, and surrendering to the sensation was all she wanted to do.

Wiggling her hips as his hands moved down her skirt, she wrapped her legs about him and pulled his body against hers. Her silky panties slid against his briefs.

"You're so hot and wiggly," Tor said. He suddenly put a hand along her jaw and held her there. She peered into his eyes. "You need to know there's a battle going on inside me right now."

"I know, I know. It's the one where the guy in the suit wielding the stake says this guy right here with the tousled hair and hard-on shouldn't be getting it on with a client."

"You read my mind. Must be a witch thing."

"Trust me, it's a woman thing. I wish I had a spell that would put you in your heart and not your brain, but I don't." Mel sighed and spread her arms out across the mattress in frustration. "I want this, Tor. It doesn't have to be forever. Or even any commitment. Let's have fun. We're both adults. We can have sex with one another if we want to. Do you want to have sex with me?"

"I do. And you're right. I need to get out of my brain."

"I know how to make that happen without magic." She reached down and found a firm hold on him. The man moaned and bowed his head to her chest. He nodded and made a few positive groaning noises, and she knew she had won the battle.

"And don't worry about protection either," she added. "I've got a birth-control spell activated, and it's very effective under the full moon."

"I'll take your word for it." He slid her panties over her hips. "Right now, I want to fall into your lush world of softness and girlie sighs."

Mel sighed for him. "Then come inside me, lover. Come inside."

He kissed each of her breasts. At first he moved slowly, reverently, as if worshipping her skin, her heat, her very being. Then his tongue dashed faster and more firmly, twirling about her nipples, and his lips suckled her to wanting moans.

When he reached for his cock, Mel kept a grip on it, and together they guided him inside her. Tor's body shuddered above hers. Mel's core tightened and shivered as his fingers slicked in her wetness and moved up to circle slowly about her aching, swollen clitoris. As he pumped deeply inside her, the man matched that rhythm with his finger. It was a heady touch that surprised her with its sudden and exacting intensity. He knew just where to touch her to raise up every shivering, delicious, humming thread of pleasure. Her thighs began to shake and her breaths came as gasps.

And when she could no longer cling to the delicious distraction of being almost there, Mel released and her body pulsed upward against Tor's. Together they came in a clutch of panting moans and cries of triumph. Heartbeats racing one another, they shared the high until Tor collapsed beside her and reached for her hand. He lifted it to his mouth and kissed the palm.

Mel turned and nuzzled up against his impossibly fiery warmth. Seeking all of his heat, she stretched a leg across his and tilted her hip closer to make their bodies snug tight against each other.

"That was good," she said in a whisper.

"It's only the beginning." His chest heaved from exertion, and Mel spread her fingers across it. His heart thundered beneath her fingers. "You make me hungry for more, Mel."

"You can have as much of me as you want."

"Good." He turned her onto her back and glided a hand down to between her legs. "I'm going to kiss you right here…" He swirled his finger about her aching clit. "…until you come again."

Chapter 19

While the shower pattered in the next room, Mel lingered between the sheets. Tor had jumped out of bed ready for the day. And when he'd encouraged her to join him, she had made the tough decision to remain in bed. It was only 7:00 a.m. Who even opened their eyes before eight?

Now she spread her hand over the spot where he had lain next to her through the night. She nuzzled her face against the pillow where his black-cherry-tobacco scent had imbued into the fibers. That had been some good sex. Awesome sex. The kind you wanted to do again and again and again. Which they had. She was blissfully exhausted.

How could the man even think to leave her alone and wash her off in the shower?

"His brain must kick in with the sunrise," she muttered, then smiled to herself.

She figured waking up in a woman's bed, not in the comfort of his ultra-tidy and organized home, had to be a challenge in and of itself. How could he even function without a stroll through his closet and a pressed shirt and tie? He'd have to wear the same clothes today, until he found a moment to run home and recharge his OCD uniform.

Again, she smiled. She liked him exactly as uptight and methodical as he could be. Because she'd seen his lighter, loose side. Singing and dancing. And oh, his kisses. Everywhere on her. Her mouth, her breasts, her pussy. Mmm...

And she would have to give that up. Because right now, she realized what sacrifice she could offer to make her dark magic effective.

Tor.

She swore and buried her face against the pillow. It wasn't fair. And yet it was. A sacrifice wasn't that unless it was great and it hurt and the person sacrificing would feel the effects for long after. She hadn't known Tor long, but excising him from her life would feel as though she were cutting out an organ and tossing it aside.

And she knew exactly how to do it. He'd mentioned something about a memory spell. She would give him that. She'd mix it up this morning and then try her hand at dark magic again. If it worked, she would know her sacrifice had been acceptable.

But until that spell was mixed, she intended to indulge in the man. To make memories that she never intended to dispel. So she returned her thoughts to his kisses skating over her skin. His lips brushing her gently and then firmly, followed by the hot lash of his tongue.

She could feel him glide down her belly and dash his tongue against her clit. Pushing her fingers through her curls and between her thighs, she found that swollen bud humming with want. She gasped as a hint of orgasm teased. She could come with a few strokes, and so...

Mel curled down her head under the sheet as her body shivered minutely and the tingles of a soft, sweet orgasm scurried through her being. She heard someone enter the room and ask what she was up to. With a giggle, she tugged down the sheet and crooked her finger at the man who wore but a towel about his hips.

"Yeah?" Tor's big brown eyes glinted. His hair, still wet and tousled this way and that with droplets of water, shone in the ridiculously bright morning sunlight. He released the towel and dropped it to reveal a sizable interest in her suggestion.

When Mel lifted the sheet to invite him into bed, her phone, which lay on the nightstand, suddenly rang. She pouted and patted the bed. "Just ignore it."

"Sure, but..." He leaned over to read the screen. "It's from your dad. Way to kill a good hard-on."

"Oh shoot." She grabbed the phone and before answering gestured for Tor to put the towel back on. "Or it will distract me," she whispered dramatically, then answered, "Hey, Dad. What's up?"

Her dad's voice was frantic, gasping in between his rushed words. Mel immediately understood what he was asking from her. "I'll be right there. Twenty minutes, tops."

Tearing away the sheets, she flew out of bed and grabbed the first piece of clothing she saw, which was a pair of gray leggings flung over a chair.

"What's up?" Tor picked up his shirt from the floor.

"My dad needs me. My sister is going at Mom like crazy, and Dad is desperately trying to get her out of the house and away from her. But in cat form, Mom tends to hide under the couch or in places that are hard to reach.

I have to distract Amaranthe so he can get her. Can you give me a ride?"

"You bet I can." He grabbed his pants and shimmied into them. Threading his arms through the shirt, he picked up his tie. "Let's go."

"I love you for this." Mel pulled on a flouncy red shirt and grabbed her bag of magical supplies.

She caught his hesitation and decided a kiss was necessary. Tor held her fiercely as she took a moment to find her place in the kiss and reassure him that all would be well.

"You're my protector," she said. "And I am my mother's protector. Or I'm helping my dad as best I can. Night of the full moon today! We've got a busy day ahead of us. There's lots to do. Sacrifices to make, on both our parts."

"You figure out what you're going to sacrifice?"

"I did."

"You going to share?"

"Nope. I think it'll lessen the efficacy of the dark magic if I do."

"Fair enough. But both of us? What do I have to sacrifice?"

"Well, you *are* bringing me to my parents' home. You know what waits there."

"Right." His brows furrowed together.

"Don't think about it too much."

Grabbing his hand, she led him down the hallway. Bruce hovered near the door and when Mel paused before her familiar, he dropped a small round piece of jet onto her palm. A stone to protect against evil, and help one accomplish goals. It also worked well to connect one to the spirit world.

"Thanks, Bruce. Now I'm ready."

Mel clasped Tor's hand and led him toward her parents' building. They lived on the entire top floor of a six-story structure in the 16th arrondissement that had been remodeled by Haussmann in the nineteenth century. It was old but sturdy, and she loved the open style and the industrial furnishings. Massive iron beams and support structures framed all the exposed ductwork and piping high above. Add a touch of dark magic, and the place had always felt like home to her.

Until Amaranthe had begun to haunt her mother, Star.

The accident that had taken her sister's life had happened two years ago. The first year following, Amaranthe's ghost had been weak. The family hadn't realized the knocks and sudden window closings were ghostly activity. Until Star had dreamed one night about the incident for which she would forever blame herself. An accident she had not purposefully made happen. It had been just that—an accident.

In cat form, Star had been fleeing the neighbor's rottweiler, which had chased her into the street. An oncoming car, driven by Amaranthe, speeding at a reckless forty miles an hour, had swerved and crashed into a street pole. The pole had sliced down the middle of the car as if it were a knife halving a sandwich. Amaranthe, the doctors had reported, had died upon impact.

But Star had learned differently in her dream. Her daughter had lived for twenty minutes following the accident, trapped in a broken and dying body, unable to scream for help, yet fully aware of the black cat who had paced on the wreckage of the car's hood as the emergency team had pried the woman's body out from the vehicle.

Star had not died the morning of the accident. But the rottweiler had not relented. Later that evening, Star had gone out to run off the intense sadness that had consumed her after losing her daughter and, blinded with grief, had also become victim of a car's overwhelming power. She'd been struck and tossed thirty feet through the air to land against a brick wall, dropping dead to the ground before the confused rottweiler.

Thoroughly and Mel had mourned two family members that day. Only Star had come back to life, unaware of the family she'd been a part of, a family she had helped to create. It had been trying times for both Mel and her father.

But her father had gone through Star's death many times previously. Thoroughly Jones knew the routine. However, it was not something with which he'd ever grown accustomed to or, in any way, at ease with. It had been different that time, with the added grief of having lost one of his daughters. He had been inconsolable, yet quietly strong in reassuring Star. Mel had volunteered to plan her sister's funeral. Together they had buried her at a crossroads near some family land in hopes she would rest in peace.

Not so. This spring was when Amaranthe's ghost had started to gain strength, and—for reasons Mel could only guess were that she assumed Star had purposely run in front of the car—her sister now haunted their mother with a misplaced death wish.

Star, having recently died three weeks earlier after the fall from the roof, was still having difficulty gaining back memories of her family, her loving husband and one remaining daughter. But to add to that the haunting by an angry ghost? To say the fragile familiar was nearing a complete breakdown was not far off.

Now Mel clutched Tor's hand as she stopped before the building and stretched her gaze up to the rooftop.

He kissed her hand and brushed the hair from her cheek. "Want me to go up?"

She shook her head. "I need to go in alone. If Amaranthe knows who you are or senses anything about you, terrible things could happen. I just need to distract her long enough so Dad can get Mom out of the loft."

"I'll stand guard down here. If you need me, call out. I'll be at your side in seconds."

"I know you will."

She took a step onto the first of three stairs leading up to the entrance. Clutching her fingers into fists, she closed her eyes and exhaled. She'd avoided her parents' home these past several days because she didn't want Amaranthe to get a read on her, to learn that something was up. Not that that particular *something* was going at all well. When would she find time to concoct the memory spell? She had to do that. Today. But she needed vervain. And courage. This whole situation had gotten so out of hand.

"Mel?"

Tor called her back to the moment with his sure, calm voice. And back into the reality that hurt her heart. "I'm not sure I can do this, Tor."

"Of course you can." From behind her, he slid his hands down her arms. Nuzzling his cheek aside hers, he pulled her into a hug. All his crazy hard lines and muscles worked in tandem to comfort her. He was a wall of strength to her wobbly, weird jumble of hope, fear and utter panic.

She shifted a hip against his, and the talisman nudged against her. She slid her fingers over the warm, crystal clear quartz.

"I wonder if it can protect you?" he said.

She shook her head. "Probably not. Talismans are very personal."

"Still. It might give you the strength you require to cross the threshold and face what lies beyond the door."

He unhooked the crystal from the D ring at his belt and placed it on her palm. "Take it."

"But…you never go anywhere without it. This is…it's personal to you, Tor."

"I'll get it back from you as soon as you come down. Think of it as my way of being close to you."

"Okay." She tucked the talisman in her pocket, and the heavy weight against her hip felt right. Yes, he could accompany her in this way. "You'll wait down here in the lobby?"

"I will. But I can follow you up and wait outside the loft."

"No." She opened the building door and, feeling the strong wards her father placed on the entrance shiver through her veins, sucked in a gasp and stepped across the threshold. "I have to do this."

And she marched onward, up the first flight of stairs, not turning back to say anything more to Tor. With his fear of ghosts, she knew argument wasn't necessary to keep him at a distance. And she didn't need him—well, maybe a little—but she truly did fear the consequences should she attempt to bring him along with her. Sliding her hand in the pocket, she curled her fingers about the talisman. It was his magic, and she did feel his presence as a repeat of that reassuring hug he'd just given her.

The stairs were creaky, and yet she never took the elevator. No magical reason, just the remembered fear of being trapped in the tiny one-person box for five hours that one summer when a lightning storm had taken out the building's power.

On the sixth floor, she stood in the vast harlequin-checked foyer before the Jones residence and sucked in a breath. A tear spilled from her eye. She missed her sister. Everything about this situation sucked, big-time.

And tonight—if she thought now was difficult, tonight would only prove insurmountable.

Could she do this?

Glancing down the stairs, she wished to see Tor standing there on the landing, his kind brown eyes offering her strength. But he had his own ghosts with which to deal. Another stroke of her fingers over the talisman reassured her. Mel sucked in a breath and walked up to knock on the door.

Her dad answered immediately. He held the handle of an empty plastic cat carrier in one hand. With his other arm, he swept it around her shoulder and pulled her in for a hug. "Thank you for coming, Lissa. This has gotten out of hand. None of my repulsive magic is effective either. She's getting stronger."

"It's not your fault, Dad." She hugged him tightly. Melting into his arms had always felt so good. But now she felt him tremble and could feel the sad energy leaking out of him. "Where's Mom?"

"Under the couch. She knows what I'm trying to do, but she won't put out more than a paw."

"Where's Amaranthe?"

"Somewhere near the couch. I think." He glanced over his shoulder. The couch was across the vast loft, pushed up against the windowed wall. "You know I've no magic to ward off my own blood. Ghost or not. If you could just call her to you."

Mel nodded. "I've got this. You focus on Mom. Soon as you have her, run out of here."

"I intend to." He gave her another quick hug. "We can do this. Tonight it will be over."

"Yes." Mel sucked in a deep inhale.

Tonight would bring peace to the Jones family. If she

got her act together. And sacrificed the one really great thing that had happened in her life.

Wandering in behind her dad, Mel searched the air, knowing she wouldn't see her sister's ghost. Amaranthe had never apported into corporeal form. But she could sense her presence by a coolness to the air—there.

The side of her neck prickled, and it felt as if an ice cube had sluiced down her shoulder and to her elbow. She gripped Tor's talisman. It helped him to *not* see ghosts? If only she *could* see her sister's ghost. Still, the inspiring sense that Tor was close, perhaps just behind her, bolstered her courage.

She could do this.

"Amaranthe?" Mel whispered. She closed her eyes. Focusing her senses beyond her body, she tapped into the air about her. "I miss you, sister."

Wavery whispers that she could not interpret slid over her scalp and tickled her ears. It was a faraway call, a fleeting scream for help. But since Amaranthe's death, they'd never been able to communicate with words. Unfortunately.

Not wanting to call attention to her parents, Mel turned the opposite way from the couch and walked over to the window. There, she breathed on the glass and then quickly traced a heart in the condensation. A sudden slash marked the fading heart, startling Mel at the power her sister possessed. Yet behind her, she was aware of her father moving swiftly toward the door, the cat carrier clutched to his chest, and inside was the hissing cat she called Mom.

Cold air chilled Mel's cheek as she felt her sister's ghost rush toward the closing front door. The door slammed, and the light fixtures rattled angrily. Her dad had successfully escaped.

Now to face her sister's wrath.

* * *

Tor paced the lobby's marble floor, arms swinging wide and meeting before him with a fist to his palm. Back and forth, slap. Back and forth, slap. When the man in dark clothing carrying a cat carrier descended the stairs in a flurry and stopped before him, Tor swallowed.

"She did it?" he asked, knowing it was a stupid question as soon as he'd opened his mouth.

TJ nodded. "Why aren't you up there with her?"

"I, uh…" Because there was a ghost. And— "Mel asked me to stay down here."

"I thought you were protecting my daughter?"

"I am, but…"

TJ shook his head, disapproving.

"Is she still in the apartment? Alone? With the…"

"I'm not sure what Amaranthe will do. She's dangerous. I can't believe someone who calls himself a protector would allow a woman to walk in on a volatile situation. Alone."

"She said it wasn't wise—" Argument was stupid. And not fair to the family. "You're right. She needs me. I'll take care of your daughter, Monsieur Jones. I promise. How's your, uh…wife?"

The cat in the cage hissed at Tor.

"Frightened. I'm taking her to my brother's for the night until Lissa can invoke the spell. You will accompany her for that?"

"Of course. That's what she hired me to do." Tor took off toward the stairs. "I'll keep her safe!"

"You will," TJ called, "or you will know the Jones family's wrath!"

That was more than enough motivation to quicken Tor's pace. He took the stairs two at a time, not sure why Mel had not taken the elevator. While waiting, he'd seen a man with a briefcase exit it, but—well, magic and elevators. There was something to that combination that he didn't want to test.

While pacing in the lobby, he had struggled with his fear of ghosts and why he hadn't insisted on accompanying Mel upstairs. And yet she had been firm, and he hadn't wanted to cause problems with the ghost. But now he realized she needed him no matter what.

At the front door, he lifted his hand to knock, then paused. He leaned in close and listened, and heard... crying. Opening the door quietly, he stuck in his head and searched the chilly air in the loft, which was two stories high and open to the rafters. He wasn't sure what he expected to see—well, yes, he was. He would see specters. Ghosts. Haunts.

Nothing.

Had the sister fled after TJ had escaped with Star? Or was she standing over Mel right now, tormenting her? He saw Mel, sitting on the floor, back to him. Her head was bowed and she was sobbing.

Rushing inside, Tor plunged to the floor beside Mel. Before taking her in his arms, he checked her expression. She didn't appear to be frightened or tormented, but she was crying. Perhaps she was not haunted right now. He took her in his arms and pulled her into a hug.

"Tell me what you need me to do," he said.

She shivered against him and sniffled. "She's here."

And he did know that. The instant he'd run inside, he'd felt the cold air, the knowing presence of another.

"Where?"

"Not sure. She won't speak to me. I can feel her anger. Why is she so angry? Why won't she believe that Mom had nothing to do with her death?"

Her mother had not purposely sought to harm her

daughter, but fact remained, she had run in front of the car. Perhaps the ghost could not get beyond that. She might only carry the knowledge she had from the moment of the accident, which had been that the cat had run before the car. And when she died, she could have never learned that it had been an accident. Maybe?

Tor didn't want to have a conversation with the entity to learn why.

"Your dad has left the building and your mom is safe," he said. "Let's get you out of here."

She nodded and, with his help, stood. Wrapping an arm about her shoulder, Tor realized she felt smaller, more delicate and so cold. When they neared the open door, it suddenly slammed shut and a gush of icy wind raked through his hair.

"You need to get out of here now," he said, fully planning to follow her out. He gripped the doorknob. The icy metal stung and he hissed, but he managed to pull open the door. "Go!"

"Wait!" Mel paused on the threshold. "I need vervain. I'm out, and Dad said he had some."

"I'll get it." Another gust of wind pushed on the door, and Tor struggled to hold it open. "Where is it?"

"With Dad's spell stuff around the corner."

"Go!" Tor yelled, just as the door slipped from his white-knuckle grasp and slammed shut.

Turning and facing the open space of the loft, Tor darted his gaze about the room. A trickle of cold air brushed his eyelids, yet it wasn't as threatening as the door slamming had been.

"Vervain," he whispered.

Around the corner? He located a kitchen and found what looked like an ancient apothecary's desk and cabinet heaped with vials and bottles and candles and potions. A massive handcrafted book sat splayed open on the center of a wood table carved with ancient sigils that caused the hairs on Tor's arms to stand upright.

He swallowed. "A dark witch's grimoire. Not going to touch that thing."

Tor scrambled over to the shelf and studied the conglomeration of vials and bottles and boxes. Everything was dusty and arranged chaotically—did no one have a sense of order in this family?

"Vervain. What does vervain look like?"

"It's in the jar labeled Vervain."

"Thanks." Tor grabbed the small jar, then swallowed roughly. "Ah, shit." He spun to face a blonde woman who looked a lot like Mel, save her eyes, which were rimmed with dark shadows. And her lips were bloodred. "Amaranthe?"

"You can see me?" The entity floated toward him.

Tor nodded, clutching the vervain to his chest. He slid his other hand down to his hip where the talisman—was not there.

When the ghost raked an icy hand through his hair, he dropped the glass jar, which she caught in a wispy hand that morphed from foggy smoke to a fully formed corporeal hand.

"This," she said, "is going to be fun."

Chapter 20

The room was so cold Tor's breath fogged before him as he breathed, ever so shallowly, and took a step back from the ghost. She had assumed corporeal shape. Flesh-and-blood real. And she looked so much like Mel, except with blond hair. The same big blue doe eyes.

Bollocks. He'd seen far too many ghosts in his lifetime, but never had one been so solidly formed.

"You see me," Amaranthe said, "because the veil between you and my world is nonexistent."

"State the obvious, will you?" he tried.

"Are you mocking me, mortal man? Who are you? Why does a common human enter my parents' home and look about for things that he should not have reason to use?"

"The vervain is for…" He wouldn't give the ghost any more fuel. He had to keep her calm. And get the hell out of here before his insecurity paralyzed him.

"Vervain is for releasing things from the heart and the soul. Hmm…" The ghost tapped a finger on her lips. "For whom? My father? My mother? Or…" Her brow arched in evil triumph. "My sister. You and Lissa are lovers. My sister is fucking a human."

He would not reply. Must not look at her overlong. She was beginning to lose the darkness around her eyes, the only thing that gave her a skeletal appearance, and her hair was changing to brown and growing even darker. Her bright blue eyes widened. Just like Mel's. Impossible. But nothing was impossible in the paranormal realm. Tor knew a specter could assume the guise of another with little effort.

"She just needed some vervain," he tried. "Silly spell stuff. You know."

"Magic is never silly. Tell me why Lissa gives you the time of day?"

"I, uh… No. I'll just take this…" He grabbed the small glass jar the spirit had set on the desk and stuffed it in his pocket. When he turned back to the ghost, Mel loomed before him, her long hair flowing and her doe eyes beaming at him. There was even glitter on her eyelids. Lemons and lavender filled his senses.

"No," Tor whispered. His jaw tight, he uttered, "You're not Mel. You're not."

"You call her Mel?" The ghost tilted her head. Crimped the edge of her upper lip in disgust. "Strange. Of course, she never did like Lissa. I always called her *twerp*. She's the older one, you know? I have always been younger. More beautiful, yes?" She quickly took on her own persona with the blond hair, and her skin remained young and fresh, not shadowed or dank.

She was beautiful. For a ghost.

"Star did not mean for your death to happen," Tor said.

The ghost snarled and slashed clawed fingers at him.

He didn't feel the cut of her fingernails on his skin, but he could feel the tug to his very being as she connected with him on a metaphysical level. Damn it, he should not have left the talisman with Mel. He'd never allowed anyone to touch it, or worse, borrow it. What had gotten into him?

But he was here now. And he wasn't about to run from a figment, a projection of a former life. The soul caught in this mortal realm was merely wearing a costume of what she'd once been. And that soul was a cruel, violent being who was trying to kill her own mother.

"Amaranthe Jones, why don't you give up and go to the light?" he asked. To use a person's full name had power; it drew them to the moment, crystal clear reality. And the dead never liked to be reminded of their status.

"The light? Ha!" Amaranthe spread out her arms, and at the ends of her fingers green sparks snapped. Ectoplasmic remnants? Or some sort of ghostly magic he did not want to deal with? "You know nothing about me, human."

"I know you're dead. And the dead do not belong in this realm."

"Says the one who has been dallying with nothing but the dead ever since meeting my sister. Oh, I know. I tapped into Melissande's thoughts when she was here. She is enamored with you. And you are of her. It isn't fair!" The ghost cried, clenching her fists. "She gets everything. Mom always did like her better!"

"That…is ridiculous. I've not met your mother but—"

"Which means you don't know anything about her. Star was the reason I will never walk this world in corporeal form. Never again will I know love, or the touch of a man's mouth on my lips."

Her figment hovered before him. Tor veered away, but

she leaned in, putting their faces inches from one another. "Would you kiss me, human?"

If he touched her, he would never be the same. Tor had made physical contact with the spirits he'd seen over the years. Not by choice. Each time, he felt the lingering remnants of a soul settle into his skin and deep into his very bones. And one so angry as Amaranthe would surely foul his very being.

"You deserve all that and more," he said, avoiding the deep blue irises that sought to pull him closer, to lure his hands up to caress her hair. As if she were Mel… "You are a soul, Amaranthe. You can live again. But you need to leave this realm first. Do that. Let your soul begin another journey."

"That's death, asshole."

He shrugged, then winced because she was right, and he had never been faced with trying to spin his way into convincing a ghost to leave this realm.

"There is nothing here for you," he tried. "Just…you will be free."

"I go nowhere without my mother's last life!"

He was not appealing to her morals, and he didn't want to make things worse for the family. Tor knew when to cut his losses and run. Slipping quickly around the ghost, he aimed for the front door.

"Your family loves you!" he called.

But as he gripped the icy doorknob, Amaranthe coalesced into form and he ran right into her. The fusion of her death-chilled essence to his warm, living flesh burned him. With a yelp, Tor shoved away from the door. He could feel her essence enter his skin and bite at his nerves.

"You're a conduit. Open to the spirit realm." The ghost stalked toward him. "I could use you."

For what, he didn't want to know. To return from whence she came? He could only hope.

Now her eyes were white and her mouth opened wide as she yowled a wicked, otherworldly cry that shattered the glass candleholder on a nearby table and broke glasses in the kitchen.

Tor's nerves twanged and his body went rigid. He wanted to swing out in an attempt to push her away, but even as he had the thought, he knew he couldn't allow himself to hurt a woman. Mel's sister, by the gods. And right now, frozen by her wicked essence, he could barely stand, let alone move an arm.

"I won't rest until she stands beside me in this strange Beneath," Amaranthe announced. "My mother murdered me."

"She didn't," he forced out through his tight jaw. The pain was incredible. He yelped, and that utterance worked to release some of the tension in his body. He bent forward, catching his hands on his knees. A shiver seemed to shave off some of her heavy residue. "She was just a cat running away from a dog!"

A slash of Amaranthe's clawed fingers streaked a burn across Tor's cheek. She stood ten feet away from him, but he touched his face and felt the blood. She was gaining strength, a strange power that he was unable to repel without the talisman.

With another unearthly shout, the ghost plunged toward him.

Tor dodged to the floor, rolled onto his back and under the charging ghost, and came up to his feet. He grabbed the doorknob and opened the door. As he crossed the threshold, he tripped on nothing more than air—or more likely, the ghost's aggression. He slid into the foyer, facing the open doorway.

Amaranthe eyed the opening with a glint to her white eyes.

"Shit." Tor lunged to his feet and reached in to grab the doorknob, and as he pulled it shut, he felt the ghost's iced fingers claw through his hair. He pulled it shut with effort and stepped back, stumbling against the wall and choking at the icy hollow in his throat.

Waiting, peering about him, he sensed she had not escaped the loft. Perhaps bound to the home, perhaps not. But she'd not been able to leave. Yet.

A prickle of hot pain clutched at his system, and he closed his eyes and huffed out breaths, trying to find a calm place instead of surrendering to the tightness the pain coaxed him toward. Panting, he heaved and then turned and caught his palms against the wall, pressing his forehead there. He'd done it. He'd faced down a volatile ghost. And…he was still in one piece. He hoped.

Shaking his arms out at his side flaked off the remaining sludge from the specter. It wasn't tangible, but Tor felt his muscles lighten. Whew!

Patting his pocket to ensure the vervain was still there, he took the stairs rapidly downward and didn't stop until he plunged into Mel's arms outside the building. Inhaling her citrus scent did not reassure him as usual. It only reminded him of what he'd just escaped.

"You're bleeding?" She touched his cheek. "What did she do to you? Oh, Tor, you saw her. The ghost of my sister?"

He nodded. "I'm good."

"I don't believe you." Her eyes pooled with tears.

"Mel, it's okay. Trust me. Just need to walk it off. Get her completely out of my system." He flung out his hand, shaking it, and then, stepping back from Mel, did the same with his other hand. A few jumps shook the lingering tendrils of nerve pain from his body as if sifting out toxins. "I saw her, plain as day. She's beautiful. Like you. But she's very angry."

"You had a conversation with her?"

"She believes your mother murdered her."

"That's wrong."

"I know that, but for some reason she doesn't. You have the talisman?"

"Oh, my mercy. I'm so sorry! You didn't have it on you. No wonder you saw her. And that must be why she was able to touch you. To hurt you."

"I'll survive."

She slapped the heavy crystal into his palm. "I've been clutching it desperately. You have to cleanse it with salt when we get home."

"First thing on my list." He glanced upward, toward the top floor of the building. The ghost had been inside him. He had felt her fingernails claw across his cheek. Her touch had entered his bones. "She can't...get out of the loft, can she?"

"She has when the door has been left open, or a window. But we only have until midnight to make it all stop. I need to go home and practice the spell, and there's the other thing—did you get the vervain?"

He patted his pocket and nodded. "Let's head home."

Mel had asked for a few hours alone in her spell room to go over the spell for tonight. She handed him a pink plastic container of black sea salt for the talisman, so he put it in there to cleanse.

With nothing to do but wait, Tor raided the fridge and found—situated around the plastic tub that held a dead witch's heart—an abundance of fruits and vegetables, which he had no idea how to cook or bake or whatever a person did to make them look fabulous like Mel did. But he was hungry, so he'd figure something out.

He grabbed a few carrots and a kiwi, then found a baguette and some soft cheese. Cutting and slicing, he ate until he was full while he prepared a plate, then set that plate by the entrance to the spell room. Calling out for a delivery, he left before the door could open and headed outside.

After finally shaking off the heebie-jeebies that had been riding him since facing the ghost of Mel's sister at the Joneses' loft, he tightened his tie and wandered up the sidewalk to the van, parked in front of the property. From the back, he pulled out one of the pressure-release titanium stakes that had been designed by Rook for the knights in The Order of the Stake.

He considered it a great sign of trust that Rook had gifted him with a few of these weapons. In preparation for later tonight, he tucked that inside his vest. He always made sure his tailor added special pockets and slip inserts for storing weapons. The man, who worked on Savile Row in London, never asked questions. He was good stock. Yet aging quickly. Who would make his suits in another few years after the old man had passed? Tor didn't want to consider the snappish Parisian tailors.

Shaking his head and laughing because he could actually find something to think about other than impending doom—and it happened to be bespoke suits, of all things—Tor surveyed the van's inventory.

The machete he'd used the other night gleamed. One of his go-to weapons. He gave it some consideration.

He shouldn't need it here at Mel's place. As far as he knew, she hadn't made a sacrifice to add efficacy to her dark magic, so he was on guard. He'd reserve the wicked blade for later, when they were on-site. Instead, he took out a pistol loaded with salt rounds and then closed the van doors.

He scanned the neighborhood and took in the small yet idyllic green yards, the brick and limestone house fronts, terra-cotta chimney pots, and tight boxwood shrubbery that had been tamed to the horticulturist's will. There was old money here in the 6th arrondissement. He assumed Mel had a trust fund, because he was never sure how witches made a living. She had mentioned something about being between jobs. The most enterprising paranormal he'd ever met was a billionaire werewolf who donated all his money to charity. But he'd come by his money through faery magic, not any sort of knuckles-to-the-grindstone work.

The world needed all sorts of workers, craftsmen and handymen. And women. He wouldn't question or argue his place in that hierarchy. He'd done what he knew how to do all his life. And now he was ready for a change, so he'd make that transformation. He could live a normal life. He just had to do it.

And yet tonight he would accompany a witch on a quest to invoke dark magic to raise a person—her own sister—from the dead. There should be something wrong with that. And yet there was nothing whatsoever strange or unusual about it when compared to his usual routine.

And that was the kicker. His normal was severely cocked up. He lived beyond slightly eccentric, or even wild and adventurous. Which was why he didn't have friends. How to have human friends when a man could never engage in conversation about a day at the office but instead about the night out cleaning up dead paranormals? He'd always been a loner, and…it wasn't all it was cracked up to be.

A night at a friend's house tilting back some brews and watching a game? He couldn't imagine it. But he'd like to.

"Yep," he muttered as he strode up the walk to Mel's house. "Ready to leave it all behind."

Mostly. Maybe? Hell, he wasn't sure anymore. Because, by staying in the thick of things for a few more days, he'd met Melissande Jones and now…

Now he really liked her. He could go so far as to say he had fallen for her. He couldn't imagine not having run into her. His life would have a hole in it without her. How crazy was that?

Mel represented the part he wanted to excise from his life. So what was he thinking? He couldn't have it both ways. Normal life and witch in his life. It just couldn't work.

Rook had been right to suggest he utilize a memory spell. If he couldn't remember ever having met Mel, then he could do this. It was absolutely the only way he could do this.

Tor nodded. It would be tough, but he'd do it. He had to.

Instead of going back inside the house, he decided to patrol around the perimeter. It was sprinkling, and clouds had darkened the sky. Most of his jobs occurred during the night, although the rush jobs were generally because some creature was stalking during the daylight—or had been found dead in a place where any human could stumble onto it.

A job in an accounting office would keep him out of the sun, as well. Tor could do the math. An office job wasn't nine to five, but usually eight to whenever a guy

could drag himself away from the desk. He'd miss the physical activity his current profession afforded. He'd have to request the tailor take in his shirts to compensate for muscle loss.

Who was he kidding? He'd up his workout program. He wasn't going to abandon these guns just because he worked in a cubicle.

Would his target skills decrease? And what about his machete-throwing skills? How about his time for cleaning a dead werewolf? Or his knowledge of which chemicals removed blood and dissolved fur and bones the fastest?

He did possess strange and esoteric knowledge. But he didn't know a thing about the flowers of which he currently strolled beneath. A canopy of soft pink petals dusted his head. They hung from a wrought iron trellis connected to the kitchen side of the house. Tor closed his eyes and drew in the scent. Sweet as Mel's kisses.

A duck's quack startled him, and he stepped out from under the trellis and into the backyard. "Hey, Duck. What's up?"

He'd just said hello to a duck, and…had started a conversation. Without so much as a blink. Tor ran his fingers through his hair. That witch. Did he really want to forget she had been part of his life?

Sitting on the edge of the concrete patio where a patch of moss tried to climb over the stone and take over, he picked a long blade of grass and remembered how when he was a kid he'd used it to whistle. Placing his thumbs together with the grass between them, he managed a screeching yet wobbly whistle. Duck tossed him a wonky look (as wonky an expression as a duck could manage, anyway).

"I'm much better at wolf howls," he said to the fowl.

"But I don't want to call any werewolves to the neighborhood."

"Why not?" asked a male voice from under the floral canopy.

Tor jumped to a stand, pulling out the pistol, and aimed it at the smirking werewolf.

Chapter 21

Mel combined the vervain and black salt and the whiskers from a hairless cat. Crushed rose petals soaked in rosemary oil topped the concoction. She whispered the words that would imbue the potion with a spell that would take away memory of which all things a human should not be aware.

It was the worst spell she'd ever concocted. But it had to be done. If Tor intended to walk away from this life, from this world she had always occupied and would continue to live in, then he couldn't know about her. It would be too painful for her if he ever returned and she knew he didn't want to have a relationship with her because of what she was.

Half an hour later, the memory spell settled in the thin glass vial before Mel's disappointed gaze. She was upset because it was complete, and it had proven to serve her what she'd needed: a sacrifice. By concocting the spell with the intent of giving it to Tor so he could take it—to forget about her—she had given the dark forces of magic what they desired most.

And she knew that because the dead ivy currently climbing along the inside of the spell-room window turned greener and more vital with every second. She'd performed a dark magic spell to bring something back to life. And it had worked. Too well. Next, she'd recloak the heart for even more practice.

Which meant tonight she should have control over the dark magic she needed.

But at what cost?

"Him," she whispered, then tucked the vial into her skirt pocket.

"This property is warded," Tor announced. "How the hell?"

The wolf crossed his arms and leaned against the trellis support beam. He was as tall as Tor, yet a wrestler's build beefed up his torso and widened his shoulders beneath a loose T-shirt. Dark brown hair clung close to his scalp, and a nick in his left eyebrow suggested an injury that he might be more proud of than upset about. Wolves rarely scarred, so this had to have been serious. On his neck, a tattoo of two small red spots resembled bite marks and—maybe they were actual bite marks. Because Tor had never met a werewolf who wasted time on tattoos. It wasn't like the ink stayed put on a shapeshifter's skin. Get a tat of *Mom* in the center of a heart? A couple shifts later, friends would question who "Norm" was.

His finger not moving from the trigger, Tor asked, "Who are you?"

The wolf thrust up a placating palm. Tor didn't sense

aggression from him, but he wasn't going to let down his guard.

"Name's Christian Hart," he offered. "I was in the neighborhood and got some squicky feelings coming from this house. I like to keep an eye on the old neighborhood. Keep things calm. But I see you're on the job, eh?" One of his nostrils flared as he breathed in the air. "You're just human though."

"And who is Christian Hart?" Tor asked.

"Just a regular guy."

"A werewolf who likes to get bitten by a vampire," Tor guessed, and lowered the pistol, but he wasn't going to tuck it away.

"You think you're so smart?"

"I am. Those are bite marks on your neck."

The wolf shrugged. "Maybe so. My girl's a vamp. No way around it. But you're avoiding the obvious. What's going on here?" He shook out his arms like a prizefighter readying for a fight. "I can feel death creeping up my spine. Feels like I've got it watching me from every which way."

"Got it under control," Tor said. "The hounds can cease and vacate the property."

Hart lunged and gripped Tor by the tie, snarling to reveal his thick canines.

"Settle," Tor said. He slid the barrel of the pistol aside the wolf's hip. "The heart is making you wild. My suggestion is you leave the area, and quick, wolf."

"The heart?" His eyes searched Tor's, but he didn't release him. And Tor felt his growing anger. He could smell it. He shouldn't have used the hound reference. Werewolves were so sensitive about being called dogs. "What is *the heart*?"

"It's a…witch thing."

Hart released him and stepped back. His gaze quickly took in the garden and then the back of the house. Like an animal, he saw it all and probably smelled it all, too. "This is a witch's place?"

Tor nodded.

"I don't like witches." The wolf mock shivered. "They are a nasty bunch."

"Then you should leave. And I won't have to see how well salt rounds work on werewolves." Tor waved the pistol warningly.

"I could take you out with one swipe, human."

"Yes, you probably can. But you won't, because the aggression you're feeling now? It's not you. It's a crazy dried chunk of muscle that once belonged to an ancient witch that's attracting all the dead things to this yard, and—I'm not sure why it attracted you, but like I said, if you leave you'll feel much better. So why don't you slowly back away and get the hell out."

The wolf looked over Tor's shoulder and narrowed his eyes. Tor saw his biceps tighten and his jaw pulse. Just as he sensed he would leap, Tor lifted the pistol. Hart soared toward Tor, but his aim was high and he cleared Tor's head and landed on the vampire who had stalked up behind him.

The wolf scuffled with the vampire, snarling and growling too loudly for Tor's peace of mind. This was a populated neighborhood—though Mel's shrubbery was higher than his head. It had gotten darker, and now the rain threatened to become a downpour. He needed to make whatever this was end. Right now.

Tor pulled out the stake and stalked around the two battling creatures. Apparently, the wolf was on his side.

Maybe? He could have let the vamp attack him from behind, so Tor gave him the benefit of the doubt.

Surprisingly, the vampire managed to fling the wolf
off his shoulders and toss him into a nearby shrub pruned
in the shape of a cat.

Yes, a cat. Oh, the irony.

But Tor didn't take any more time to snicker over it.
Plunging the stake against the vampire's chest, he compressed the paddles, and the titanium stake entered the
asshole's heart. Ash formed about the stake's entry point,
but the rest of the body merely shivered, convulsing.

"A bloody revenant," Hart said from the ground. He
was tangled in the cat's shrubbery tail. "What the hell?
How do you kill one of those things?"

"Keep an eye on it!" Tor called as he swung out of the
backyard and around the side of the house. Should have
grabbed the machete after all. He secured the weapon
from the back of the van and sped around to the site
where the vampire lay convulsing. The werewolf stood
over him, growling.

With one swipe of his arm, Tor brought the machete
down. The vamp's head severed from its body. The whole
thing finally ashed into a pile of steaming gray flakes.
Rain pattered the pile, sluicing it into a sludgy mess on
the grass.

"How do you know that one was revenant?" Tor asked.

"Because I can smell its stench." Hart tapped his nose.
"Superpowers, don't you know?"

"You know a lot for a wolf."

"Yeah, but what I don't know is, Why was it here?
What did you do to attract that thing? Was it that heart
you were telling me about?"

"Dead things are attracted to what the witch inside is
using for a spell."

"Yeah? Well, I'd like to lodge a protest against dark magic in this neighborhood."

"Good luck with that. Thanks for having my back. Literally."

"No problem. And you are?"

"Torsten Rindle." He made to offer his hand, but the wolf flinched as he raised the machete, so he transferred it to the other hand and then made the offer. The wolf had a good, steady clasp.

"I've heard of you," Hart said. "And it wasn't good. You caged a friend of my girl's a few years back. Domingos LaRoque. Vampire."

"I remember him. Poor guy. But I didn't cage him." That vampire had been tortured by werewolves and now had an extreme aversion to sunlight. Not necessarily a bad thing for vamps. But, as well, he was not always there in the head. *Crazy* was putting his condition gently. "I helped him after his escape from the pack who had tortured him."

And that was all he'd say about that. Client confidentiality was key.

"I should get going," Hart said. He tossed his head sharply, flicking the rain from his face. "You're right. The vibes coming from this house are beyond wicked. But how long will it last?"

Tor tilted the dull side of the blade against his shoulder. "Should be over by morning. Full moon tonight—" He glanced skyward. Rain spattered his cheeks. Clouds covered the moon, which would later be shadowed by the earth. "But then, you know that. Which begs the question—what are you doing in the city?"

"I'm headed out to our château later," Hart said. "But I'm sticking around town as long as my growly side will allow it. My girl's due to give birth any day now and has been staying with a healer in the area who's keeping a close eye on her. I want to stay close, as well."

"Congratulations." Tor could hide his wince like a pro. A child born of a vampire and werewolf? Yikes.

A scream from inside the house alerted them both. Tor ran onto the patio and opened the glass door. Behind him, the werewolf followed close on his heels. "I got this," Tor called as he raced through the living area.

"Yeah, we'll see," the wolf muttered, still following.

Tor ran down the hallway and into the spell room, then stopped abruptly at the sight of the vampire holding Mel against his chest. Fangs glinting, the bastard gripped Mel tight about the neck. And when Hart joined him and hissed a curse, the vampire cracked a bloody grin.

"Keep your distance, *mes amies*," the vampire said. "I want the heart. But if you're not careful, I might have to rip out her carotid and use it to tie the two of you up to keep you out of my way."

"Cocky—"

Tor caught Hart against the chest with an elbow when he felt the wolf try to rush forward. "Chill, man. Let's have a conversation with the nice vampire, all right?"

"Another revenant," Hart said.

Tor eyed the vampire keenly. The wolf was right. The vampire's eyes were red—not like a demon's, but as if a blood vessel had burst, almost obliterating the whites. He also...smelled. Tor could scent earth on him. As if he'd risen from a grave? That he could smell him, above and beyond the herbs and other scents in this room, was remarkable.

"First, I want to know how you were able to enter the witch's home without a proper invite."

Vamps could not cross a private threshold without an invite.

Mel cleared her throat. "Mortal realm rules are not relevant to a dead thing."

The vampire tightened his clutch on her.

"And," she continued, "my wards are down while I, umm…sealed the sacrifice."

Tor winced. He wanted nothing more than to tear Mel away and decapitate the vampire, but he wasn't a fool. And the vamp was closer to Mel than he was. For now.

"Is there a revenant tribe in Paris we don't know about?" Tor asked.

The vampire tilted his head against Mel's. For her part, Mel appeared calm, but Tor kept an eye on the vampire's hand, wrapped under her chin. One quick slash of those long fingernails could end the witch's life.

"I didn't come to chat," the vampire said. "And tribe business is private."

Which confirmed the question about a tribe. Rook had been correct to make such a guess.

"So is the part where I slayed half your number the other day alongside an Order knight also a secret?" Tor volleyed.

The vampire hissed. "You were the one?"

Tor waggled the machete at his side, but not too boldly. The vampire held his girl.

"You won't use that on me unless you also want her head rolling on the floor beside mine," the vampire taunted. "I've been sent for the heart. Where is it?"

If the vamp knew it was a heart, he could have only learned it from another vamp in the know. And that could only have been the one Tor had let go the other night in the alley after he'd stolen Mel's bag. His mistake.

And in that streak of lightning were illuminated the dozen faces that stood outside the windows looking in.

Revenant vampires.

Chapter 22

"Get the heart out of the kitchen," Mel muttered from behind the vampire's foul grip. The creature smelled, and she was pretty sure it was because he was dead. But if Tor was going to grandstand and waste time joking around with the strange werewolf, she was not having it. "Please, Tor!"

"I'll keep an eye on him," the werewolf said.

Where he had come from was beyond her, but she couldn't worry about that right now. She'd already tried to zap the vamp with repulsive magic, but her nerves made that impossible. She should have recloaked the heart. Fortunately, the vampire couldn't sense it so close because of the dried wild roses hanging overhead. They were a powerful block, and sometimes even repellent to vampires.

"Fine." Tor took a step back, but made a show of taking in the windows.

A dozen sets of eyes, most with white irises, peered

in, giving Mel the creeps. She could handle one vampire. Maybe. Probably not. Her nerves wouldn't allow her to even whisper a repellent spell right now. But she felt safe with Tor and the werewolf close. But if the other vampires got inside? Tor had said he wasn't a slayer. He was just the cleanup guy.

"Hurry," she managed to say.

Tor nodded and slipped around the corner. A whistled tune echoed down the hallway and into the kitchen. How the man could sing at a time like this—then Mel realized it was his fuel. He was whistling a song she recognized: "Call Me Irresponsible," about a man who realized he'd fallen in love.

Damn it, she was probably falling for him, too. Not even probably. She'd fallen hard for the guy who had killer dimples and a soft heart for levitating frogs.

The revenant's grip loosened a bit, and Mel could breathe more easily. She wouldn't move though. She wasn't stupid. But she was—curse her—curious.

"What are you going to do with the heart?" she asked. "Every dead thing in Paris has been after it. I don't understand. What use will it serve you?"

"It gives life to the dead," the vampire said. "Who wouldn't want it?"

"In case you haven't noticed, Monsieur Revenant, you *have* life. And you are dead. What difference is the witch's heart going to make?"

"Don't you understand? With the heart's power, I will be alive, not dead. No longer a revenant."

"Go for it," the wolf encouraged. "That will make you easier to kill. Beheading unnecessary." He crossed his arms high on his chest and kept his gaze to the windows. "Once you're like all the other vamps? Just a stake will do."

"He has a point," Mel said, crimping her brow as she realized she was agreeing with a werewolf. A strange, wet werewolf she had never met before. "Don't you like having the added failsafe your current status of undead provides?"

"Do you like me, witch?" The vampire nudged his nose against her ear. His hot breath wilted across her cheek. His scent resembled earth upon which mushrooms had spoiled and rotted into the ground.

"I generally do not like men who are mean to me, and who threaten to kill me," she said. "So, my answer is *no*. And you smell."

"Not my fault. Death does that to a man. Among other things, like being unable to get it up because some things are just…" He started a sigh but then caught himself as he again tightened his grip about Mel's neck. "You see why I want the heart?"

"Got it!" Tor reentered, wielding a pink plastic container high. He gave it a shake and something inside sloshed around. In his other hand, he had not let go of the machete.

Mel couldn't figure out what he might have put in the container. The real heart was under the table right now. She just hoped the vamp didn't peek inside the decoy container before taking off.

"Give it to me," the vampire commanded.

"Let her go first." Tor held the container before him in a teasing waggle. "She gets to move to the other side of the table, away from you. Then I hand you the heart. That's the only way it's going to work."

The vampire roughly shoved her away. Mel caught her forearms on the spell table, sweeping a spray of black salt to the floor. She quickly sidled around to the opposite side, but when she started toward Tor, the vampire hissed.

"Right there," he commanded. "Until your boyfriend hands over the goods."

Tor tossed the container, and while it was airborne, the vampires outside the windows clawed at the glass and made a hungry ruckus. Mel shivered. She couldn't wait for this night to be over. And this was only the preshow.

The vampire caught the container, then made to open the cover.

"Uh!" Tor put up a finger. "That thing needs to be kept on ice, and you shouldn't expose it to the volatile herbs and chemicals here in this witch's spell room."

The vampire gave the warning some thought.

"Hey." Tor shrugged. "If you want to render the thing useless, by all means, open it and give it a look over. But the heart has been on ice ever since she obtained it."

"Then how am I supposed to use it?" the vamp asked.

Mel looked to Tor for another fast retort, because she had nothing right now.

"That's your problem, thief."

The vampire snarled. The crew outside the window pushed against the windows, and the glass panes creaked.

"Keep it on ice," Tor said as a means to quiet the possible invasion. "And to use it? Just being in its vicinity activates it."

"So right now I'm growing more alive?" The vampire caressed the container greedily. "I *can* feel it."

"I suppose. But it won't last for long." Tor winked at the werewolf.

Mel furrowed her brow. What were they up to?

"It'll last as long as I keep it on ice," the vampire decided. He turned and hefted the container over his head to show his minions.

Outside, cheers rose.

And Mel could only be thankful the neighbors were away on holiday.

"I'll be going, then. I do thank you." The vampire bowed and exited out the back door into the yard.

"Stay right here. Put up a protection ward," Tor ordered Mel.

"Where are you going?"

He brandished the machete boldly before him. "Can you use vampire ash for your spellwork?"

"Always."

"Then Hart and I are going to harvest a batch for you."

The werewolf bumped fists with Tor, and the men headed out the back door.

And with the first vampire's yowl, Mel winced, but then she smiled. With a few spoken wards, she put up a screen of protection around the house and extended it as far into the yard as she could. And then she dipped to look under the table. Hecate's heart was still there, safe, nestled amidst the wild roses and…soon to prove much more harrowing than this experience had been.

She whispered a cloaking spell using her newly acquired dark magic. A shivering hug enveloped her body and she gasped. Dark magic was now hers.

And that made her more fearful than ever.

Tor thanked Hart for his assistance as the werewolf kicked a pile of soggy vampire ash on his way out of the backyard. But Hart paused and turned to count the piles.

"What?" Tor asked.

"I have a suspicion we missed him."

"Who?"

"The head vamp. The one who had your woman in his clutches. There's a dozen piles. We got all the minions, but I don't recall beheading the bastard who stole the heart. Did you?"

"No. Bollocks."

"And where is the heart?"

"It wasn't the real thing. I put a chunk of watermelon inside a plastic box. Figured it would provide the weight and size of a heart. But you're right. I don't see the container anywhere."

"He's still out there."

"Yes, but hardly dangerous. I'm not sure how deadly a vampire and his box of watermelon will prove."

The werewolf snickered, but then winced. "Still."

"Right." Tor glanced to the patio doors. Mel had been shaken by the vampire. He needed to go to her.

"I'll sniff him out," Hart said. "You take care of your woman. You said this would be over soon?"

"If all goes as planned, midnight will end it."

Hart checked his watch. "Got a few hours to go. There's a lunar eclipse tonight. Blood moon."

"I know. Not like it couldn't have been performed at high noon. You know how witchcraft works."

The werewolf visibly shuddered. "I'd better set to the trail, and check on my sweetie. See you later, man."

"Great to know you, Hart!" Tor called as the wolf left the property.

He had no worries that the man would not track down the rogue vampire. So he strode up to the house and tried to open the patio door—but was forcefully repulsed. His body landed in the wet grass just off the patio. A sludge of vampire ash oozed near his head.

Tor could do nothing but chuckle. "Good going, witch." Her wards were back up.

From inside the living room, Mel shouted, then opened the door. "I'm so sorry! Just wait." She drew a sigil in the air and recited two words. Tor felt the air noticeably change. In fact, his whole body relaxed on the ground.

He'd better enjoy it while he had this opportunity.

"Oh, my. That's a lot of vampire ash. That'll keep the Jones family in stock for a long time. Even wet, it will prove useful."

"That werewolf has some masterful claws. Hell of a lot easier than my machete to remove a vamp's head. He's a good guy."

"Where did he come from?" Mel stepped out and offered him a hand to help him stand. She brushed off some ash smudges from his vest and shirtsleeves. "I don't know the guy."

"He used to live in the neighborhood and was attracted to the heart. We talked it out. He's on our side. It's been quite the day, hasn't it? I'll be glad when tonight is over. What time is it?"

"Eight."

"When do you want to head to the crossroads? Is it far?"

"It's about an hour out from the city. We should leave a little after ten. I suppose you'll want to change your uniform."

He shrugged. "I'll dry off."

He kissed her then, and it didn't matter that he was covered in ash from revenant vampires or that he'd pulled a muscle in his thigh and it ached with every step. Or that he was even more determined to walk away from this lifestyle. Mel was in his arms. And that made everything better. The world in all its wrongness slipped away. He could hold her always.

"You taste like ash," she said, and then laughed. "But you also taste like Tor." She wrapped her arms about his

chest and hugged him fiercely. "Thank you for everything. I need you to know that before tonight's spell."

"Why? Do you expect something to go wrong?"

"No. Maybe? I don't know. You know how my magic
seems to have a mind of its own."

"It'll be good. I know it will. This is something you
are determined and focused on. Nothing will go wrong.
And I'll be there in case something does."

"And what about after?"

"After?"

"You're heading off to your normal life, right?"

"Uh, right."

She shook her head. "I understand that. I'd like to
change your mind, but I am the last person to want to
change another's mind. In proof, I, uh…made this for
you." She slipped her hand in her skirt pocket and pulled
out a vial. Without handing it to him, she instead slid it
into his shirt pocket and gave it a gentle pat.

Tor placed a hand over the pocket. "What's that for?"

"It's a memory spell. It'll make you forget everything
you know about the paranormal. It's all done by inhalation. Might make things easier."

"Oh. Uh, thanks." He winced and rubbed the shirt
pocket. "Do you want me to do that?"

"No." She stepped back, nervously swaying side to
side. "Yes. Tor. I…I don't want you to leave my life. But
if you have to do it, then I don't ever want to have been
in it. It'll be too hard for me."

"Then maybe you're the one who should take the
memory potion?"

Her heavy sigh hurt his heart. "It doesn't work on a
nonhuman. Besides, it's… Oh mercy, it's my sacrifice,
Tor. I made it for you and now it's done. My dark magic
now works. And I know it because I've been able to

anoint the heart and do some preparations. And I know the cloaking spell worked this time. So, yeah. That's what I did."

Hell. Him leaving her life was a sacrifice to her? He hadn't realized how much he meant to her. But he could understand, because she meant as much to him.

How was he going to walk away from her? Waltz out of her life after tonight's big finale? He didn't want to do that. But if he had to, a loss of memory might prove the wisest course. Then he'd never have to regret having known Mel and walking away from her.

Bollocks. This sucked.

"Thank you," he said quietly.

"Thank you for not questioning me or refusing the spell, or for making this harder than it has to be. I've fallen for you, Tor. I had to say that so you would know it. At least for a few more hours, and then you'll forget it all. Oh." She kissed him quickly. "I wish we could have sex."

"We can always have sex." He would prefer a shower before tumbling into bed with her, but if she was in the mood, and they did have time…

"I want to but I also need to store up my energy for the spell. Sex with you would leave me a panting, depleted witch. A very happy witch. But in no shape for spellcraft. Especially the dark stuff."

"Then I probably shouldn't kiss you anymore."

"Oh, no, kisses are great. They activate my root chakra and ground me in my power."

"I'm not sure what you just said, but it works for me."

Lifting her into his arms, Tor carried her into the living room, and with the heel of his shoe, closed the sliding glass door behind him. He set her on the edge of the couch and leaned in to give her another kiss that would activate her root—hell, he just wanted another kiss.

Mel pulled him against her, and together they tumbled onto the couch amidst her giggles. He kissed her quickly, again and again, as if to capture each bright giggling tone. His anger at witnessing the vampire holding her captive fell away. Thankful to have her safe and in his arms, he luxuriated in their connection. It was truly magical, being lost in her strange witchery.

When Mel nudged him to the side and then showed him her palm, covered with vampire sludge from his clothing, Tor sat up and pulled her up to kiss the crown of her head.

"I'm going to take another walk around the yard, make sure we got everything," he said. "You okay in here by yourself?"

"I am."

"Did you have time to go over the spell?"

"I did. I'm as ready as I'll ever be. I'll make us something to eat before we leave, yes?"

"Sounds good." He kissed her again. "Thank you."

"For what?"

"For finding me when you needed help."

She nodded.

I can't imagine my life now without you in it. That's what Tor wanted to say, but instead, he kissed her on the forehead, then headed out to the yard.

While Tor forked up the salad she'd made, Mel left him alone in the kitchen. She told him she wanted to do a last check through her supplies and a once-over on the spell. Inside her bag, she'd packed all the accoutrements required for the big event.

But how to concentrate on the spell when all she really wanted to do was tug him into her bedroom and make love to him and wish it all away? Wish that in the morning they would wake, never having gone to the cross-roads. That her mother would never again be haunted by her sister. That Tor could forget his goals of having a normal life.

"Normal." Mel shook her head. "It'll never fit him."

But she couldn't deny him the opportunity to give it a try. Because if she did somehow manage to convince him to remain in her life, he would always wonder what could have been.

She'd never been in love before. Not the sort of love where her toes tingled and her belly swirled and her smile always jumped out before she knew she was happy. But that's how she'd felt the past few days. When Tor was around, she felt silly-happy. Goofy, even. Filled with the possibility of whatever could happen between the two of them.

Who would have thought she could fall so quickly?

It was meant to be.

Best to end that tonight and move forward tomorrow.

Hooking her bag over a shoulder, she flicked off the lights in the spell room and wandered out to the kitchen.

"You packed and ready to go?" Tor cleaned his dishes in the sink, then turned, wiping his hands on a dish towel. He'd changed to dry clothing and now sported a bright red tie with his white business shirt and tweed vest. "What will my role be, exactly, when we get there?"

Mel's thoughts veered to everything she wished could happen. Like the spell being unnecessary and her mom being safe from her sister's wrath. And her falling into her protector's arms and living happily ever after. "Oh, just looking handsome."

"Huh?"

"I mean—" Shoot. That was wrong. This story was not going to give her a happily-ever-after if she wanted to help her family. And she did want that. "Well, you are handsome."

"Handsome isn't going to protect you."

"Seems to be working fine so far. But seriously, I'll need you to be on guard. I'm not sure what is going to happen. Or what creatures will be drawn to the heart while it's in use. I'll have to uncloak it for the spell. The crossroads should repel most, but you might want to load up on weapons."

"Got it. This could be a challenge for both of us."

Most especially the witch, who wasn't sure she wanted this night to end the way it would. Which could only be with Tor walking away from her.

And leaving her with an unhappily-ever-after.

An hour later, Mel sat on the passenger seat, clutching the bag of her spell supplies while Tor navigated the country gravel road. She'd dressed in an ankle-length red dress that tied in the back with black corset ribbons. It reminded her of a Victorian-style dress, but with a touch of Goth to it. It felt…ceremonial. And she needed everything she wore, touched and spoke to set the mood and tone for tonight.

The rain had stopped and clouds had cleared. The moon, blocked by the earth's shadow, was tinged with a red-orange sheen, and sat full and bright in the sky. The blood moon. She could feel the heart pulsing within the bag. It was almost as if it were aware that something momentous was going to occur.

Or something evil. And dark. And so wrong it could never be right.

Don't think like that, she cautioned inwardly. She could do this. She could. She…

"I don't think I can do this!" Mel burst out.

Tor pulled the van over to the shoulder of the road and turned to give her his full attention.

"It's crazy," she said in a panic. "I thought I could. And I really do have to. No one else in the family has the blood bond to Amaranthe like I do. But—oh." She sought Tor's gaze in the shadows. "I don't think I can kill my sister tonight."

Chapter 23

Tor shifted into Park. He turned on the van seat to face Mel. And said, "Wait. What?" He shook his head, knowing perfectly well he'd heard her clearly. "Let me get this straight."

She nodded, her big eyes gleaming in the darkness. Somewhere the full moon hung in the sky, but it didn't light up the cab.

"First, I learn you've stolen a valuable artifact that attracts revenants like the plague."

"Zombies. But yes."

"Zombies." As much as he hated to admit it, zombies did exist. Unfortunately. "Then, you tell me you're going to invoke necromancy. I was cool with that."

"Because you're a cool guy."

He did have that going for him. "But then, you tell me about the ghost. Which I had a very firm rule about not working with. It took me a while to come around, but I did."

"I forgive you for your reluctance."

Tor opened his mouth, but nothing came out. She was so…oblivious sometimes. And yet it was a cute obliviousness that he couldn't seem to resist. Heaven help him; he adored the woman.

And yet.

"But now you tell me not only are we going to raise the dead. And deal with a ghost. But also then…kill her?"

"It's how the spell is designed. Oh, but, Tor!" Mel caught her face in her hands and shook her head. "I can't do that. I can't kill my sister again."

He swallowed and forced himself to pat her on the shoulder. "You're not killing her again. It was an accident the first time. I mean…you haven't killed her before. Unless there's something you haven't told me about?"

"No! I would never raise a hand to my sister. Dead or alive."

"I didn't think so." Exhaling, he leaned to the side, his shoulder nudging the seat. Just when he thought things could not get any weirder, they did. Should he have expected as much? Probably. Mel had a way of keeping him on his toes, like it or not.

And he did like it.

"I think I've done a good job of keeping up with your antics so far, but I have to say, you're losing me here, Mel. Dare I ask why you want to end your sister's life a second time?"

"Don't you get it?"

"If I did, I wouldn't be asking. Explain. Please?"

"I can't let her live! Once the spell is invoked, Amaranthe will come to this realm not as the ghost she's been. I will literally raise her up from the grave. And the number one rule of witchcraft, even dark witchcraft? One should never raise the dead."

"Then why do it?"

"Because that's what the spell requires. I must call forth the wounded party and demand she cease her actions."

"You really think a conversation with your dead sister is going to get her to stop tormenting your mother? She didn't seem very amenable when I spoke to her at your parents' place."

"She will. I'll tell her she has to believe the truth. Oh, but Tor. How can I do this? After we've talked and she's agreed to leave Mom alone, then I have to return her to the grave in the most peaceable manner. And that involves…" She reached into her bag and drew out a crystal blade. "…this."

So much for peaceable.

She shuffled forward and bowed her head to his knees. Sniffles filled the van. And Tor, for once in his life, was without words. He didn't know what to tell her. This job had jumped the cliff that first night he'd found her waiting in the van. And since then they'd been struggling to keep their heads above the current. But now he could only see them going down, down, down a swirling whirlpool to hell. Or Beneath, which the paranormals called it.

This dark magic stuff was not for the weak of heart. And Mel's heart was full and wondrous and pink and fluffy and filled with all things good. If she invoked such magic tonight, she would never again be the same.

He didn't want to lose her to the dark side. *But you're going to lose her anyway when you step over to normal tomorrow. She gave you a freaking memory-loss spell as a sacrifice!* And if he didn't use the spell, would her sacrifice have been in vain? How would it affect her dark magic? For all purposes, it would work tonight. But tomorrow, what foul deeds might be reversed if he didn't drink the spell?

He stroked her hair. Midnight was twenty minutes away. If she didn't invoke the spell, her mother would forever be tormented by her daughter's angry ghost. Or only so long as she was still alive. If Amaranthe had her way, she'd see her mother dead sooner rather than later.

"Maybe we should think about this," he offered. "If your father could keep Star away from your sister's ghost—"

"Seriously? You saw Amaranthe. You know what state she's in. As well, my dad is barely holding it together. He almost strangled you. Tor, this has to be done. Tonight, under the blood moon. Did I tell you? Mom is on her last life."

"The ninth?" Things just got better and better. Not.

So that ruled out a slow and thoughtful approach to the situation. Which Tor felt sure the family had already considered long enough. This was a last-ditch effort to save the mom's life. And to put the sister to rest peacefully.

With a crystal blade.

Thoroughly Jones had warned Tor that whatever he'd expected to happen with Mel would not. He never could have foreseen this job ending in the witch needing to kill her sister. Dark magic or not, it was not a task he wished upon Mel.

He gripped Mel's wrist and she lifted her head. "I'll do it," he offered. "You speak the spell, then I'll plunge the knife through your sister's heart. You don't have to take that darkness into you. I've done it enough. Another—"

Mel lunged forward and kissed him. Deeply, lusciously. And for a while he forgot about the foreboding situation that faced them. He'd found a good one. Rather, she had found him. And he did not want to walk away from her. To…forget her.

How to make things different?

When she pulled away from the kiss, tears in the corners of her eyes glinted due to the sparkles that dotted the black liner curling out from each eye. She forced a smile. "You're my hero. But you can't do it." She held her palm up to show him the scar. "I'm the one with the connection to Amaranthe. And the spell maker has to be the one to do it."

"I'll speak the spell. You just tell me what to do."

"You can't enter the consecrated circle with me. And I need you to stand guard for whatever zombies or revenants come crawling up to get their hands on the heart. It's uncloaked right now."

"But, Mel, I don't want you to get hurt. Or get your hands dirty with this dark magic. You're not sure of yourself. I know that."

"I'm not. I know I don't want to be a dark witch. I'm perfectly happy with unicorns and sparkles. But it needs to be done. And I've made the sacrifice, so I don't want that to be in vain. And…I love my mom. And my sister. I want Amaranthe to rest peacefully. If I can give her that, I will." She blew out a breath. "I guess that means I'm doing it. Whew! I might need a drink after this is over."

"I've got a bottle of vodka in the back."

She quirked a brow.

"It's a good flame starter when I need to burn evidence. Also, I have been known to need a shot or two before a job. And after."

"You do the things no one else will do," she said. "And yet you remain a kind and generous man. So maybe I can do this thing tonight and the dark won't harm me too much?"

"Turning dark or remaining light at heart—I believe it's always a choice. If I didn't keep a good attitude about things, my heart would have turned black years ago. Hell, I wouldn't be alive today, I know. It's a strange balancing act."

"I can learn so much from you. The world will have lost a great protector when you walk away from it."

"Tomorrow," he said, "isn't here yet."

"Right. Do you have the memory spell on you?"

He patted an inner vest pocket.

She bowed her forehead to his. "I don't want you to take it, but I don't want to be the one to make that decision for you. I'm giving you the option, like it or not. I... Tor, you mean a lot to me. I know we've only known each other a few days, but...I think I love you. I've fallen for you."

"I know exactly how you feel."

"You do?"

He kissed her then. Slowly, lingering in the warmth of her mouth. He felt right here. With her. Sitting in the center of a world teeming with danger. This strange witchery had lured him to the edge. Now, to step over it or cringe and turn away from it all?

"We'll take it one minute at a time," he said, and tucked the vial into the change holder by the driver's seat. "Yes?"

She nodded. "Let's get this show on the road."

He clasped her hand and bowed his forehead to hers. "You look so beautiful this evening. I'm a lucky man. And I don't want you to worry. I'll be close to you always. If you need anything, you call out. Got it?"

"If I call out...?"

"I'll come running. Promise."

Mel hefted her spell bag over a shoulder and followed Tor toward the crossroads where, two years earlier, she and her family had buried her sister. They'd chosen the crossroads because her death had been violent. They had hoped—with a spell designed by her father—to keep her at peace and buried.

That hadn't happened.

So now she would rectify that. Even though her heart was crumbling inside her rib cage right now. Someone had to do it. And it couldn't be Tor. Though she loved him for offering. If there had been a way for her to hand over the reins and let him do the dirty work, she would have done so. But magic didn't work that way. He wasn't a witch. Nonwitches could perform a few simple house-witch spells, but the real magic could only be innate, and soul deep.

Gravel crunched under their footsteps. Long grass sprang up along the edges of the old road. It smelled green and lushly fertile. Tor gestured for her to stay put while he walked the next ten feet and stood in the cen-ter of the crossroads. Two old gravel roads intersected here in the valley not far from Versailles, but far enough out that this was actually a private area that rarely saw humans. It was on land owned by Mel's dad and uncle. Someday the family may build here. She would love to live out in the country.

Tor hefted an altered rifle over one shoulder, having explained to her that it shot salt rounds, regular bullets (silver encased) and even flames. In his other hand, he wielded the machete. At his hip he wore a belt with knives and other weapons attached to it. The crystal talisman caught the moonlight. He looked like a warrior—in a three-piece suit. He'd removed the coat, and the tweed vest was dark gray. His red tie was neat, and his shirt-sleeves were rolled to his elbows. He looked all business.

If a man's business were kick-assery.

Which it was.

Mel felt his intensity as a visceral warmth in her muscles. Something about a man in a suit ready for battle really did it for her. But now? Whew! If she wasn't preparing to raise the dead, she'd go after that sexy man and have her way with him.

With luck, all would go well and they could head home early and spend the rest of the night making love.

After pacing two full turns and scanning the area, Tor gestured for her to approach the center point where the barely used road formed a cross of grassy tufts between the tire ruts.

"You ready for this?" he asked.

Never! "Yes. I can do this. You think we're safe?"

"No. But I'll make sure nothing approaches while you invoke the spell. What's just beyond that forest?"

"It's an old family graveyard—oh."

Both met each other's gaze with the intense knowing that caused a sinking feeling in their guts.

"Really?" Tor asked, with all the frustration of the past few days punctuating that one word. "A graveyard. Bloody perfect."

Just the right breeding ground for more zombies. Bloody perfect, indeed. Not.

"Will you make it snappy?" he asked.

"I will work as speedily as the threat of a zombie invasion will allow."

"You going to lay down a protection circle?"

"Yes, I'll get that ready and I'll ward it so you, and nothing else, will be able to enter it while I'm invoking the spell."

"Good. Make it ironclad. I'm going to wander toward the graveyard to check out that potential nightmare. Don't worry, I'll keep you in my eyesight."

"I'm not worried," she lied. "You'll have my back. It's what you do best."

"For another few hours, anyway," he muttered.

Right. And then he'd drink a memory-loss spell and walk away from her forever.

"I'm going to take this off." He unhooked the talisman from his belt and handed it to her. "Best I see whatever comes our way."

"Are you sure?"

"Positive. Just because I can't see the danger doesn't mean it's not there. It's about time I faced up to that which most disturbs me. I'll never be able to begin a new life if I don't do that."

He had gotten wise about that. Unfortunately. Mel tucked the talisman into her skirt pocket, and before she could argue, Tor turned and wandered off.

She wished he would have kissed her before striding away. Standing beneath the moonlight at the center of the crossroads, she suddenly felt so alone. A thin cloud crept across the moon's crimson face. Crickets chirped in the long grass, but she sensed no other animals nearby, not even a squirrel or bird. Tor's footsteps *shushed* through the grass, but he was already out of sight, for the trees shadowed his position.

Midnight would toll in ten minutes. Mel set down her tapestry bag and knelt by it. She had a lot of work to do. First she took out the crystal tiara and placed that on her head. Inhaling and exhaling, she centered herself and cast a thin violet light around her. Nothing too strong. She would need access beyond her physical body.

Next she poured the salt circle about ten feet in diameter. It would provide enough space to work, and… for two people to stand in. As she finished the circle, she said a blessing, then closed her eyes to invoke the protection wards and seal herself inside. Spreading out her arms and tilting back her head, she whispered to the universe to hear her summons and join in her magic this night. It may be dark magic, but she honored all kinds and respected the elements required to make this work.

"And ye harm none; do as thou wilt" was the witch's rede that she respected. Even dark witches.

As she closed the circle, the moonlight seemed to swell and beam down upon her. Everything felt electric, from the air brushing her cheeks and hands to the glitter of moonshine on the grass blades. Mel glanced about to spy Tor walking around the circle thirty paces away, gun over his shoulder, machete swinging in the other hand, alert. When his eyes met hers, he nodded, then gifted her with a dimpled smile.

She had fallen in love with that man. And he had confessed the same to her. But would tonight's events make her lesser in his eyes? The nature of his job required him to do many evil things. Or if not necessarily evil, then bad things that needed to be done to protect the greater good. Vampires had to be slain if they proved harmful to innocents. Same with werewolves, and others. Evil was all in the perspective. So was bad. And dark. Someone had to partake of it.

As she would do now.

Pulling her supplies out of the bag, she set them on the grass. A crystal athame given to her by her father, carved from smoky quartz, had darkened over the years as he had used it in his own magic. She could feel the immense power within it, and had rarely used it herself, for it was dedicated to the dark arts. Beside that she set vials of rosemary, sage and hyssop. Red salt and a black candle. A cloth bag of tiny bones from various animals such as mouse, frog and rat. She'd left Bruce home tonight because she hadn't wanted to risk his life. There was no telling what would occur within this circle. She would invoke a willing elemental to use as a familiar for this spell.

And finally, she drew out the plastic container within which the heart pulsed. It cast a red glow from inside the blurry plastic. Mel peeled back the cover and the thing thumped as if it were inside someone's chest. Hecate, the goddess of magic and witchcraft. And necromancy. How appropriate that her heart was required for this spell.

"I honor you, Great Mother," Mel said as she placed the heart on the grass before her. It continued to beat and grew redder and glowed brighter. After arranging the rest of the items and then lighting the candle with a snap of her fingers, Mel had it all ready to go.

A tug to her dress smoothed out the skirt around her legs. A sweep of her hand brushed the hair from her face. And she felt the clock tick into the witch's hour as a tightening in her muscles and a knowing in her soul.

"All's clear!" Tor called. "Weirdly."

Yes, that was weird. But she wouldn't question a good thing. Everything could change on the turn of a thin gold euro.

Adjusting the crystal tiara on her head, Mel then began the spell with a whisper. She'd memorized the incantation. It was simple. Slowly she found a rhythm. The words were few and Latin, and must be repeated over and over until she reached a crescendo and a beat that thundered in her ears.

Gripping the crystal athame, she stood over the candle and drew the blade across her palm to drip her blood to mingle into the wax. Tilting back her head, she called up the elements of earth and fire to assist her this night of a dark summoning.

* * *

Tor altered his attention between the vast darkness that surrounded their little circle in the middle of nowhere, and the center stage where the witch with whom he had become enamored was enacting a vile and repulsive spell. Hecate's heart glowed like a beacon. He thought, if any paranormal creatures could *not* hear the witch's chants, then surely they would be alerted by that glowing organ.

To think about witches and all the crazy things they used in their spells would make him question his sanity for engaging in such an alliance. So he didn't. Instead he kept one ear cocked for movement in the darkness. One finger on the trigger. And one eye on the beautiful witch in the breathtaking red gown.

Her chants mesmerized. Her body swayed as if with the wind. She created a dance to the sounds of her incantation; her jet hair fluttered in waves about her shoulders and elbows. The athame she waved through the air traced a red line of light that lingered long after. She drew sigils that he did not recognize, but could feel in his soul. For they made him uncomfortable and his mouth dry.

Pausing in his pacing, Tor witnessed the sudden burst of grass being mown flat in the circle center and radiating out up to his feet. Mel stepped aside, nudging the heart over with a toe. The candle flames burst to a length nearly as high as Mel's hip. And with a slash of her athame over the newly broken ground, a hand burst free from beneath.

Tor heard a growl from the darkness behind him. He spun around to face glowing red eyes.

"Bring it," he muttered.

Chapter 24

Aware that Tor had fired at something in the dark, Mel did not take her eyes from the woman who had clawed her way up from the earth to stand before her. Blonde, slender and dressed in her ragged black burial dress, Amaranthe shook off the dirt from her arms and hair. She was Mel's younger sister by eleven months. Looked exactly like her, save for the hair she'd consistently bleached since her teenage years.

Pale dead skin gleamed like moonstone under the blood moon. Even the dirt smudges and bruises discoloring her arms and neck could not alter her beauty. She embodied a tattered glamour. Or, as her father might say, a glamorous evil. Mel's eyes dropped lower. Her sister's hip bone poked out through skin and torn silk fabric.

When she finally looked at Mel, Amaranthe's blue eyes brightened momentarily with recognition. And then she snarled. "What have you done to me?"

In the distance, a creature yowled. Tor's gun echoed a few shots. And—was he whistling Sinatra?

Of course he was.

Mel clutched the glowing athame to her chest. "Amaranthe, I love you."

"Love me? You—you've raised me from the grave! How dare you? Is this the vile punishment you wish to bestow upon me?"

"For tormenting Mom? I should," Mel said defensively. Then she deflected her sudden anger. She'd not come here for a fight. "But I am not so cruel as death has made you."

Amaranthe tilted her head to the side and her neck cracked, leaving it at an unnatural tilt. "Star killed me. And now she will suffer."

"Mom did no such thing. And you know it! She was being chased by that nasty dog from Apartment B on the ground floor. You know how frightened she was of that big ugly beast. She had no idea you were driving down the street."

"Yes, well, I was driving, wasn't I? I was so angry at him!"

Mel swallowed. The reason her sister had left in a huff that evening was to go to her boyfriend's house and ask him if what her family had told her was true. Amaranthe's boyfriend had made a pass at Mel. And when Star had tried to convince Amaranthe that the fledging wizard was no good for her, she'd accused them both of lying to her.

"It was my fault," Mel said. "I never should have told Mom what he did. But he creeped me out. He suggested… things."

Amaranthe snapped up her head and looked down her nose at Mel. "It was true. That bastard had a roving eye for other women. But that doesn't change the fact that I am no longer alive, and it was because of my mother.

I can still feel the moment of impact. The metal slicing through my skin and bone. Tore my leg clean off." She slapped her exposed hip bone, and her entire body wobbled as that joint threatened to give free and collapse her. "Damn it! Curse you, witch! I will rip out your heart if you do not restore me to the grave in which you laid me."

"In due time," Mel said as calmly as she could manage.

Her sister was a mess. And truly, she was torturing her by allowing her to exist in such a state. She felt the energy within the circle cringe and quickly redrew the warding sigil in the air. It lingered near Amaranthe's head in a brownish-red light that mimicked the moon's shadowed glow.

"Protection from what?" her sister asked with a sneer at the glowing sigil. "The idiot over there shooting at anything that moves?"

"Tor is protecting me while I perform this spell. It is to put you to rest peacefully, Amaranthe. And to save Mom. She has only one life remaining!"

"I know that. And she is so frightened of my incorporeal spirit. It is comical how easily I can get that feline to shiver."

Mel lifted a hand, prepared to slap her sister, but she refrained.

"Don't want to slap my head clean off?" Amaranthe retorted. "Considerate of you. What are you doing? Practicing dark magic now? Who do you think you are? I was the one following in Dad's footsteps. You and your silly light magic should know your place."

"Seowen," Mel recited.

Red thread sewed shut Amaranthe's mouth.

Mel bit the corner of her lip. She must hurry, or she would faint from utter horror. Indeed, the dark arts were not to her taste.

"Forgive Mom," she commanded. "Admit you loved her when you were alive. She is your mother. You are her daughter. Give her freedom. That woman would never harm a soul. She chases mice and then lets them flee. She loves you so much, Amaranthe."

Her sister scratched away the threads closing her mouth. "She doesn't even remember me. Or you!"

"She does. Dad teaches her and she remembers. I know she does. It is innate in us all to know our family and those whom we love. Please, Amaranthe, I love you. And I forgive you for scaring Mom off the rooftop."

Amaranthe's switchblade smile cracked her mouth open a little too high on one side.

Tor backed toward the circle, gun in hand and a stake in the other. "Almost done?"

Amaranthe turned and looked over him. "You again? I can show you things that'll make your stomach turn—"

Tor stopped and looked down. His shoes almost touched the salt. He shuffled backward.

"It should have been me!" Mel suddenly said.

Amaranthe spun to face Mel. "What did you say?"

"I should have been in the car that day," Mel said. "I know it. You know it. Your beef is with me, not Mom. I should have driven to Jacques's house and told him to leave us both alone. I should have protected you. My little sister."

Amaranthe straightened her neck with difficulty and lifted her chin. "You always did that. Put an arm around me, step in front of me when the bullies showed their might. Jacques was using me. Oh! He confessed it all when I went to him that night. Wanted to blood bond with me to gain my dark magic. He said he'd tried to take some of yours."

"I know that," Mel said quietly. She hadn't intended to

tell her sister that. Jacques had chased her and attempted a binding spell on her. She'd only wanted Amaranthe to leave the man, not hate her for his wayward attentions.

"I was so angry," Amaranthe said. "Driving home in such a fit...without paying attention. I'm sorry I didn't believe you about him right away." Amaranthe bowed her head. "We always trusted one another. It's what sisters do."

"Then do one last thing for me," Mel said. "Forgive Mom and set her free. And then I will help you to rest peacefully."

The candles flickered. A cricket chirped somewhere nearby. Yet the air was heavy, as if a storm could crack open the sky at any moment. And over it all, the red moon was witness.

"I miss you," Amaranthe said. "And Dad and Laith and Vlas. We had such fun times with our cousins. And... Mom," she breathed out on a whisper.

"I think of you every day," Mel said. "You are always in my heart. And here." She splayed open her hand.

Amaranthe did the same to reveal the matching scar on her palm. Then she glanced to the glowing heart on the ground. Behind them, Tor spun and rushed to fire at another approaching predator.

"Is that Hecate's heart?"

"It is," Mel offered.

"How did you get that?"

"I stole it from the Archives when Uncle CJ wasn't looking. He's quite angry with me."

"You try so hard to be bad, Lissa. You'll never be a dark witch. You couldn't have made a sacrifice."

"I did." Mel held up her head, trying desperately not to sink into a flood of tears. She'd done what had to be done. "I can invoke dark magic," Mel said, "if it means enough to me. Like you. You mean the world to me, Amaranthe. I wish you were still alive so I could hug you."

Again, Amaranthe glanced behind her to Tor. When she turned to Mel, the look on her face was unreadable.

Her sister nodded over her shoulder. "He calls you Mel?"

"Yes, and I like it. I like him. I might even love him. I never thought a person could fall in love so fast, but it feels real."

"You never dated that often, but when you did, it was with your whole heart. He will hurt your heart, Lissa. Mel."

"That man is incapable of doing such a thing." Unless, of course, he intended to walk into normal the moment they'd finished here. "Tor is a real hero."

"Maybe. Maybe not. You need to know what he is made of before you lose your heart to him."

"He's trustworthy and brave. What more is there to know?"

"He has a secret."

"I know about the woman who killed herself."

"All of it?"

What was she up to?

"Oh, sister." Amaranthe bowed her head on her crooked neck. "I'm tired. I do want to rest. To move on."

"Then do what you must. And I will do what I must."

Amaranthe reached to touch the athame Mel held, and it glowed red when she did so.

"I don't want to do it," Mel said. "I'm pretty freaked about all this, actually. But you know me."

"You couldn't harm a fly. Don't worry. It won't hurt. And you're right, it will give me peace. I'm sorry. I've harmed not only Mom but the entire family."

"Mel!" Tor shouted.

Over her sister's shoulder, Mel sighted a gang of zombies charging toward her protector. They were much more agile than one would expect from the undead. In but moments Tor would be inundated.

No time to waste.

Mel plunged forward to hug her sister, and her hands went right through what she realized was a figment. Not even a zombie. "Do it now," she said. "Say what needs to be put into the universe. Make it real."

"I forgive Star for what I'm not even sure was her fault."

"Amaranthe."

"Very well. It was an accident. Not planned. I was in the wrong place at the right time. Curse that bastard Jacques. I love Mom," Amaranthe said. "I do."

Tor's shout indicated he was not winning, but rather, was in pain. He wasn't holding the machete. In fact, Mel saw it on the ground, far from where the zombies now surrounded him.

"I will give you peace," Mel said to her sister.

"And I will leave you with a parting gift. It has to be done. It will reveal his darkest truth. And then you can determine if he is worthy of your love."

"I don't understand."

"You will. Goodbye, Melissande. I love you. I will see you in our next reincarnation."

"Promise. *Nox restitutio!*" Mel recited, and then plunged the athame into her sister's chest. At the same time, the scar on her palm opened and began to bleed. Tears spilled from her eyes and she cried out. She'd felt the resistance of blade entering muscle. Like her sister was not a ghost but—

"Thank you," Amaranthe said. Her bleeding hand swept over Mel's hair. And then she was nothing. Not even ash or mist. Mel simply stood there holding nothing in her arms.

She sniffed at oncoming tears. Smelled blood in her hair. Squeezed her fingers as the blood dripped onto the ground. At her feet, the heart, spattered with her blood, had settled its glow. It looked rather dark and desiccated. And then she heard Tor's shout again.

Racing out from the salt circle toward the machete abandoned on the ground, she grabbed it. It was so heavy! She needed both hands to lift it.

A zombie snarled at her and pounced.

Mel used her kinetic magic to thrust the blade through the air toward Tor. A zombie leaped for it and missed its target. The machete dropped, landing in Tor's grasp. The growls surrounding him were silenced as the zombies realized who now held the power.

With a flick of his wrist and a spin of his hips, Tor cut the weapon through the multitude of zombies. Howls and yelps accompanied the ones able to run away.

With determination carving his features fiercely, Tor marched toward Mel. Just when she was close enough to hug him, he pushed her behind him with one arm and raised his gun in the other, aiming toward the zombie who crept toward the salt circle—the glowing heart was in its hand.

"No!" Mel pushed Tor's arm, and his aim missed the zombie. "It'll damage the heart! If you destroy it, all the witches in the world will die."

He met her frantic gaze. "Bollocks." Dropping the gun, Tor rushed the zombie and jumped onto its back. The heart wobbled and fell onto the grass.

"Duck!" she heard, and instead of looking for her pet, she did as she was told. A zombie soared over her head.

Tor stomped past her, stake in one hand and the machete in the other. He jumped onto the fallen zombie and staked it in the heart, then drew the blade across its neck.

Stumbling backward, he dropped the stake. His foot landed on uneven ground, toppling him to a sitting position. And for the first time, Mel noticed how torn-up and battered he was. He bled from a cut on the forehead. His shirt was shredded. A long slash down one thigh bled onto the ground.

The beheaded zombie body convulsed on the ground as it dechunked.

"Don't look!" Tor called. He turned and pulled himself up, then caught her and turned her back toward the circle. "You don't need to see that."

Mel nodded. Not like she hadn't seen worse. But his concern bolstered her. And his embrace reassured her like nothing else ever could. In his arms, she was safe. And loved. Now to keep that feeling for their short time that remained.

"Is your sister at peace?" he asked.

He clung to her, and she realized it was for support more than anything. Mel nodded. "She is."

"You did good."

"So did you."

"There's cleanup to do. Gotta bury the remains. I'll need some time."

"You want me to help?"

"Nope. This is what I do. Or did do."

Please, no. She didn't want him to leave his life behind. And her.

But that was not her choice.

"I'll gather my things and wait in the van," she quietly offered.

"Give me twenty minutes."

Mel nodded and started toward the salt circle. But she

stopped when the pale woman in a long white tattered dress bent over the salt and picked up the pulsing heart. "Oh mercy. Tor!"

Her protector rushed up behind her.

"There's one left," Mel said.

"Not this," Tor said on a gasp. "Charlotte?"

"Who's Charlotte?" And then Mel remembered. She was the woman who had killed herself because Tor had not been there to rescue her from the ghost haunting her tormented soul.

This was her sister's parting gift.

Chapter 25

Tor swallowed and reached for the crystal talisman—that he'd handed over to Mel because he had thought he was beyond the need for it. And he had been. But he'd not expected to see the one person who had given him reason for the safeguard in the first place.

How could she be here? He'd never seen her before as a ghost. Of course, he'd always worn the talisman.

"Charlotte," he said on a heavy breath.

The specter stood in the salt circle, clutching the pulsing heart to her chest as if it were a wondrous child's toy. Her short red hair flitted about her head and—she didn't look like a decaying zombie, but her skin was blue. Tor could still remember finding her body that cold February morning. He hadn't believed a person's skin could be so blue. And her lips, as well as the bruising under her eyes, were purple black. She'd worn a floaty white dress, one she'd once told him had been her first-communion dress.

The ghost standing in the circle suddenly noticed

him, her attention veering from the heart but her fingers clutching deep into the pulsing muscle. "Tor?" Her lips struggled with a smile. "Is that you? What are you—you can see me now?"

He nodded. Behind him, he was aware of Mel's presence, but she stood off to the side. He had slain all the zombies. He hoped.

Not sure what to do, he stepped toward the circle. "Yes, I can see you, Charlotte."

"You've avoided me for so long. You terrible, terrible man. Why did you do that? I've been pleading for your attention. Tearing my hair out to simply get you to notice me. Did I disappoint you when I did as I was told and cut my wrists in the bathtub? Such a peaceful death, that."

"No," he said calmly. He had no desire to fast-talk his way out of this one. He needed to face her. But his knees grew weak and his fingers trembled at his sides. He didn't notice the machete had slipped out of his hand. "I was never disappointed, Charlotte. I loved you."

"You don't anymore?" She crushed the heart, and blood dripped down her white dress.

"If she destroys that heart…" Mel hissed from behind him. "Tor!"

Charlotte took in the witch with a sneer. "I've been watching you with her. You notice her. You love her. Why could you never love me like that, Tor?"

Another squeeze of her fingers against the heart pushed out more blood from the thing. Its pulsing had slowed.

He approached cautiously, fully aware that he should not step into the circle with her. That would give her the ability to connect with him on a visceral level. "Charlotte, you should set down that heart. You don't need it."

"But it will give me life." She hugged the thing tightly. "I can feel it."

Behind him Mel groaned.

Tor turned to look over his shoulder to find Mel had fallen to her knees, and she clutched her throat. Was Charlotte's squeezing the heart taking away Mel's life? The life from all witches?

"Please, Char, you can't have life. You'll never be as you once were. You'll always be like this."

"What's wrong with me, Tor? I'm like all the other ghosts you can see. Are we not your closest friends? Don't you like me now? Am I not pretty enough for you? Why did you never want me as a lover? I was so in love with you."

He'd known that, but he'd only ever felt Charlotte was a friend, and hadn't been in the frame of mind to start a romantic relationship with another screwed-up person who could also see ghosts and who was slightly mad. Yes, he'd had a bit of better sense back then. Unfortunately, he'd never had the courage to tell her that and had allowed her awkward flirtations. A cruel manifestation of his own cowardice.

"You are so beautiful," he offered. "But you must stop squeezing that heart. It's getting your dress all messy. And if you break it, it won't work anymore."

She bowed her head over the fading heart, and a teardrop spilled onto it and dripped off in a bloody splat onto her bare blue foot.

"You can have it." She thrust it toward him.

Tor took a step, but at Mel's groan behind him, he realized his toe touched the salt circle. He wasn't sure if it was keeping Charlotte in, and didn't want to test that theory by breaking the line.

"Toss it to me," he said. "I hurt my leg and it's hard to walk." It was true. And blood did stain his pants leg. But as Charlotte bent to study his thigh, she clutched the heart to her chest again, keeping it well out of his reach and inside the circle.

Charlotte looked up at him and lifted a haughty chin. "You're protecting her, aren't you?"

"Of course I am. She hired me to do a job. I told you about my work."

"And look how well you are doing that job. She lies on the ground near death. You can't take care of any woman, Torsten Rindle. You fail us every time."

Indeed. And even more reason to step away from the protection business. Who was he to believe he could make a difference by swinging a machete or wielding a stake? Ridiculous. The spirit was right. Mel would be better off without him in her life.

"Failure," Charlotte repeated. "As a friend, a man and even as a protector." The ghost let out a throaty chuckle that tightened Tor's skin and lifted the hairs all over his body.

And with that, Charlotte hoisted the heart high. Blood drooled down her wrist and forearm. A squeeze made it glow brightly, and then she thrust it toward Tor. He leaped to catch the thing in his hands, finding it was difficult to grasp the slippery thing. He stumbled and went down, landing on his back near Mel.

But the growl from inside the circle rolled him to his side. Charlotte's visage changed, her skin brightening to an unreal blue and breaking open to beam out brilliant red light from within. Her eyes glowed white and her mouth opened to snarl with a toothy maw.

Managing to tuck the heart against Mel's chest, he

heard her whisper, "You have to sacrifice for the dark magic to take her down."

"Sacrifice? But what? How?"

"She needs to die before the heart does."

"I've never slain a ghost. I'm not sure…"

"Your sacrifice will give her the peace she deserves."

A bone-crunching howl filled the air. Tor scrambled up to a stand, limped toward the machete and grabbed it. In the distance, he saw movement near the graveyard. "More zombies," he muttered. "Can a bloke get a break?"

Charlotte's ghost had increased in bulk and muscle and now stomped the ground outside the circle. The grass browned under her steps. Mel swore and whispered an incantation.

The ghost slapped down a hand on the grass, and it burned a flaming path up to Mel. Her skirt ignited. The witch screamed and scrambled away, leaving the heart lying but inches from the fire. Tor jumped to extinguish the flames.

When Charlotte approached him, he pressed the tip of the machete to her chin. The blade moved through her figment, a useless weapon against an incorporeal specter.

The ghost gripped the sharp blade, and it turned red as an ember. Tor felt the heat of the metal permeate the hilt, and within seconds he was unable to hold the burning weapon. He dropped it.

"Tor!" Mel yelled.

He looked over his shoulder and saw the crystal talisman soaring through the air toward him. He reached to grab it—but at the last second, retracted his hand.

Not seeing Charlotte wasn't going to change anything. And it would only piss her off all the more. It was time he faced his demons.

The crystal talisman hit Charlotte in the chest, and instead of going through her, it lodged there. She yowled and slapped a hand to it, but couldn't get it out of her chest.

Tor wasn't sure what it would do to her. It had only been charmed so he couldn't see ghosts and protect himself from their attack. It symbolized that which had most frightened him. His greatest fear was now standing before him, and…

He stepped up and grabbed Charlotte by the face, one hand to each side of her head. His hands did not go through her figment, but instead he felt her as a solid, cold being radiating with a fiery heat that must be from the crystal.

"I loved you then and I love you still," he offered. "As family. As two souls who needed one another. We both know ghosts have power, Charlotte. And your mind was half in and half out of the two realms. They would have gotten to you sooner or later, no matter if I had been there that night or not."

She struggled against his hold, but he held her firmly. The talisman in her chest beamed brightly and he smelled sulfur, as if the demonic were burning its way out of her.

"Take the peace you deserve," he said. "But if you choose to stay as you are, I will accept that. And I promise you I will never wear that talisman again. I will see you always. I will allow you to haunt me as you see fit."

The ghost's eyes teared up, and now her smile was genuine. "You would do that for me?"

He had to. He would. Tor nodded.

She touched the crystal, and now her whole body glowed a brilliant white. "I can feel you in this. Your kindness. Your strength. Your compassion. It's taking the darkness from me. The spirit that haunted me has been inside me since my death. I haven't been able to get free from it. Tor…you have released me."

"I don't understand."

"Your unselfish ways have helped so many. I love you." She clasped the crystal and pulled it from her chest.

As Tor stepped back, he watched a great spume of black smoke trill out from Charlotte's chest and dissipate in the air above her head—as if a demon being exorcised.

"It's gone." She dropped the crystal onto the grass, and then her figment flickered and dispersed.

"Charlotte!"

Tor dropped to his knees inside the circle and bent over the glowing crystal. And in that glow, he felt the years of friendship they had shared bubble up like laughter. It felt giddy in his heart and lightened him. And he smiled as he wrapped his arms across his chest.

"Be at peace, Charlotte. I love you."

Who would have thought the one thing he'd carried with him for years could be the thing to set both him and his lost friend free? He picked up the crystal. It felt light, and it sparkled as if dunked in faery dust. Over the years it had taken on the shadows and dark vibrations of all those ghosts he'd not wanted to deal with. And now…it had been cleansed.

He hooked it at his belt and pushed up from the grass. Brushing the salt from his palms, he shook his head and looked up to the moon. It was lighter now, white and bright, no longer red. It was as if the moon had also been cleansed.

He stepped backward, and his foot crushed the machete blade into the ground. Turning to pick it up, he then saw Mel lying on the ground beneath a spindly maple tree, her eyes closed, the red skirts splayed out like blood. The heart beside her did not pulse or glow red.

"Mel!"

Plunging to the ground beside her, he shook her head, but she didn't respond. The hem of her skirt had burned, but he didn't see any damage to her leg. Frantically, he bowed to place an ear over her heart. He could still hear her heartbeat, but she felt cold and lifeless.

"No, it can't be like this." He grabbed the heart, which resembled a hunk of dried meat. He shook it. "It's not broken." He examined it and found there were no cuts or breaks where he'd earlier seen the blood ooze out when Charlotte had squeezed it. "It's fine. It was just a squeeze." There were no burn marks on it from the fire. "Mel?"

The sudden chirring whine of a cicada sounded, and from the tree above dropped an insect that landed on Mel's chest. Tor watched it crawl slowly across the red fabric up to her shoulder, where it paused and seemed to look at him. He swallowed. A smile was irrepressible. Really?

With a spread of its wings, the cicada rose into the air for a few seconds, then landed on the heart he held. Tor lifted the organ to study the insect more closely.

"I wish I could have known you. I have loved you all my life."

In response, he felt an overwhelming warmth flood his chest. The meaning was unmistakable. Tor nodded. "You love me, too? I know you do."

With that, the cicada took to flight, a slow journey that wobbled her over the salt circle and higher into the air until Tor could no longer see her wings glint with moonlight.

"That was freakin' cool."

He turned to the smiling witch beside him. "You're alive?"

"Of course I'm alive. What? Did you think I was dead?"

"Yes. The heart. When Charlotte squeezed it…"

"It felt like my heart was being squeezed. It's possible every witch in the world felt it. But if I'm alive, that means we're all alive." He set the heart on her lap and it began to glow. "You did it, Tor. You saved the world."

"I didn't save anything. You're the witch with the amazing dark magic. You gave your sister peace."

"And you gave Charlotte peace with the sacrifice of your need to be safe from ghosts. We both did all right."

"That we did." He kissed her, then stretched onto his back to lie beside her.

She tilted her head onto his shoulder, one hand gently clasped about the pulsing heart. "I love you. Is that weird to say? We've known each other just a few days, but it feels…real."

"It is real. As real as the cicada that landed on your chest and made me understand that my mom is always watching over me. I love you, too, Mel."

They clasped hands and looked up at the star-speckled sky. It was difficult to see stars when in Paris. One had to travel out to the country, away from the city lights. And tonight dazzled with a thick constellation of starlight, with the moon as the spotlight.

Mel turned and looked at the side of his face while he stared up at the stars. "You know something? I don't feel all that dark right now. I actually feel pretty good that I was able to help my mom and sister. But I couldn't have done it without you."

"And I couldn't have given Charlotte her freedom without your support. And this." He waggled the quartz talisman above them. "It cleansed her of the evil that had been inside her since before her death. Amazing."

"You do know that a talisman is just an object. It's the belief of the owner that provides the real magic."

"I did not know that."

"You did it all by yourself, Tor. With or without a chunk of crystal. It was all you."

It was an interesting concept, and it would take him a while to accept it. Tor hooked the crystal at his belt loop, then took Mel's hand again. "We should date," he said. "We're kind of perfect for one another. You balance out my extreme side."

"You tolerate my goofy side."

"You make amazing smoothie bowls."

"You are a fashion rock star. I've never been so attracted to a man in a tweed vest in my life."

"You have weird pets."

"You have OCD."

"You like to talk to flowers and sing to the sky."

"You have a talent you don't recognize."

"I recognize it. I'm just…" He sighed. Though the vial tucked in his pocket was virtually weightless, he felt it heavily upon his heart now. "There is that goal of mine."

"I know. We both know. And we're ready for it. Like it or not, it's how the universe wants us to be. We should get on the road. It's late. Or rather, early."

Tor checked his watch. "Really? 4:00 a.m.?"

He had four hours before his interview.

As the two stood and turned to the van, Tor picked up the abandoned crystal tiara and put it on Mel's head. "Wear this. Always. Sparkles and unicorns. It's you." He kissed her. "I'm not tired. I think I'll head home for a quick shower and straight on to the interview."

"Sounds like a plan. But we have one problem to take care of before we go anywhere."

"What's that?"

She pointed toward the van, where a werewolf crouched on the top and growled at them.

Chapter 26

Mel had just enough energy to summon a repulsion spell, and combined with the infusion of dark magic she'd worked, she had never felt more powerful. However, when she thrust out her hand toward the werewolf standing on top of the van and opened her mouth to recite the spell—Tor grabbed her wrist and spun her around to face him, effectively obliterating any magical energies that may have zapped the predator.

"Holster it, Mel. I know that wolf."

"You do?" She squinted at the beast now crouched and peering at them with big gold eyes. How could a person determine one werewolf from another? They were all hairy and ugly, and their heads were wolflike while their bodies were sort of still human, except übermuscly and—so much hair!

"That's Christian Hart. You met him earlier."

"Oh." She put down her casting hand. "You sure?"

"Hart!" Tor waved to the beast.

The werewolf jumped from the van, landed in a crouch, then stood. As he strode toward them, he shifted in a matter of seconds. His head grew smaller and human shaped, and arms and legs conformed to the normal human length. Hair disappeared from his body to reveal pale skin and...no clothes.

"Whoa!" Tor put a hand before Mel's eyes, but she tugged it away. Because that was a sight. "Bloke, would you mind the lady?"

"Sorry." The wolf, now completely in human form, covered his erect penis with both hands. "That happens when I come back to were shape. Clothing never shifts with us. It's just the way things work."

Tor slid off his vest and handed it over to the man. Hart took it. It would not wrap completely about his waist, but he was able to hold it before him and clasp it at his hips.

"What are you doing out here?" Tor asked. "Hunting grounds?"

"You know it. If I'd known you were headed this way, I might have gone the opposite direction. What's going on here?"

"You didn't see the zombies?" Mel asked. The moonlight had a certain way of highlighting the man's incredible muscles, and she pulled in a sigh at the flex of his biceps. Did they glisten? Ahem. "They almost killed Tor."

Tor cleared his throat. "I had things under control."

"I thought you were going to stop the dead things from wandering about?" Hart asked.

"We did!" Mel hugged Tor with glee. "It's all over now. Hecate's heart has served its purpose."

"Yes, but we still have to secure that thing under lock and chain," Tor said, then asked the werewolf, "Did you ever track down the vampire from the yard?"

"Crying over a box of watermelon. Ha! That was a sight. He's been dealt with. But…I can still feel it." Hart pointed to the heart Mel hugged to her chest. "And other things do, too." He looked over a shoulder, scanning the darkness. "You two should probably get the hell out of here while the getting is good. Might be more zombies…" The werewolf sniffed the air. "That is the rankest scent. Maybe just one though."

"Then you can handle that. You've experience." Tor clasped Mel's hand. "Let's give CJ a call and tell him we're on our way with the heart."

"He won't appreciate being woken up so early."

"It's either that or the zombie apocalypse."

"A phone call it is!" Mel started toward the van, yet managed a look back at the werewolf. Yep. Nice ass. "We'll have to meet when there aren't zombies or revenants, Hart!" she called as she crossed in front of the van to the passenger side.

"I agree! Good luck to the both of you. Uh, Tor, you want your vest back?"

"Nope. You keep it."

"Doesn't fit." The wolf rubbed it back and forth across his groin.

"Really not interested in wearing it again," Tor said. With a wave, he sent off the werewolf, who dropped the vest and, as he ran toward the darkness, shifted to a four-legged wolf.

Tor slid inside and started up the van.

"I could wash the vest for you," Mel offered.

"I have others. And did I notice you were drooling over a certain wolf?"

"Well, come on. He was naked!"

Tor chuckled. "The guy does have some muscle on him." He wrinkled a brow as he thought about that statement. "So! On to the Archives. You call your uncle. And I'll prepare to face the dark witch's wrath yet again. Good times tonight. Good times."

Forty-five minutes later, Certainly Jones met them at the Council headquarters, which housed the Archives down a long, narrow alleyway that no one would ever suspect led to anything so fantastical as an organization that collected magical objects and was dedicated to policing paranormals of all breeds and species. And that was exactly the way they preferred it.

CJ strode down the alleyway, stopping Tor and Mel before they got close to the entrance. Mel figured her uncle wasn't about to let her get inside the building again. Fair enough.

She handed over the plastic container, and CJ whistled as he shook his head. "I can't believe you slipped this out without me noticing."

"Yes, well, I do have my talents."

"Thievery?"

"It did serve a purpose. Mom is now safe. Our family can finally begin to mend."

CJ glanced to Tor, who was looking the worse for wear. Blood was caked on his brow. A slash in his trousers revealed thigh, and his frayed shirt would have to be trashed, but he was smiling. Mel squeezed his hand.

"What repercussions should we expect?" CJ asked as he tucked the container under an arm. "Where did you perform the spell? What, exactly, was the result?"

Tor reeled off the latitude and longitude of the crossroads. "Just east of Versailles."

CJ nodded. "Our family land."

"I was able to talk to Amaranthe and get her to forgive Mom," Mel provided. "Then I gave her peace. And then Tor saved the heart from getting crushed by his dead girlfriend."

"Friend, not girlfriend."

"Crushed?" CJ rubbed his throat. "That explains a lot. A few hours ago, I thought I was suffocating. Was trying to figure who was working a spell on me. I warded myself quickly, but it lingered."

"That was the heart. It was almost destroyed. But it's all good now." Mel rapped the plastic box with her knuckles. "Put this in a steel box and throw away the key."

"Your visiting privileges have been revoked," CJ admonished.

"Oh, come on! I love researching spells in the stacks. That's how I learn. I promise I won't ever steal from you again."

CJ's look did not indicate trust. "I will consider it. But at the very least, you'll be grounded from the Archives for a good six months."

Mel pouted. "Fair enough."

"You call your dad?" CJ asked.

"Texted him. Didn't want to wake him. I would have texted you, but Hecate's heart really does need to be put away. Now."

Tor glanced behind them down the alleyway. "Yes, now."

"Got it." CJ shook a finger at Mel. "I don't approve of your methods, Lissa, but I am glad you got the job done. Your poor mom and dad needed this. You stepped up. You've done the family proud."

"Thank you. But I, uh…"

CJ tucked the plastic container under an arm and gave her his full attention.

"I'm not so sure I'm cut out to be a dark witch,"

Mel offered. "It's not me. At all. But Dad would be so disappointed—"

"No, he won't." Her uncle clapped a hand onto her shoulder and bent to meet her gaze. "TJ loves you, Lissa. No matter what kind of magic you practice. And hell, maybe the family needs a light witch to balance out the dark, eh? Vika once practiced only light. I say you should honor the witch you are and don't try to be something you are not. You want me to talk to your dad about it?"

"Thanks, CJ." She hugged him, then tapped the container. "We should leave you to tuck that away. I've seen more than enough zombies in the past few days for a lifetime, thank you very much."

CJ extended a hand to Tor, who shook it. "Thank you. You've kept my niece alive. The Joneses owe you for that."

"You'll get my bill," Tor said.

CJ disappeared into the building, and the twosome strolled toward the van, hand in hand. Tor checked his watch. "Ah, hell."

"What?"

"It's already seven thirty?"

"Your interview is at eight."

"I don't have time to run home and change." They stopped at the van, and he opened the door for Mel and helped her up inside.

"Does that mean you're going to skip it?" she asked.

"I would never miss an appointment."

"Oh." Her shoulders dropped. She wasn't going to mention the memory potion. She'd seen him tuck the vial back in his shirt pocket. She'd lost him after all.

Her heart fell in her chest. But she lifted her head and did her best to keep back the tears.

"Besides…" Tor reached up to adjust the tiara on her

head. "I know exactly how this is going down, and I wouldn't miss it for the world."

But she wouldn't mind missing it. Mel nodded and forced a smile. "Onward?"

"Buckle up. We have to make the city limits through the crazy morning rush-hour traffic."

The office building was situated in the center of La Défense district, nestled amidst the tallest structures in Paris. It gave off the closest atmosphere to New York, Tor had once decided of the busy metropolitan area.

Having easily passed by the snoozing security guard in the building lobby, he now strolled down an aisle between cubicles that led toward the conference room, where the receptionist had directed him and where the meeting was to take place. As he passed the desks, workers turned to stare, openmouthed, hands to chests. A few gasps were audible.

When he neared the room, which was open, he straightened his tie and slid his hand down the length of it—which stopped midchest thanks to the zombie who had managed to slash a claw through the imported silk.

Shit happened.

"Monsieur Demengoet?" He entered the conference room and spied the bald man sitting at the end of a long table with a few file folders spread out before him. "Torsten Rindle. At your service."

Tor pulled out a chair. He set the machete he'd had tilted over a shoulder onto the glossy wood table, placed the gas mask he'd hooked at his belt next to it, then sat, put up his shoes on the table and offered a smile to the stunned interviewer.

"Monsieur Rindle, what is this?"

"Uh, the machete? It's standard gear for beheading

vampires and zombies. It's sweet." He patted the weapon, then glanced out the doorway. Down the hallway, a bunch of heads observed, like gophers popping up from their holes. "It's a tool of my trade."

"This is highly uncalled-for. How did you get past security?"

"I strolled in. Don't worry. I'm not going to use it here. I just got off a job. As you can see. A bit untidy, but you know, that's what the job requires. And I am a man who goes all-in, full-out, whenever he's called to do the task. Would you like a list of my skills? Not only am I an expert with the blade, but my marksman skills are exemplary. I'm also keen on the chemical compositions required for proper crime-scene cleanup. I can twist any story to make your head spin. And…" He tugged a vial out from his shirt pocket and set it on the table before him. "I'm not afraid to use magic when necessary."

The man sputtered and slammed the file folder shut. "I don't know what sort of charade you are trying, *monsieur*, but I have had enough. Vampires and werewolves? You are a lunatic!"

"Far from it. I am a necessary asset to society. I make sure people like you don't believe in all the bad things that could happen to them, especially the bad paranormal things. If I didn't do my job? There would be chaos."

"Then why are you seeking a new job?"

Tor leaned forward onto his elbows. "You know, I thought I needed a change. To walk away from that which I have embraced all my life. Call it a ghost story. A silly fear. And toss in a bit of love story, as well. But I've overcome that, thanks to a helpful, weird and breathtakingly gorgeous witch."

"A witch—"

"She made me understand that I do what I do because I can, and because I enjoy it. Which I do. Can't lie. Taking out a clutch of zombies is incredibly satisfying. You've never seen something until you've watched a dead thing dechunk."

"I am going to call security."

"No need." Tor stood and propped the machete over his shoulder. "I just had to come here and put myself in this atmosphere. To know that it wasn't right. And it's not. I could never function enclosed in one of those confining beige cubicles. I need to remain freelance and ready for action."

He picked up the gas mask.

"Now, I know what you're thinking. If this guy is so good with spin, how's he going to spin an entire office building into believing he was never here? That he didn't march in with a big-ass machete and make a spectacle of himself?"

The interviewer merely huffed.

Tor clasped the vial. "Sometimes a guy has to rely on witchcraft. Thanks for your time, Monsieur Demengeot. Just hope you never see me in the future. Because the only way that'll happen is if the big bads have come for you. And if they do? I'll know. Have a nice day."

With that, Tor pulled the gas mask over his head and face. Next, he flicked the cork out of the vial and then waved it around in the room. As he strolled back down the hallway, he waved the vial before and behind him. Everyone dodged this weird action. One man fainted.

"Stay safe!" he called as he grabbed the door handle. Tossing the vial into the garbage can broke the thin glass. The spell would suffuse the room and overtake everyone in the vicinity with a memory relaxer that should erase what they believed to be paranormal. And since he was toeing the line of all things strange and paranormal, it should obliterate memory of his visit, as well. "Fight the good fight!"

He pumped a fist in the air and wandered out to the curb where the van was parked. Mel had moved into the driver's seat, so Tor hopped in the passenger side.

"You get the job?" she asked as she pulled away and onto the main road.

"Absolutely not." Her double take made him smile.

"Oh. Are you, uh…you bummed?"

"Nope. You got any more silly questions?"

"One more. Did you use the memory spell?"

"I did." Tor set the machete behind him on the van floor. When he looked up, Mel gaped at him. "When I was wearing this." He waggled the gas mask and then tossed it in the back. "The whole office will forget any strange talk of zombies and other creatures. But I will not."

"So that means you…don't want normal?"

"Absolutely, without question, no. That would be the most boring, obnoxious, unexciting existence I could imagine."

"And…" Her words were barely a whisper. "…us?"

"You still up for dating?"

She nodded eagerly. "You want to come home with me and crawl into bed and have wild sex until we both fall asleep from exhaustion?"

"Absolutely."

Epilogue

A week later...

Sinatra sang "Witchcraft" through the radio speakers while Tor held Mel in a close dance hold. The twosome swayed on the patio, their heartbeats synced, breaths tinged with the excitement of holding a lover. The sun had set and the night flowers had opened to release their heady perfume.

Bruce levitated near a red candle that flickered in the middle of a rose-petal circle. Duck waddled over the grass, plucking at unfortunate snails.

Off in another Parisian arrondissement, Thoroughly and Star Jones were packing their things in preparation to move out to the countryside and build a retirement cottage. They intended to enjoy every moment of Star's last life. In the safest way possible.

And somewhere in the neighborhood, a werewolf and

his vampire lover were cooing over their newborn daughter, who would grow into a half vampire/half werewolf, who would someday fall in love with a man who was her complete opposite in every frustratingly impossible way, and with whom, after much trial and romance, she would live happily ever after.

"Do you believe in happily-ever-after?" Mel asked Tor as she snuggled closer to his warm, hard, muscled chest smelling of sweet cherry tobacco.

"I want to."

"I'm not sure it's so easy to have."

"Wouldn't be worth having if it was easy."

"I don't know. I kind of like pushing the easy button every now and then."

He tilted her into a sudden, heart-pounding dip and bowed to kiss her. "I can give you *easy* every now and then." He waggled his brows and pulled her up and into his embrace.

"I like you easy. I also like you hard. Really hard." She hugged her hip against his groin, and Tor moaned as his erection tightened. "I like you any way I can get you, as long as I get you."

"You have me, witch. Two weirdos who will always be chasing normal—"

"But who never want to catch it."

"Exactly. I think Bruce is getting too close to the flame. Bruce!"

The frog ribbited and adjusted his angle to barely avoid the candle flame. Bruce then hovered away, but not without casting Tor a look of disdain.

"That is the most judgmental frog I've met," Tor said.

"He likes you."

"He tolerates me."

"I'll have a talk with him. You'll be spencing a lot more time here?"

"You won't be able to get rid of me. Though I did get a text right before we came out to the patio. Something about a missing book on werewolves. The text was sent from the Agency CEO, Dez Merovich, in the States. Smells like trouble."

"Sounds intriguing."

"Sounds not normal. Just the way life should be."

"The normal stories are never very interesting."

"I prefer my stories weird."

"Here's to our weird story," Mel said. "May it be filled with adventure, romance, hot sex and that elusive happy ending."

Her lover bowed to kiss her and a flutter of sprites sparkled up from the grass to circle their heads, while off in the yard, Bruce levitated near Duck. If a man knew how to speak amphibian, he may have guessed the familiar's croak to have been, for once, approving.

* * * * *

Thoroughly Jones and Star's story is
This Glamorous Evil.
If you are interested in CJ's story, please read
This Wicked Magic.
Christian Hart's story is Claiming the Wolf.
Domingos LaRoque's story is Beautiful Danger.
And Rook's story is Beyond the Moon.

Author Note

I hope you enjoyed this, the final story for Harlequin's Nocturne line. It's been such a joy to write paranormal stories for this line, and it is with great sadness I say goodbye to it. I wrote one of the first Nocturnes, *From The Dark*, and over the years have created a world I call Beautiful Creatures. All my Nocturnes (save a few) are set in that world, and while you don't have to read them in any particular order, they do all mix and match characters and families that are related. I've tried to list at the end of each book which secondary characters also have stories. For a complete downloadable pdf book list, visit my website at: MicheleHauf.com.

This is not my final paranormal romance by any means. I will continue to write in my world. As well, I will be writing for Harlequin's Intrigue line and get to exercise my love for romance, suspense and action-adventure (I'll try to keep vampires off the pages of those stories). For updates on my new releases, do follow me on social media:

Facebook.com/MicheleHaufAuthor
Twitter.com/MicheleHauf
Instagram.com/MicheleHauf
Pinterest.com/toastfaery
HaufsBeautifulCreatures.tumblr.com

Here's to a weird happily-ever-after!

Michele